# Hell Week

ALSO BY ROSEMARY CLEMENT-MOORE

*Prom Dates from Hell*

MAGGIE QUINN: GIRL VS. EVIL

# Hell Week

a novel by

**Rosemary Clement-Moore**

DELACORTE PRESS

Published by Delacorte Press
an imprint of Random House Children's Books
a division of Random House, Inc.
New York

This is a work of fiction. Names, characters, places, and incidents either are the product of the author's imagination or are used fictitiously. Any resemblance to actual persons, living or dead, events, or locales is entirely coincidental.

Delacorte Press and colophon are registered trademarks of Random House, Inc.

www.randomhouse.com/teens

Educators and librarians, for a variety of teaching tools, visit us at
www.randomhouse.com/teachers

Library of Congress Cataloging-in-Publication Data
Clement-Moore, Rosemary.
Hell Week / Rosemary Clement-Moore.—1st ed.
p. cm.
Summary: While working undercover on a series of stories for her campus newspaper, college freshman Maggie reluctantly endures mixers, rites, and peculiar rules, but soon learns that members of the sorority to which she has pledged have strange powers and a terrible secret.
ISBN 978-0-385-73414-1 (hardcover)
ISBN 978-0-385-90429-2 (Gibraltar lib. bdg.) [1. Greek letter societies—Fiction.
2. Universities and colleges—Fiction 3. Journalism—Fiction. 4. Demonology—
Fiction. 5. Horror stories.] I. Title.
PZ7.C59117Hel 2008
[Fic]—dc22            2007007438

The text of this book is set in 12.5-point Filosofia Regular.

Book design by Angela Carlino

Printed in the United States of America

10 9 8 7 6 5 4 3 2 1

First Edition

In memory of
Trini

*

May heaven be full of Frisbees and
unguarded dinner plates.

# 1

Bright teeth flashed; I fought the instinct to recoil. Perfectly white, perfectly even, possibly once human. Coral pink lips pulled back all the way to the gums, giving the smile an unfortunate equine quality. "Soooo . . . ?" The owner of the teeth and lips drew out the word and flipped it up at the end in a question. "What's your major?"

"English." An untruth. I don't tell them, as a rule, but I'd been asked this question five times in the last hour, and the lie rolled off my tongue now with ease.

"Gosh, you must have to read a lot, huh?" Another blinding smile; I hoped my squint passed for an answer.

"So, Maggie. What made you decide to go through Rush?"

She pronounced it with a capital $R$. Five rounds of the cattle call officially known as Sorority Formal Recruitment had run together in my banality-numbed brain, and I couldn't remember where I was. I glanced around the crowded room for a clue. The noise was formidable, the chatter of a hundred or more coiffed and groomed girls like purebred dogs at a show, their yelping echoing from the walls.

Just like every other sorority house I'd been to in this first series of parties. Here, though, the décor was Cotton Candy Pink and Tampax Box Blue. Verily, I had reached the lair of the Delta Delta Gammas.

"Well, Ashley . . ." My slightly breathless drawl mimicked hers. "I thought Rush would be fun. Get to know people, you know."

She laughed, her eyes squinched up in two half-moons of insincerity. "Soooo? Which dorm are you in, Maggie?"

She kept checking my name tag. At every house, the girls had used my name exhaustively, making me feel as though I'd wandered onto a used car lot.

"I'm living at home." This much was certainly true. "I grew up here in Avalon."

"Oh." Her smile, and I use the word loosely, was forced. "Well, at least you know your way around. You probably have a car, too. What kind is it?"

Her segues could really use a little polish. "It's vintage."

"Oh, really?" She raised her brows with renewed interest.

"Yeah. A Ford Pinto."

"Really." Beneath her carefully applied self-tanner, the

corners of her mouth were white with strain. "Your parents live here in Avalon?"

It would be hard to live at home and go to school here if they didn't. But smart-ass wasn't my persona here at the International House of Snobcakes, so I merely answered enthusiastically, "My dad works here at Bedivere University. He's an engineer."

"Is he really? Mechanical or civil?"

"Custodial."

"O-kay." She glanced at her watch, then searched the room for rescue, or maybe just an avenue of escape. "Well, it's been real nice meeting you, Maggie. I need to go . . . um . . . talk to these girls over here."

She took off; I knew from my research that leaving a rushee standing alone was a big fat no-no. Unless, of course, you'd rather invite a chimpanzee to join your sisterhood. And no one in the Delta Delta Gamma house looked like Jane Goodall to me.

But since I'd been deserted, I reached into my purse and turned off my microrecorder. No sense in wasting megabytes.

$$\ast \quad \ast \quad \ast$$

The *Avalon Sentinel* is an independent small-town paper, which is almost an anachronism in itself. The historic Main Street offices smelled of ancient cigarettes, even though the place had been smoke-free for twenty years.

I sat in a hard wooden chair that had been squeaking beneath anxious backsides for decades. My colleagues—or rather, the guys I'd stepped and fetched for all summer during my internship—kept making excuses to walk past the office, peering into the windows as the editor-in-chief read my submission.

Ethan Douglas was probably thirty, but he had pale skin, freckles, and flaming red hair, all of which made him look more like Opie than Spencer Tracy. Like me, he had journalistic aspirations beyond the *Avalon Sentinel,* but—also like me—he had to start somewhere.

He lifted his eyes from the paper and gave me a dubious look. "You made this stuff up."

"I swear." I raised a Boy Scout salute. "The only stuff I made up was the lies about my dad being a janitor. Oh, and I don't drive a Ford Pinto."

In a skeptical voice, he read what I'd written: " 'I'm an English major,' I said for the umpteenth time. 'I wish I was an English major,' said Sorority Sue. 'I mean, I speak it already, and everything.' "

Laughter from the doorway behind me. Ethan glared in that direction, not terribly menacing with his freckled choirboy face. The guys from the newsroom went back to work, and I got down to business, too.

"You said if I brought you a story that no one else here could, you would give me a shot."

I was uniquely qualified to infiltrate Rush, being that I was a girl and an actual college freshman. I might as well use it to my advantage.

Anyone who drove by the frat houses on a Friday night could tell that fraternities evaluated their future pledges based on their ability to chug beer and score with the coeds. But the closed-door secrecy on the distaff side of Greek Row lent a certain mystery to what was, in essence, about as exciting as six successive tea parties with your grandmother and her septuagenarian friends.

Not *my* grandmother, of course. When the mood struck her, Granny Quinn could put on the doily better than anyone. But tea with Gran might mean anything from an authentic Japanese ceremony to a formal reading of your tea leaves. Gran had "the Sight," as she called it. So do I, though for most of my eighteen years I didn't consciously acknowledge the fact.

But then I had to rescue my senior prom from a ravenous horde of demon spawn. I learned the hard way there's nothing like a supernatural smackdown to make you wake up and smell the brimstone.

Ethan Douglas rubbed his chin, which was slightly red and shiny from his morning shave. "I'll give it to Janey and see if she has a place for it on Friday."

"Lifestyles?" I tried to tone down my unprofessional indignation. "With the pumpkin recipes and 4-H announcements?" Not to mention that Janey Cotton still displayed pictures of her college chums in a Delta Zeta picture frame. My story would run between the obituaries and the funeral home ads, if at all.

"Where else would it go?" Ethan said, annoying me with the truth. "It's more social commentary than scathing exposé."

"But . . . ," I sputtered, with no real argument. "The pretension and the elitism . . ."

"Maggie, females of all ages have been throwing hoity-toity parties and shunning the inferior for centuries. I shouldn't have to tell *you* that."

I wasn't sure if I'd just been insulted or commiserated with. But he was right about one thing: He didn't have to tell me about the rabidity of the alpha bitch in defending the social hierarchy. I had the bite marks to prove it.

"Okay, what about the perpetuation of an outdated system of stratification and false superiority . . . ?"

Ethan handed the copy across the desk. "If that's your point, the story isn't done. You've only been to one round of parties."

I stared at him in dawning horror. "You mean . . . I have to go *back*?"

"Bring me the story that I don't know." He spun his chair to face his computer screen. "That is, if Professor Quinn lets you live when he finds out you made him a janitor."

I'd been dismissed. Folding the rejected story into thirds, I stuffed it into my satchel and headed out of the office, then down the stairs. Out in the bright September morning, I paused on the Main Street sidewalk, lifted my face to the sunshine, and breathed deeply. The too-warm breeze stirred my short, dark hair across my eyes, hiding their childish watering.

Stupid to be so stung, when Ethan had only told me the truth. The rejection smacked me, deservedly, in the pride. Ace reporter for the high school paper was about as real-world applicable as presidency of the local *Star Trek* club. My first taste of Small Fish and Big Pond went down badly.

The clock in the square struck the hour, and I blinked away self-pity, mentally squaring my shoulders. *Never give up, never surrender.* That was my new motto.

Besides, what else was I going to do? I lived at home and

all my friends had gone away to school, including my best friend, Lisa, who was halfway across the country. The guy I was nuts about hadn't called me since he spent the entire summer doing an internship in Ireland, and none of my freaky intuition could tell me why not. Because *that* would be useful.

My wicked psychic powers didn't give me winning lottery numbers or insight into pork futures. No, what I got was the inspired idea to strap on a push-up bra and infiltrate the Delta Delta Gammas.

Let's face it. The saddest thing about this whole undercover sorority thing was that I really didn't have to *pretend* to be that much of a loser.

# 2

"Maggie Quinn," said my grandmother, her Irish accent deepening in familiar exasperation. "Saying that you are just a little bit psychic is like saying you're just a little bit pregnant."

"Gran!" I glanced around the coffee shop. The over-stuffed couches and scratch-and-dent-sale chairs of Froth and Java were full of Bedivere University students, but hopefully we sat far enough from the midmorning caffeine zombies that her comment had gone unheard. The last thing I needed was word getting around campus that I was psychic. Or pregnant, for that matter.

"You either are, or you aren't," she continued, lifting her mug of tea. "The only question is how noticeable it is."

Gran had called me right after I'd left the *Sentinel*'s offices, before I'd even reached the Jeep; fifteen minutes later she met me in F and J, where she listened to me whine, then told me to get over myself.

Besides being psychic, my grandmother was trim and trendy, and busy with her volunteer activities, which included the altar guild at St. Stephen's Catholic Church and teaching yoga to senior citizens at the Spiritual Enlightenment Center. (Avalon was small but eclectic, rather like Gran.) It must have been New Age day, because she wore a sage green cotton jacket and pants, her bright red hair all perky.

I slouched across from her, cradling a paper cup of caffeinated goodness between my hands, dressed in my least ragged jeans and a fitted oxford, shirttails out. I'd ironed both my shirt and my hair in an attempt to look more polished. The pale yellow cotton had held its press longer than my sable bob; I could feel the latter reverting to its usual cappuccino froth by the moment.

The wavy brown hair I got from my mother; the rest of me was all Quinn. In addition to the Sight, I'd inherited my grandmother's green eyes, pixie-shaped face, and pointed chin, as well as a certain broadness in the beam I could live without.

"I thought you'd be happy that I've accepted my freakitude."

She rolled her eyes. "Somehow I'm still sensing a lack of true commitment."

"I wonder why that could be. Maybe because last time, following my instincts almost got my friends and me killed?"

Pained guilt deepened the soft lines of her face. Gran still hadn't forgiven herself for not sensing the depth of trouble I'd been in last spring. I wished she'd cut herself some slack. The things under your nose are the hardest to see, in any sense of the word. Plus, I'd gone to some pains to keep the whole truth from her, and I suspected other forces might have been doing the same. No proof, of course. Just a hunch.

But that was the thing about my . . . whatever you wanted to call it. Most of the time, it didn't *feel* any different from simple—if eerily strong and accurate—intuition. I kept hoping for an instruction manual, but the best I'd been able to do was a copy of *ESP for Dummies* that I found on the bargain table at Barnes & Noble.

I hunched over my coffee cup, breath running out in a sigh. Just the smell of Froth and Java usually made me feel better, and I was trying hard to follow through on my resolution to drop the drama. "I just wish I didn't feel so stupid. When I had that dream about the Greek letters, I thought there would be a story there." That was how my psychicness had first shown up, in the nighttime, when logic couldn't override the subconscious. "I thought, just once, my intuition was picking up on something useful."

Gran clicked her tongue and cast her gaze heavenward. "What did you think you would discover in one night? Don't they arrange these things to get more in-depth as the week goes on?"

"Yes." Nice of my gran to join the Maggie-is-an-idiot refrain. "It's a good thing I didn't burn all my bridges."

"See." She smiled over her paper cup. "Your intuition did tell you something useful. So where will you go?"

I fished in my satchel for the e-mail I'd printed that morning. Mom had been appalled. Apparently, when she went through Rush—my own mother; I'm so ashamed—their invitations to the next round of parties were delivered to their dorm rooms. On silver platters, for all I knew.

During the past Friday's orientation—excruciating in length and level of enthusiasm—I learned about "recs" and "bids" and "legacies." All the talk of leadership and sisterhood was, considering we'd all shelled out registration fees, sort of like trying to sell us a car after we'd already made a down payment.

Rush—Recruitment, I should say—worked by double elimination. In the first round, which took two days, you went to all ten houses for the short torture sessions I'd described in my article. Then six tonight, four tomorrow, and two the last night. At each round, the sorority could choose to invite you back—or not, in which case you were "cut"—while simultaneously you had to narrow your choices. Theoretically, I could have had to choose six out of ten houses to visit for tonight's second round. Needless to say, I faced no such quandary.

"Maggie Quinn?"

The speaker had a rounded, evening-news sort of voice. I turned, looked up, and up again. A tall, thin blonde stood beside our table, the light from the window behind her. I answered warily, "Yes?"

Her hair was pulled back in a tight ponytail, which bobbed as she looked me up and down. "*Where* is your name tag?"

"Uh . . ." I recognized her now, and the other young woman with her, carrying a tray of drinks. Both were Recruitment guides, or Rho Gammas, as the Panhellenic Council—the organizational body of sororities on campus—called them. Which said something about the pretentiousness involved, if "Panhellenic Council" wasn't your first clue.

There were fifteen Rho Gammas, representing all the different houses, and though it was supposed to be a secret, some of them were easily identifiable. The blonde was Hillary, and I had her pegged for a Delta Zeta—aggressive perfectionists. Their party had been orchestrated to the millisecond with robotic efficiency. The girl with the drinks was Jenna, who wasn't so easily pigeonholed.

"Potential New Members are supposed to wear their name tags at all times," said Hillary, with a gravitas that implied I'd left the space station without my helmet. I'd also noticed that the tendency to speak in capital letters seemed to be a Greek trait.

"Sorry. I'm having coffee with my grandmother, and she already knows my name."

Her instructions were brisk and sober. "The selection process goes on twenty-four-seven, Maggie. The houses will be watching to see how the Potential New Members comport themselves on campus, in class, in the cafeteria, and even off campus."

"Like Big Sister?"

"Exactly!" she chirruped, pleased I'd seen her point. I thought I heard Jenna snort back a laugh, but I couldn't be sure. I know I heard Gran chuckle. "Is that your schedule for the next round?" Hillary asked.

"Yes, ma'am."

She took it from my hand, her eyes flicking over the e-mail. "Only four invites, I see. At least you don't have to make any choices tonight."

"Yes. Considerate of so many houses to cut me."

She scanned the list. "Epsilon Zeta. Yes, that figures. Theta Nu. Zeta Theta Pi and . . ." Her brows made an eloquent arch of surprise. "And Sigma Alpha Xi. How . . . interesting."

She said "interesting" like she meant "unfathomable."

"Maybe they're filling a dork quota."

"Of course not," Hillary demurred, in a tone that said, *That explains it.* "You must have impressed them with your wit and charm." Behind me Gran chortled again as Rho Gamma Blonda handed me back the schedule. "Put on your name badge as soon as possible. And you know the dress for tonight?"

"Black tie?"

"A simple sundress will be fine." She turned toward the door, beckoning the other young woman after her. "Come on, Jenna, before the mochas get cold."

The other Rho Gamma didn't follow right away. She was more subtle all around. Her brown hair had expert highlights, like strands of gold woven through chocolate-colored satin, and if she had on any makeup, I could see no sign of it on her flawless skin. With a secret little smile, she sized me up. "That's funny. I didn't see any Ford Pintos parked outside."

I cleared my throat. "Well . . ."

"Also odd—I had Professor Quinn for history last year."

Gran looked from her to me and back again. "Maggie, just what were you telling them?"

"Um."

Jenna intervened with a friendly grin. "Nothing too bad." She offered her hand. "I'm Jenna Nichols. You must be Maggie's tea leaf–reading grandmother." Her amused glance slanted my way. "Or was that a lie, too?"

"An embellishment, really." I avoided Gran's glare; she disapproved of lying. "I thought you Rho Gammas weren't supposed to talk to the sororities about the rushees."

"We're not. But rumors get around." She grinned and lifted her cardboard tray of drinks. "I've got to go. You're all right with your schedule? No conflicts with classes?"

"No, I'm good." The parties would all be in the evening, and I had no night sections. "Thank you for asking."

"That's what I'm here for." She smiled at Gran. "Nice to meet you, Mrs. Quinn. See you later, Maggie." Then she made her retreat to the September sunshine.

I heaved my satchel over my shoulder, stuffed the printed e-mail into the front pocket, and, grabbing my half-full cup, I turned back to Gran. "I gotta run. I'm meeting the school newspaper adviser to ask about joining the staff."

Her annoyance evaporated quickly. There are advantages to being the only granddaughter. "Take care of yourself, Maggie. Tell your mother I hope she's feeling better."

"I will, Gran." I leaned forward and kissed her soft cheek. "See you later. Thanks for the coffee."

I turned to go, but Gran's lilting voice stuttered my step. "Oh, and tell Justin I say hello."

Slowly, I pivoted to face her, and I could feel my cheeks beginning to heat. "Justin?"

"Yes. He's back from Ireland, isn't he?"

My brain slogged through a morass of mixed emotions that had churned throughout the summer—hope and affection tamped down by a growing weight of worry, and thickened into a soup of romantic uncertainty. "I suppose he must be, since classes started last Thursday."

"Well, don't worry, dear. You'll see him soon. And then you'll get everything straightened out."

Vision, hunch, or wishful thinking? I wove through the tables and shouldered open the door. Matchmaking grandmothers were one thing; matchmaking *psychic* grandmothers were a whole other level of irksome, even when you loved one as much as I did mine.

✳ ✳ ✳

Part two of *Maggie Quinn, You're Not Special* featured Dr. Hardcastle, possibly the most boring journalism professor ever. I'm not saying that Media and Communication is the most fascinating thing to begin with, but it takes a new level of tedious to make me struggle to stay awake in a journalism class.

He was also the adviser for the *Ranger Report*, Bedivere University's newspaper. I had made an appointment with him during his posted office hours and brought along my sample articles and photographs. A wasted effort since as soon as I told him why I was there, he said, without looking up from his computer: "I don't take freshmen on the *Report* staff."

I stood stupidly in front of his desk, the portfolio hanging from my hand. I didn't know how he could see anything; the room was dim and cluttered and smelled as though he had his lunch there a little too often. Or maybe that stale smell was the professor himself. He had a Grizzly Adams thing going for him.

"Never?" I asked.

"As close to never as makes no difference."

*Never give up, never surrender.* "Here are some samples of my work." I opened the binder to an eye-catching photograph of the Avalon High star forward making a spectacular jump shot. "And in addition to working on the AHS paper for three years, I was an intern at the *Sentinel* this summer."

Dr. Hardcastle glanced at the picture and flipped dismissively through a few pages. "Not bad."

"I can write captions, do layout, proofread, whatever you need."

But Professor Hard-ass had gone back to Web surfing. "Come back after you have six hours of prerequisites."

"I'm already enrolled in six hours of journalism—"

"Then come back after you finish them."

He wasn't going to budge. I didn't need to read minds to see that.

"Okay," I said, because there was no point in pissing him off. "Thanks for your time."

I slumped out of his tiny office and leaned against the wall, weighed down, for a moment, by self-pity. It was right next to the journalism lab, where they put together the paper. I could hear the familiar click of multiple keyboards, smell the printer toner and film developer.

Dismissed again. Would the suck never end?

Someone touched my shoulder, and I spun around with a stifled squeak.

"Sorry." The speaker was a young man with intelligent eyes and a Byronic shock of thick, dark blond hair falling across his forehead. He had a friendly smile, and as my brain transitioned from grouchy, grizzled professor to cute young guy, he took the binder out of my limp hand.

"I overheard your conversation with Hardcastle. By which I mean I shamelessly eavesdropped. Let's see what you've got."

"The journalistic clap, apparently." I cracked wise to calm my nerves as he leafed through the pages. "No one wants to touch me this morning."

He raised one brow. "You tell me that after I'm already holding your portfolio?" Then he smiled and gave it back. "I'm Cole Bauer, editor of the *Report*. Anytime you want to submit something to me, go ahead."

"Really?" My roller-coaster day took an upswing.

"Sure."

Belatedly I remembered my manners, and held out my hand. "I'm Maggie Quinn."

"I know." He nodded at my name tag, which I'd dutifully put on when I returned to campus. "How's Rush going?"

I touched the plastic-covered card self-consciously. "Actually, if you'd really like to know . . ." On impulse, I slipped my hand into my satchel and pulled out the folded article.

Both his brows went up at that. "You don't waste time, do you?"

My cheeks heated. "Not when I have a feeling about

something. I think I may have written that for you without realizing it. Er, for the *Report,* I mean."

He nodded. "I know what you mean." Unfolding the pages, he gave them a cursory glance. "I'll read it and let you know."

"Thanks." I felt a quick shot of relief. I'd offered it; he hadn't laughed. Now I just had to let things shake out. I took a step backward, making my exit. "I'll be in touch."

Waving the pages, he moved to do the same. "Or I will. See you."

He turned and disappeared into the newspaper lab, and I headed for my next class in that fog of abrupt reversal, when things take a quick turn and you're not sure you're responsible for it. I don't know if it's the instinct talking, or fate or whatever. But I never know where that left turn is going to take me.

✳   ✳   ✳

Case in point. For eighteen years I'd planned to go away to school, much to my parents' frustration. Bedivere University is a small old liberal arts school with stiff admission criteria and an excellent reputation, which attracted students and teachers from all over and kept Avalon from being more small-town backward than it could be. In fact, the whole place—college and town—felt connected with the rest of the world but slightly out of step with it, making the name seem more than coincidence. It's a great school, I could walk from home if I wanted, and my professor dad got a tuition discount.

That said, the reason I am not, in fact, attending the University of Anywhere-but-Here, despite having been admitted and financially aided, lay with my parents, who could not behave like respectable, decently middle-aged people.

I knew my mother was pregnant before she did. In the pharmacy one day, with one of those half-aware impulses I get, I had picked up a plus-or-minus test and put it in the cart. Mom was surprised, to say the least. "Something you want to tell me, Maggie?"

"It's not for me," I said.

"Do tell." Her calm was admirable, under the circumstances.

"Really. Unless the Angel of Annunciation dropped by to leave a message while I was out, it's for you." As soon as the words left my lips, the feeling went from hunch to certainty. Not even the fall of Mom's face, the paling of her cheeks, could dim it.

She firmed her mouth and put the test back on the shelf. "Don't be ridiculous. That's just not possible."

I returned the pink and blue box to the cart. "Humor me."

My only-child status had not been my parents' choice. Memories of those stressful years of roller-coaster disappointment are fuzzy, and I don't know when, exactly, they gave up hope. But now I was about to have a sibling, even if Mom didn't believe me until she'd started the daily puke.

As for my staying at home, I don't remember making a conscious decision; one morning I woke up knowing that Avalon and Bedivere was the right choice. Gran says that sometimes people like us are led where they need to be, if we just listen to our inner voices.

I tend to think inner voices are only good for getting a person locked in a padded room or burned at the stake. And

I'll tell you right now, I am no saint, because I'm not sure I would have listened to my mental Jiminy Cricket if Justin weren't returning in the fall.

Justin, who still hadn't called me, even though I knew he'd been back in town for a week.

# 3

I arrived at the Epsilon Zeta house breathless and wind-blown, my cheeks hot with exertion. I'd had to rush—no pun intended—home to change after class. I'd brushed my hair and powdered my nose, too, though the effort was wasted by the time I drove the Jeep to Greek Row, found a parking spot, and hightailed it to where my group had assembled, cool and composed despite the warm September afternoon.

"Sorry I'm late!" I gave an exaggerated roll of my eyes. "But you would not believe my professor, wanting us all to stay until the end of his lecture. Can you imagine?"

The buxom brunette beside me shook her head. "I

know! We have all semester to go to class, but Rush only lasts one week, and affects our Entire Lives!"

Sadly, she spoke without irony. Up on the steps Jenna rapped on the door, telling the Epsilon Zetas that the next round was assembled, and beside her, Hillary looked at me with no small disapproval. I reached up and smoothed my hair with my hands, an involuntary reaction.

Such was the power of the Rho Gamma stare. In addition to shepherding our group from house to house, they ran herd on the rushees throughout the day, enforcing the rules. Besides the mandatory wearing of name tags, we weren't allowed to talk to "actives"—that is, sorority members—outside of the parties.

My name tag was dutifully pinned to the bodice of my sundress, where it scratched the pale skin of my bare arm, and the only sorority girls I'd talked to today had been Jenna and Hillary, which was, obviously, allowed. But I was pretty sure writing pithy articles skewering Rush traditions was against the Rho Gamma rules.

✳ ✳ ✳

Two houses later, my brain and my butt were both numb.

Every round had a theme, and tonight was the philanthropy round. Every sorority chooses, at the national level, a pet cause or organization, and each chapter is required to do an annual fund-raiser to justify the other fifty weeks of purely self-indulgent social activities. And for the past eternity, the rushees had been required to hear about it, mostly through video montages and PowerPoint presentations.

The propaganda also showed the house's personality.

The Theta Nus had managed to work their GPA ranking into their presentation. The Epsilon Zetas had lots of guys in their pictures, always with arms thrown around the girls. I'm not saying the Epsilon Zetas were a sure thing, in any sense of the phrase, but . . . well, when your house is called the EZs maybe it's just inevitable.

Dusk was sitting heavy and humid in the sky as Jenna and Hillary escorted us to the next house on our agenda, the Zeta Theta Pis. The curvy brunette from before—Miss Entire Life—drew up alongside me. "I like your outfit," she said as we walked. "It's kind of sixties retro."

It was. Gran never got rid of anything. Yellow and red, with splashes of orange, the frock had useless little spaghetti straps and a full, pleated skirt. I wore ballet flats and a Band-Aid on my ankle where I'd cut myself shaving. "I raided my grandmother's closet for something to wear."

"Grandmother's Closet?" she echoed. "I've never heard of that store."

"It's, uh, very exclusive." There was another girl, a redhead, stuck with us behind the rushee bottleneck on the sidewalk. I caught Red stifling a smile, but the brunette was oblivious.

"Anyway. Great dress. I'm Tricia, by the way."

"Thanks. I'm Maggie."

We reached the Zeta house slightly ahead of schedule, earning a restorative break. Lip gloss tubes and compacts appeared for synchronized primping. Only Red-haired Girl and I abstained, and lounged against the stair rail to wait.

She reminded me of an Irish setter, in a good way. Her dark red hair fell, slightly feathered, to her shoulders, and she had a rangy, athletic grace. She looked as if she would be more at home on a ball field than a sorority house.

"What houses are you interested in, Maggie?" Tricia asked. She had whipped out a little battery-operated fan and was using it to blow her long brown hair from her flushed face.

I mimicked Hillary's ultraserious tone. "How can I possibly decide when I've yet to hear all the philanthropies?"

Irish Setter Girl smirked. Tricia looked suspiciously between us. "What's so funny?"

"Nothing. Except that 'Recruitment'"—I made little quotes in the air—"is like comparing the gas mileage of a Mustang and a Corvette. You say you're being practical, but all you really care about is which one looks best for picking up guys."

Hillary strode past us; along with her black T-shirt with its green *RG*, she wore pressed khaki shorts and sneakers that had never seen a workout. She glanced at me on her way up the steps. "I see you managed to find your name tag." Then she stopped, her blond ponytail swinging as she stared with narrowing eyes at my chest. "*What* did you do to it?"

I glanced down at the tag, which now said: *Maggie Quinn. English major. Lives at home.* "I thought this was more efficient."

Tsks and titters from the rushees. Irish Setter Girl snorted, in a laughing-with-me kind of way.

"Prospective New Members," said the scandalized Rho Gamma, "are *not* supposed to alter their name badges!"

"Oh. I didn't know."

Jenna climbed the porch steps past us. "Don't worry about it, Maggie. We'll get you a new one tomorrow."

Hillary bit back her opinion on that, and followed her up. "We'll see if they're ready for you."

As soon as Hillary and Jenna turned to the door, the red-haired girl hissed at me. "Hey. Have you still got the pen?"

"Sure." I reached into my little handbag and fished it out. She pulled the paper from her plastic holder. Under her name—Holly Russell—she wrote "ΣΑΞ Legacy" while I peered shamelessly over her shoulder.

"What's that?" I asked.

"Efficient." She grinned at me and folded the card back into its sleeve.

"Why efficient?" I asked. I knew from the interminable orientation that a legacy was someone whose close relative was a member of a certain sorority.

"Spares everyone the trouble of making nice when it's a done deal."

A legacy wasn't supposed to be an automatic in, but that didn't mean it wasn't. "I guess that explains why Zeta Theta Pi asked me back."

"You're a Zeta leg?" She handed me the pen. "Write it down. It'll impress the other houses. Everyone loves the Zetas."

"Really?" I glanced at the double front doors, emblazoned with ZθΠ. I'd been there yesterday, of course, but those parties had been short and the houses pretty much blurred together. "Why?"

"Because they're cool, why else?"

I tried to picture my mother in a cool sorority and failed

utterly. My mother is an accountant. "What about the Sigma Alpha Xis?" I pointed to Holly's name badge. "Did you write that to impress people?"

She sighed. "No. I wrote it so they won't feel they have to bother being nice to me. No SAXi leg goes anywhere but SAXi."

"What are they, like the mafia?"

She barked an Irish setter laugh. "No. Not exactly."

The Zeta doors opened before I could ask her anything else, and we flowed in, carried by the inexorable tide of Sisterhood with a capital *S*.

✳ ✳ ✳

Our merry band left the Zeta house as the sun dropped low in the west.

"Didn't I say?" Holly shortened her strides and we hung at the back of the pack along with Tricia, making our way toward the SAXi house near the center of the block.

"You did." The Zeta Theta Pis exemplified cool: effortless, amiable, seemingly unconcerned with status or social hierarchy. That unforced confidence reminded me of my friend Lisa. She'd gotten tagged with the nickname D&D Lisa during the role-playing phase of her youth, but by the time she graduated summa cum laude, it had become more of a title. Uniquely beautiful (once she emerged from her Goth cocoon), smart, and sarcastic, she wasn't part of any group at Avalon High, but she had an impressive network of minions and a small fiefdom of friends.

She'd be pissed to think she had anything in common with a sorority. Maybe I just missed her because there was so much on Greek Row worthy of mockery, and I had no one to share it with. I hated that she was so far away, and hated even more that we'd argued before she left.

"I would totally pledge the Zetas if they gave me a bid." Tricia bounced with excitement, which was a brave thing for a girl with her generous bosoms in a strapless dress.

"I thought your heart was set on Delta Delta Gamma."

"Well, all my friends from home, who have already finished Rush at other schools, they went Delta." She laughed, but there was a brittle edge to it. "I'd be the only one from the old squad who didn't, and what fun would that be?"

"A lot more fun than doing something just because your old friends are doing it." I'd gotten a fix on Tricia pretty quickly. Sweet and eager to be liked; girls like the Deltas would smell her insecurity the way sharks smell blood in the water.

Holly spoke from her other side, sounding very reasonable. "You should pledge where you have the most in common with the members here at this school." I found myself liking her, and Tricia's naïve good nature kind of grew on me, too. If we had met under different circumstances, or if I was who I said I was, I might be thinking of them as new friends, or at least potential ones.

"Maggie?"

I recognized that baritone voice instantly, though I'd last heard it distorted by a transatlantic phone connection.

Darn Gran and her stupid Sight.

Slowly I turned, conscious that Holly and Tricia had stopped, too, and were staring curiously at the tallish young man across the tree-shaded lane.

He wore running clothes, was flushed and sweaty. His

brown hair stood up in spikes and his T-shirt clung in dark blotches, which looked nicer than it sounds. Despite the utter lack of traffic, he looked both ways before he crossed the street, which was so very Justin that I felt a painful, twisty flip in the region of my heart.

I waited, feeling strangely tentative considering how much I'd missed him. A zillion questions hopped around in my brain, but something knotted my tongue. Maybe it was the way he smiled and moved as if to embrace me, but then stopped when he saw our audience.

Holly seemed to have some intuition of her own, because she grabbed Tricia's arm, spun her around, and double-timed to catch up with the group. But the moment had passed, and Justin and I shuffled in that awkward way you do when you really want to touch a person but a hug might be too much and a handshake is definitely absurd. A kiss, which was how we had parted, seemed out of the question.

"I haven't heard from you," I blurted out, because a moment like that can always use more awkward.

He looked sheepish, apologetic. "I know. Jet lag, then getting my stuff out of storage, then I had to meet with my adviser about my thesis. The days got away from me."

"Okay." I didn't point out that he'd found time for a run. I didn't point out a lot of things because I didn't want to be snide, and sarcasm is pretty much all I have when I feel this out of my depth.

His gaze took in my uncharacteristic dress, then narrowed on my name tag. "Are you going through *Rush*?"

I smoothed the folds of my skirt. The evening air was cooling quickly as the sun disappeared. "I'm undercover."

He had a crooked smile that always hit me in the gut. It turned his clean-cut, Boy Scout face into something subversively rakish. "Can I buy you a cup of coffee and hear about it?"

"I'd like that." I said it in shamelessly eager haste. "But I have to finish this first. Why don't we meet at F and J? About nine o'clock?"

He nodded, decisive. "Froth and Java, nine o'clock."

"Maggie!" Jenna called back from the group, sounding impatient and a little annoyed.

"I've got to run." I edged up the hill, reluctant to leave and break the tentative reconnection.

"See you then." He smiled and gave me a little wave.

"Yeah. See you." I lifted my fingers, too, and watched him return to his workout already in progress, wishing my psychic mojo extended to reading minds.

✳ ✳ ✳

The Sigma Alpha Xi house was in the colonial revival style, popular when the university and its nearby neighborhoods were built in the late nineteenth, early-twentieth century. The lawn sloped down from the house and the rushee herd ranged there when Jenna and I arrived; the Rho Gamma climbed the steps to the columned portico, where she rapped on the door. Holly and Tricia waited for me at the back of the group, near the sidewalk. Night had fallen in earnest, but didn't hide their avidly curious faces.

"*Who* was that?" Holly asked.

"A friend." At her disbelieving look, I sighed and tucked a lock of hair behind my ear. "It's complicated."

She made an "I'm waiting" gesture. Tricia helpfully added, "I want to know, too. He's adorable."

Holly turned to her, her brows climbing. "Adorable does

not begin to describe a guy with thighs like that." Then, swiveling her attention back to me: "So what gives?"

I looked toward the house, hoping for a reprieve. No dice. "We went out in the spring, a couple of times." An oversimplification, but—taking all the world-saving and monster-hunting out of it—true enough. "Then he went to Ireland for a three-month internship."

"So what's so complicated?" Holly asked. "He's back and obviously happy to see you—" Tricia snickered and Holly smacked her arm. "Not like that, pervert."

I shrugged, looked away, needlessly smoothed my hair again. "We e-mailed over the summer. Great, chatty letters about nothing and everything."

"That's so sweet." Tricia grinned. "Kind of like *You've Got Mail.*"

"Yeah. Only in reverse, because his letters started getting shorter, less personal, slower." I lifted my hands helplessly. "It sounds lame, I guess. Hard to explain."

They nodded, synchronized head bobs of sympathy. Holly summed it up nicely. "So now you have no idea where you stand."

"He probably got really busy with his internship." Tricia, clearly the eternal optimist. "You'll see."

"Maybe." I studied the toes of my shoes, flecked with grass and bits of pine needle. There was no point in pretending that my heart wasn't hanging in the balance; at least after meeting up tonight, I would—

Then the door to the sorority house opened, spilling light into the dusky shadows and bringing me back to the task at hand.

*   *   *

The Sigma Alpha Xi chapter room was nothing short of elegant. Hardwood floors shone beneath an oriental rug, and dark blue and deep red echoed through the décor. No one thing screamed money; it was the way everything fit together. If the Zetas had been intrinsically cool, then the Sigmas were fundamentally classy.

I had the dance down by now. The doors open and we rushees enter like cattle into a chute. One of the sorority members steps forward in a well-orchestrated move, takes a girl by the elbow, and leads her to a designated area of the room. It took me a few rounds to catch on to the architecture of the "random" party groupings and the carefully choreographed mingling.

The smiling girl who met me this time managed to make it look natural. "Hey!" she said, guiding me to an empty spot in the crowded sitting area. Like all the other SAXis, she wore a khaki skirt and a button-down blue oxford, very preppy but cute. She had short blond hair that flipped up at the ends, and freckles danced over her nose.

"I'm Devon. And you're . . ." She read my name tag and laughed. "Yeah. You'd think that we could come up with better questions than that. But your brain goes kind of numb after a while."

Her candor connected with me, and I found my cynicism—not slipping, exactly, but bending enough to concede, "I can totally see where that would happen."

Her nose crinkled with her grin. "Right. Now I'm left with nothing to ask but if you're enjoying Rush."

"Don't you mean Formal Recruitment?" I replied.

"Right. And are you?"

I hedged my answer. "It's been very interesting."

Another laugh. "How tactful of you."

"How do you stand it?" I looked around the room at the blue and khaki members, the rushees in their sundresses and sandals. "Smiling and asking dumb questions all night?"

"Wait until tomorrow. It's Skit Night."

"Oh God." The groan slipped out before I could catch it. I hadn't meant to be that honest. This Devon was either genuinely disarming or very sneaky.

"*We* all had to go through it," she said. "Think of it as a rite of passage."

I could be sneaky, too, I guess. "What do you remember most from your Rush experience?"

She smiled. "The friends I made. How overwhelming everything seemed, when you go through that door and girls are swooping down at you. Those dumb songs all the houses sing."

"Is it easier on the other side? Except for the lame songs, I mean."

"It can be stressful at some places. This is serious business. Most houses have to make a quota."

"The SAXis don't?"

"We keep a smaller membership. We're very selective, so our pressure is on finding the right girls, not just the right number."

I must have looked surprised at her frankness because Devon laughed again. "It's not money or class or GPA. It's not easy to define at all. Our members just know when a girl is right, usually early on. And usually our pledges know when SAXi is right for them."

Something about the way she said that: "just know." How many times had I described my intuition that way? I *just knew* things.

"Did you 'just know' that SAXi was for you?"

I expected a flippant, canned answer. Instead she gazed at me for a moment, an odd sort of half smile on her lips. "Yeah." Her tone was uninterpretable. "SAXi sort of chooses us, Maggie. You'll know, too."

I couldn't tell if she meant that as a good thing.

"Hi, Devon." A new girl joined us—a young woman, really, with maturity and an air of command. "Are you going to introduce me to your friend? You've been speaking together for almost ten minutes."

Devon's freckles disappeared into her flush, confirming that the reprimand hadn't been my imagination. I wondered if it was really the ten-minute monopoly, or if the other girl could read the exchange of information from across the room.

"Of course," she said. "Maggie, this is Kirby, our chapter president. Kirby, this is Maggie. She's an English major, and lives at home."

I glanced at her, expecting a smile or a wink, some hint at the shared joke. But with a smile that didn't reach her eyes, Devon took her leave, moving on in the rotation.

"How are you enjoying Rush?" Kirby asked.

"Well enough, thank you." I caught myself speaking to her like an authority figure, which was crazy and disturbing. She wasn't *my* president. "I was enjoying talking to Devon," I said pointedly.

As a member came by with a silver tray full of glasses of lemonade, she snagged one and offered it with a napkin. "Have a drink?"

I eyed the beverage as if the decorative twist of lemon might jump out and bite me. "This is my fourth party of the night. My back teeth are already singing 'Anchors Aweigh.' "

She smiled. "It's a little party trick. Gives you something to do with your hands."

"In that case." I took the glass, mostly to get her to leave me alone about it. No wonder Devon had scuttled obediently on her way.

"Now that we've been through the niceties . . ." Kirby gestured toward the wooden folding chairs set artfully around a cleared space. "Maybe you'd like to take a seat. We're about to have a short presentation on our philanthropy."

"How thrilling." If President Kirby noticed my irony, she didn't let it show. Hers was the gently imperturbable smile of a political hostess.

I slouched into a spot next to Holly. The space contained a piano and a Chinese screen, behind which I could just detect movement. "Please God, don't let it be a skit."

Holly glanced at me, saw the drink in my hand, and lifted her own. "I thought you said you were already sloshing on the way over here."

Raising a toast, I clinked our glasses. "Why are we here, if not to drink the Kool-Aid."

"Cheers, then," she said.

"Sláinte," I answered, and we drank.

A cherub-faced girl came out from behind the screen,

34

and I groaned softly. Worse than a skit—a skit by precocious children. She went to the piano. A lanky boy emerged, and to my surprise and bemusement, slipped the strap of an electric guitar over his head. A couple of SAXis moved the screen aside to reveal, along with the amp for the guitar, a small drum set with a pigtailed preteen seated behind it, sticks in her hands and a smile on her face.

A woman—older than us, but not elderly by any measure—walked to a small podium. She wore a smart, charcoal gray pantsuit, a silk scarf at the collar. Her strawberry blond hair was neatly coiffed and her smile warmly practiced.

"Good evening," she said. "I'm Victoria Abbott, one of the chapter advisers."

"She says that like it's supposed to mean something," Holly whispered in my ear.

"She's the wife of our congressman," I hissed back. Holly wouldn't know since she wasn't from here. "Nice suit."

"Well, yeah. It's Armani."

I processed this—the distinction of a three-thousand-dollar suit, and the fact that Holly recognized one. Casting my eye over her, I paid closer attention to the excellent cut of the black and white dress she was wearing.

"I'd like to briefly tell you about the Roll Over Beethoven Foundation—Sigma Alpha Xi's chosen philanthropy, not least because it was started by SAXi alum Susie Braddock."

An awed ripple moved through the group. Even a loser like me had heard that name. Ms. Abbott continued. "The Roll Over Beethoven Foundation promotes music education in schools, and funds free after-school music programs. But why don't I let the program speak for itself."

I tensed as the kids began to play. The opening bars were instantly identifiable. They were covering one of my favorite songs by—I kid you not—the Talking Heads. And they did not suck.

If I *was* looking for a sorority, for sisterhood or networking, or for mixers with the frat boys across the way, I would have totally taken it as a sign.

# 4

I arrived at Froth and Java for the second time in the same day, which was actually not that unusual for me. What had me a little off balance was a message from Cole Bauer that had been waiting on my cell phone, asking me to call him. I did, but ended up leaving him a voicemail in return. So much had changed since that morning, and I felt slightly disconnected as I smoothed my windblown hair and checked my reflection in the front window of the coffee shop, wondering if I should put on lip gloss.

Justin was already inside, staking out a pair of deep chairs good for conversation. He stood when he saw me, and we did another one of those unsure dances of greeting. Finally he took my shoulders, leaned down, and kissed my cheek. And I blushed. I could feel it spread over my skin, from the top of my dress to the roots of my hair.

"Hey," I said, brilliantly.

He stepped back and grinned as he looked at me. I still wore my sundress, though I'd taken off the despised name tag. He'd showered and changed into jeans and a green and white rugby shirt. Close up, I could smell him, clean and sort of spicy, beneath the overwhelming scent of coffee. While there might be some uncertainty to our relationship, there was no ambiguity about the way I felt when I was near him.

"You look great, Maggie."

A short lock of hair fell against the heat of my cheek, and I brushed it back. "Thanks. I've been working out."

Justin laughed, because he knew how ridiculous that was. He gestured to the chair perpendicular to his and I sat, setting my cell phone and car keys beside his on the side table.

"So, what's this about going undercover?"

"With the Future Stepfords of America, you mean?" The chair was too soft and deep. I had to balance on the edge to keep from sinking into it like quicksand. "Newspaper story."

"So how is it?"

"Interesting." I solved the quicksand problem by tucking my legs up under me and leaning on the poufy upholstered arm. "It's more of a social commentary sort of thing than hard-hitting investigative journalism."

"So nothing . . ." He gestured vaguely. "Weird?"

"Sorority girls from Hell, you mean?" I laughed. "That's so seventies B movie."

His smile turned rueful. "It does sound cliché when you put it that way. How's your mom?"

"Aside from the morning pukeathon, she's doing great."

"And your gran?"

"Good." I anticipated his next question. "And Dad, too."

He smiled that crooked smile. "And Lisa?"

"Fine, I guess. She left for Georgetown last week."

"Is she still . . . ?" He faltered, maybe because of the busy coffee shop, maybe because of the baggage it brought up.

"Studying the dark arts?" I tried to hit a droll tone, but missed the mark and landed closer to sour and dejected. "It should make her fit in well in Washington, D.C., I guess. If I wasn't worried about her moral compass before, living that close to the Capitol would do it."

"I don't know." Justin had better aim, and he struck the perfect note of comforting humor. "Georgetown University is affiliated with the Jesuits. Maybe it will be good for her."

That made me smile. Not because of any renewed hope for Lisa's ethical education, but because Justin was such a font of eccentric information.

I left the uncomfortable subject of Lisa for a happier one. "Was the internship everything you'd hoped it would be?"

"It was great." His face lit with warmth for his subject. "Hearing their folktales in Gaelic, looking into the weatherbeaten faces of those living so close to the land and the legends, and seeing the belief that's woven into the tales. And the pictures we took of the haunts of the fair folk and the giants . . . I have enough for a whole book, let alone a thesis."

"That's fantastic." I had to grin; his enthusiasm was contagious. Justin's graduate studies were in anthropology, specifically the folklore of magic and the occult. Or as I called it when we met, an advanced degree in "Do You Want Fries with That." Dad said Justin was hard to classify academically, but they let him hang out with the history folks anyway.

"After what happened this spring," I ventured, curious, "how will you write about all this in a scholarly paper? Don't you question everything now, wonder what's myth and what's real?"

He fiddled with his cell phone on the table. "I still have to record it empirically as folklore and fairy tales. We don't know which is which, do we?"

I paused, a little surprised at that noncommittal answer from Justin, the true believer. And there was that ambiguous "we." I knew he wasn't talking about me. I had the theoretical advantage of my Spidey Sense to tell me when the boogeyman was real. "No. I guess not."

He rose to his feet, dusted his hands on his jeans. "Can I get you something to drink? Vanilla latte, extra shot, right?"

"Yeah." I smiled, feeling a melty warmth inside at the fact that he remembered.

Our friendship had been a brief, intense proving ground, but romance-wise, he'd left before we'd gone out more than twice. We'd kissed—which was a little like saying Mount St. Helens had exploded once. But I suppose I could understand the "just friends" uncertainty of our relationship when he boarded that plane, and why we were starting over now.

I even understood if he'd gotten too busy, too involved with his work to e-mail me the way he did at first. Three months was a long time. He was across the ocean, building his career, and . . .

His phone rang. I glanced toward the counter, where Justin waited for the drinks. Clearly he couldn't hear his ringtone over the chatter and music. I swam out of the chair and picked up the phone, intending to flag him.

It was playing that Irish song, the one they use in every movie with a bar fight or a leprechaun. Everyone knows it's the Irish song, and Justin's phone was playing it and flashing the name *Deirdre* on the caller ID.

A vision popped in my brain—in the space of a held breath, a series of images flickered in front of my mind's eye like those old film reels where you see the blink between frames: A black-haired, green-eyed, creamy-complexioned woman trekking through a boggy field, sitting with Justin over a couple of pints in a pub with a smoky peat fire. The two of them, heads together in intimate conversation, him inclining to say something, her leaning forward to meet him and . . .

The phone clattered to the floor, falling from my nerveless fingers. Maybe I broke it, but I couldn't care. Head whirling, I tried to bring the room back into focus. My heart slammed against my ribs. What the hell had just happened?

"Maggie?" Justin had returned, drinks in hand.

"I dropped your phone." My own voice sounded flat and cold. I stared stupidly at the phone on the floor, not about to touch it again. Something was *wrong* with me.

He set down the drinks. "Are you all right? You look sick."

I *felt* sick. I was seeing things while I was awake. My freakitude had just reached a whole new level.

"Deirdre called." The words blurted out, the way the images had blurted into my brain. "I wasn't spying on you."

"What?" He blinked in confusion, brow knit in concern. "Spying? Of course not."

"I just picked it up and . . ."

"And what, Maggie?" Bending slightly, he searched my face, trying to trap my gaze. "What happened?"

But I couldn't tell him. Too many emotions had seized my brain and nailed my tongue to the roof of my mouth. I couldn't make my lips form the questions that would clear everything up. Who was Deirdre? Was she why you stopped writing? All valid questions, but I couldn't get past the part where, oh my God, I was even more of a freak than I thought.

"I need to go." I grabbed my keys from the table and he snatched them neatly from my shaking fingers.

"Maggie, what the hell is wrong with you?"

I pressed my hands to my pounding head. "I have a headache all of a sudden."

"Then let me drive you. You look awful."

"No." My latte, all three shots of it, stood on the table. I grabbed it, took a scalding drink, gasped, but felt better. The burn, like a slap in the face, calmed my hysteria. One more deep breath and I squared my shoulders. "I'm fine."

"You are *not* fine." His voice had a taut edge, from trying to keep it below the general hum of conversation and the music playing in the background.

"All right. I'm not fine." Another sip of espresso and I could lift my eyes to his and hold out a steady hand. "But I can drive. Give me my keys."

His gaze searched mine, and I wondered what he saw

there. I had no clue to his thoughts, though his confusion and worry were clear. Finally he relented. "Will you call me when you get home so I know you made it okay?"

"Fine." Anything to get him to give me the keys. He hesitated a moment longer, then dropped them into my palm. I didn't wait, but fled the coffee shop like the coward I was.

# 5

Parked in my own driveway, I called Justin and told him succinctly that I was safe at home, answering his concern. Yes, I was all right. I'd just had a long, stressful day, and my psyche was wrung out like a dishrag.

By the time I'd driven home, the warm September wind whipping through the open Jeep and clearing my head, the panic had abated, and these didn't even feel like lies. My *ESP for Dummies* book had said emotional state can affect your Sight. Of course, it talked about blocking reception, not suddenly getting an imaginary slide show, but still.

I'd justified away my intuition for almost eighteen years. I have a talent for denial that puts even my mother to shame.

When I went inside, the living room was dark, but there was light from both my parents' bedroom and Dad's study. I called a greeting, got goodnights in return, and climbed the stairs to what we jokingly call my suite. There's a study area on one side, and French doors, which I almost never close, mark the bedroom.

My phone rang as I was dropping my satchel by my desk; warily, I dug it out of my pocket. The caller ID flashed a number with the university's prefix, and I flipped open the phone and tried to inject some perky into my "Hi. This is Maggie."

"Hi, Maggie. This is Cole Bauer."

"Hi, Cole." I sat on the edge of the desk chair. "Sorry about the phone tag."

"It's all right, as long as you're working on round two."

The words went in, but my spent neurons failed to process them. "What?"

"I want a report for each round. We'll carry it through the week, with a blacked-out photo. You don't mind a pseudonym, do you? You need to preserve your anonymity."

Slowly, my brain translated. "I guess you liked the piece?"

"The way the Greeks dominate this campus, they deserve to be skewered a bit. Plus, it'll sell papers. Well, the *Report* is free, but you know what I mean."

"Yeah." Beyond my agreement, comment was unnecessary. With contagious excitement, Cole outlined a scheme of James Bond complexity for keeping my identity a secret.

"So what's my code name?" I asked, when he gave me the chance. "Can I be Secret Squirrel?"

I'd been joking, but he answered, "Morocco Mole would be more appropriate."

"But too obvious." I used the same serious tone. We agreed on the details of the rest of the week, and said good-bye.

I hung up the phone, numb and fatigued, as if the ping-pong bounce of my emotions all day had burnt out my circuits. But I wasn't quite done yet. As I dug in my dresser for a pair of pajamas, the cell rang again.

I flipped it open without checking the caller ID. "Hello?"

"Maggie?" Lisa. I must have at least one emotional circuit left, because my throat closed up at hearing her voice precisely when I needed her.

"Hey," I managed.

"What's wrong?" Her tone, always brusque, was tinged tonight with concern. "You sound weird."

I flung myself onto the ancient love seat in the corner of my study. "I've had a very weird day."

"Uh-huh." She didn't sound particularly surprised.

"How did you know?" I asked, unable to keep the wariness from my voice.

"I looked in my crystal ball, what do you think?"

That was the thing with Lisa. She joked about things like taking over the world or raising an army of zombie minions to do her bidding. Things that, in retrospect of the last year, weren't funny at all.

"Seriously, Lisa. You didn't do a spell or something, did you? Because you know I'm ethically opposed . . ."

"Look, I didn't call for a lecture, all right?"

Silence, while I weighed how much I desperately wanted to talk to her versus my conviction that her dabbling in—jeez, "sorcery" sounded so melodramatic. Let's say, my fear that her arcane studies would do nothing to obliterate the enormous blot already on her karmic account book.

Lisa broke the silence first. "I just called to chat. I didn't know you were upset until I heard your voice."

"Oh."

"I'm an evil genius, Maggie Quinn. I can add two and two without the benefit of a magic wand."

I sighed and slumped deeper into the cushions. "You're not evil, Lisa. Just . . . goal oriented."

She gave a bitter laugh, and redirected the conversation. "So what's up?"

"First I had a piece rejected by the city paper and my journalism professor is kind of a dick. Then the editor of the school paper liked my story, but it means I have to keep going through this Rush business, which is wearing on my nerves. And I finally saw Justin, but I think he might have an Irish girlfriend."

"Did you *ask* him if he had an Irish girlfriend?"

"No."

"Maggie, you idiot." She'd said that so many times over the years, I could picture the roll of her eyes, the shake of her head. "You know those books, where the only thing keeping the moronic heroine apart from the hero is the fact that they don't talk to each other? How you always want to smack the girl?"

I knew exactly what she meant, but I had new sympathy for those morons. "You don't even like Justin."

"That's not the point. You do."

"And then there's the *way* I found out." Time to turn the subject from what an idiot I was. "I had a vision."

"Like one of your dreams?"

"No. Well, sort of, but different, on fast forward or something. And awake." I explained picking up Justin's phone, and the psychic slide show. "Images and impressions, really fast. It was weird." And scary, but I didn't tell her that.

She paused, and like a lot of Lisa's pauses, it was uninterpretable. "This is a new thing?"

"Yeah. Maybe it was a fluke."

"Maybe some jealous Irish witch zapped you through the phone."

"Gee, I'm *so* glad you called to cheer me up, Lisa."

"Don't mention it." I heard a squeak, like bedsprings or a chair, the sound of settling in. "How are classes?"

"All right so far. Mostly jaunting back and forth across campus, collecting syllabuses. Syllabi? How about you?"

"Georgetown is pretty cool, but expensive. Good thing I didn't blow through my savings account after I got the scholarship. I'll need it to keep me in Diet Coke and eye of newt."

"Oh, really," I said, in the same matter-of-fact tone. "Do they have one-stop occult shopping over there?"

"No, but you wouldn't believe what you can get on the Internet."

"Don't scare me more than I already am." I meant it as a joke, but it fell flat, the way things do when they're too true.

A pause. I pictured her in a dorm room, a cramped, drab place transformed with posters and throw pillows and thrift store finds. She'd be sitting cross-legged, her chestnut hair falling around her elegant face. The only thing I couldn't imagine was her expression. Regretful? Wistful? Stubborn?

All three laced her voice when she finally spoke. "I wish you'd understand. Studying this stuff . . . it's something I have to do."

"Why?" I challenged her, not for the first time. "Because

it's there, like Mount Everest? An intellectual challenge you can't resist?"

"It isn't just idle curiosity."

"Oh, well, that's a relief. I'd hate to think you were jeopardizing your soul to satisfy a mental itch."

"Jeez, Mags. You make it sound like I'm sacrificing kittens or something. I'm making a scientific and theoretical study of occult folklore. It's not any different from what Justin is doing."

"Justin is studying brownies and green men. You're practicing spells and potions."

"Your point?" She was 100% stubborn now.

I pressed my hand over my eyes. "It's harnessing a power that isn't your own and making things *happen*. It's exactly what got us into so much trouble this spring."

"Maggie, there are things out there. Real things. Scary things."

"Things we shouldn't be messing with!" I said.

"Don't you think it's better to understand them? How the supernatural works and how to fight it?"

"No." I was adamant, but *ESP for Dummies* mocked me from the floor by the couch. "I think we were lucky the last time, and we should leave that stuff alone."

"Says the girl with the Psychic Friends Network in her head."

"*I* can't help it." Which seemed truer by the day. "*You* have a choice."

"No." Her voice was taut with sadness. "No, I really don't."

I wanted desperately to understand why she thought that, when this path could only be dangerous for her, when she knew what awful bloody things that kind of power could lead to.

"We always have choices, Lisa."

"That's what this boils down to, isn't it? You don't trust me."

Now it was my turn to pause, condemning her with my reluctance to answer.

"Right." She charged on when the silence stretched too long. "Well, you have no reason to, I guess. Except maybe that we've been friends since the seventh grade."

"I trust your *intentions,* Lisa, but—"

She cut me off. "But we all know where those lead. I'm sure Azmael is keeping my seat warm for me."

"That is not funny." I felt sick, furious at her, terrified for her, and completely freaked by her saying the demon's name aloud. "Do *not* joke about that."

"Evil genius sorcerers never joke about Hell, Maggie." Self-loathing clipped her words. "Later."

She hung up. I called her back immediately, but she didn't answer, had turned the phone off or simply ignored it. For all I knew, she'd blown it up with her magic wand.

Nothing had been the same between Lisa and me after that night at the prom. Though arguably, neither of us was the same person that we were going in. Facing demons will do that to you. We emerged intrinsically bound by the experience, but in a way, strangers to each other.

We'd tried to ignore it. But then I'd dreamed about her on Midsummer Night. I'd seen her in a circle of girls I didn't know, some kind of New Agey ceremony that seemed innocuous. I got a feeling of renewing energy, something like the smell of green spring grass or the heavy, lush scent of ripe berries. No alarm there. But from my mental perspective I could see Lisa's face, could sense her whip-smart intellect crackling behind a carefully neutral expression. And I knew that was trouble.

Our confrontation afterward was pretty well recapped in tonight's argument. I told her what I thought about her playing with fire; she insisted I didn't understand what she was trying to do. I thought I understood very well. Lisa was trying to control the uncontrollable.

I picked up the ESP book and it fell open automatically to the pages of exercises, worn and gray on the edges, the spine creased where I'd held the book open while I practiced meditations for clarity, protection, and strength. Hokey, yes. I'd felt ridiculous sitting cross-legged and still on the floor. But I did them anyway, all summer long. Clearly, I was no stranger to the need for control.

✳ ✳ ✳

Eventually, I made it to my desk chair and contemplated the blank screen of my laptop. I needed to get my Rush thoughts down while they were still fresh, but my brain churned restlessly. Opening my playlist, I looked for something soothing.

Nothing in the library appeased my frayed nerves. Barenaked Ladies—too flippant. Kelly—too power pop. Joss—too blond. Fiona, Sheryl, Sarah—all too Lilith Fair. Where was the "you've pissed off all your friends and now you're all alone" music?

Susie Braddock's name leapt out at me. I'd forgotten I had one of her songs.

In a new browser window I typed her name into Google. The search engine helpfully supplied the first ten of a gazillion entries. I clicked on the official fan page of the Grammy-winning artist, free-associated through Susie Braddock's bio, then on to the Roll Over Beethoven Foundation, and other notable SAXis. Finally I felt calm enough to do some work on my newspaper assignment and started closing windows.

The bottom page was a pop-up window; a lousy ad, though, because I couldn't tell what it was selling. It consisted of an animated GIF that took up the entire window, some kind of diagram, like a black and white test pattern made up of circles and linking lines. They pulsed slightly as I stared, so subtly that I couldn't tell if the motion came from the symbols or an optical illusion.

I went to click on the window, to make it active. But as soon as I touched the trackpad, the whole image disappeared, and a new box appeared to tell me that MS Extorter had unexpectedly quit.

Crap. The only thing I hate more than pop-up ads are ones that crash my browser. One Java applet too many, I guess, telling me how I could get bigger boobs, which I might be interested in, or see nude girls on ice, which I definitely was not.

# 6

My article appeared below the fold on the front page of Tuesday's *Ranger Report.* The Greeks were aghast, the rushees were titillated, and the Rho Gammas were on the warpath.

This was *so* much better than buried with the obituaries (no pun intended) in the "real" paper.

"Who do you think it is?"

My ears perked up while I stood at the Starbucks kiosk in the student union, watching like a vulture as the barista steamed the milk for my latte. Somehow I'd made it through my eight o'clock class on only one cup of coffee, but now I needed a high-octane infusion ASAP.

A second girl answered the first. "I think it's that skinny

girl from Sutter Hall. You know, the one with the Lisa Loeb glasses. She looks like that snobby intellectual type."

"She can't *look* like the type. That would defeat the purpose of being incognito."

"Is that what you're wearing?"

Since I'd been shamelessly eavesdropping, it took a moment to realize the question was directed at me. Turning, I saw Hillary with her hands on her hips, the *RG* on her chest standing out like a blazon. It's a bird, it's a plane, it's . . . Rho Gamma Girl.

I pointed to my new name tag. "Look. No graffiti."

Her blond ponytail whipped back and forth as she shook her head. "You look like you just rolled out of bed."

As a matter of fact, I *had* just rolled out of bed and into a clean pair of jeans, a T-shirt, and a worn Bedivere U. hoodie, then on to my eight o'clock calculus lecture. There had to be something unhealthy about math that early in the morning.

"Sorry. I guess I should have dressed up for class. Like that." I pointed to a pair of Kappa Phis walking by wearing the exact same thing I was, except their hoodies said ΚΦ and they had standard Greek-issue ponytails instead of unruly dark brown bobs.

Hillary huffed in annoyance, then waved the subject aside, back to serious Panhellenic business. "Forget it. I'm asking everyone"—she addressed the girls at the table, too, unfurling the newspaper that had been rolled up in her hand—"if you have any idea who this is."

No question who she meant, but in the interest of clarity she pointed to the anonymous silhouette beside the byline—not Secret Squirrel, to my great disappointment, but the Phantom Rushee.

"We were just discussing that," said one of the gossiping girls. They all had name tags pinned to their T-shirts. The speaker was Lindsey. "Brianna thinks she knows someone."

Brianna didn't look happy to be put on the spot. "I said I knew someone who looked like the *type.*"

"And I still say she won't be a *type,*" argued a third girl.

"There's no way she can completely hide it," volleyed Brianna. "Surely it will show."

"What will show?" I asked, figuring it would be suspicious to remain silent.

"That she's not one of us, of course."

Maybe that was the purpose of the ubiquitous ponytail—to show there were no sixes on the back of any necks.

Hillary saved me from saying this aloud and wasting good material for my next article. "Since you girls know each other best, Panhellenic is asking for your help. Just keep your ears open, and if you have any ideas who this Phantom Rushee might be, you'll tell one of the Rho Gammas."

The rushees nodded, and I did, too, projecting innocence and cooperation as hard as I could. Maybe a little too hard, since Hillary's glance lingered on me, a little too long and a little too narrow-eyed. Possibly she suspected me, possibly just disliked me, but clearly I'd better tone down the smart-ass a bit if I wanted to avoid the scrutiny of the Panhellenic Council, which was starting to scare me just by reputation.

"Where are you going tonight?" she asked me, meaning, of course, which houses had invited me back.

"The same as last night." Meaning all of them had, since I'd been on my best behavior. The only one that surprised me was the Sigma Alpha Xis, since the girl there—Devon—had said outright that they were fairly exclusive. But maybe she'd put in a good word for me.

"Don't be late this time," Hillary chided. "Recruitment is serious business, and the houses need to know if you are committed."

I nodded obediently, and she left to continue her witch hunt. No falsehood there. I certainly agreed that we should all be committed.

✳  ✳  ✳

My favorite class was History of Civilization (Part I). An honors class, it was engaging, participatory, and challenging. Also, my dad taught it, and it was the first time I'd seen him in days, even though we lived in the same house.

"Hey, Magpie." He greeted me as I came down the steps to the front of the lecture hall.

"Hi, Dad."

A copy of the *Ranger Report* lay on the podium, and he tapped the anonymous picture. "I don't suppose you know who this prankster is, do you?"

"Not a clue," I said, perusing the page.

"Too bad." There was a mischievous twinkle in his eye. "I think she's rather droll."

"I think she's rather frivolous. There are serious issues in the Greek system, and she's cracking jokes."

"Can't please everyone, I guess." Zipping his computer case, he gathered his binder of lecture notes. "Are we going to see you for dinner tonight?"

"Can't. Third-round parties." I smiled too brightly. "It's Skit Night! Oh boy!"

Dad's mouth set in an unhappy line. I'd overheard a

couple of girls saying he was good-looking in a Robert Redford kind of way. I bet they wouldn't say that if they'd ever gotten the Frown of Paternal Disapproval. The one I was getting now.

"Every year I see these girls burning themselves to a cinder before the semester is half done, trying to keep up with their classwork and this sorority business. That's not going to be you, is it?"

"Come on, Dad. You know me."

"Exactly." He glanced over my shoulder, directing a question to someone near the door. "Did you need me?"

"No, sir." Justin's voice. "I wanted to talk to Maggie a sec."

"Sure thing," said Dad, deserting me with a cheery wave.

I thought about just following my father out, and my expression must have shown it. Justin raised his hands as if to show he was unarmed. "I only wanted to make sure you're okay."

"I think so." I'd justified and compartmentalized the weirdness. My distrust and confusion, however, was unresolved.

He closed the distance so that he could lower his voice. Out in the hall a river of students went by, no strangeness in their lives. "You want to tell me what happened?"

My lips pursed as I considered it. Really, how does one say: I had some kind of psychic power spike and saw what looked an awful lot like some girl making a pass at you.

"Who's Deirdre?" I said it like that, a non sequitur bomb.

His brow knit in confusion. "How did you know her name?"

"I'm Psychic Girl, remember?" The most I was going

to admit until I knew he was still on my side. "Also, the caller ID."

"Oh." He smiled sheepishly, laughing at himself. "She was one of the other interns on the oral history project. We—all of us—worked pretty closely and got to be friends."

"Uh-huh."

He held up a hand. His eyes, warm and brown and without guile, met mine. "Honestly, Maggie."

Here's the thing about people like Justin, people that Lisa—in D&D parlance—called "lawful good." They can't lie worth a damn, and when they try, it shows, even to normal folks, not just weirdos like me.

The truth of his statement resonated. The deepest part of me knew that if he had something going on with another girl, his honor would require him to tell me about it. And I guess if I hadn't been so insecure, the shallow part of me would have realized it, too.

"Okay." My gaze wandered over the empty lecture hall and I wished we were having this conversation someplace that felt less like being onstage. "I'm sorry I freaked out the other night. I wasn't really jealous." He didn't speak, but gave me an even look that forced me to admit, "Well, not *just* jealous. It's complicated."

"Then tell me," he said, reasonably.

My eyes went to the ceiling, as if maybe my feelings would be outlined there, and I could manage to articulate them. "I just wish I knew what to think. About us. I mean, I don't know if I'm . . . If we're . . . I mean, obviously not yet, but could we be . . . ? Do not laugh at me."

"I'm not laughing." And he wasn't. He reached out and caught my hand, met my eye. "I really like you, Maggie."

Oh God, here it comes.

"But—"

I groaned, loudly, and tried to pull my hand away.

"Would you just listen?" He held fast to my fingers while I looked anywhere but at him. "I'm working so hard right now. My whole focus is getting this degree, and I've got this teaching assistant job, and the thesis, which may turn into a dissertation. I'm not going to have a life outside of school for a while."

Great. My first boyfriend was breaking up with me before he'd ever really been my boyfriend. With an audience of 150 empty seats to witness my "it's not you, it's me" humiliation.

"I know your studies are important to you," I said.

"Not just to me." He dropped his voice. "Occult folklore needs serious study and documentation by someone who understands and . . ."

"Believes in it, I know." I made his argument for him. "Preaching to the choir here, Justin. Been there, vanquished that. Trust me, I am *very* sympathetic to the time you spend doing research."

Pulling my trick, he lifted his gaze to the ceiling, looking for answers. I wondered if he even realized he was still holding my hand. "But you're also a freshman," he said, "and you should be doing all those freshman things."

"You are *not* going to turn this into a conversation about you knowing better than me what I want."

He sighed—resigned, determined—looking me in the eye as he dashed my hopes. "No. I'm telling you what I want, which is to concentrate on work without feeling like I'm taking you for granted. I want to be your friend right now."

If only he was lying, had suddenly discovered a talent for it. But he wasn't. His feelings might not be as simple as friendship, but he wasn't lying about his wishes.

"Okay," I said.

"Okay?" Finally, he let my fingers slip from his, and my skin felt colder. *I* felt colder. "What does that mean?"

"It means I like you. A lot." Gathering my books from the lecturer's table, I clutched them tightly to hide the shaking of my hands. "And I need you when things go wonky in my life. I would rather be your friend than lose you completely, so if those are my options, then fine, okay, we can be just friends."

I didn't force a smile, didn't even say good-bye. I left without meeting his eye again, but I felt his gaze follow me out of the hall. The whole thing would have been a lot easier if he'd been a jerk, or if the romantic cliché was his way of letting me down easy. But it wasn't, and I was going to have to wrap my heart around the reality of right guy, bad timing.

# 7

"If I ruled the world," I told Holly and Tricia as we walked between houses that evening, "I would ban all skits."

"I like the skits," Tricia said. Of course she would.

"You like everything." I looked up at the stars as we walked. "The skits, the stupid songs, the watery lemonade . . ."

The night was warm and still. Was it my imagination, or were even the heavens full of Greek letters? Lately I saw them everywhere—campus and store windows, and still in my dreams.

Holly walked backward, facing us, hands tucked in the pockets of her corduroy blazer. "You know, Maggie, someone *might* think you weren't having a wonderful time."

"Did *you* enjoy watching 'Mary Potter and the Half-Greek Princess' as performed by the Adam Sandler School of Dramatic Arts?"

"Well, no," she admitted. "But all of Rush is kind of hokey, you know."

"I know now." I kept more laughter in my voice than cynicism. We'd formed a kind of foxhole camaraderie, especially Holly and I, but I still had to remember my camouflage.

"What made you decide to do it?"

I shrugged, sensing nothing behind the question, but hedging anyway. "Same reason as you."

The trees that lined the sidewalk shaded her face from the moonlight, and hid her expression. "I'm going because my mother made me."

"Your mom the Sigma Alpha Xi?" asked Tricia.

"Yep." She turned forward, closing the subject. I sensed—and it didn't really take my crazy Jedi mind tricks—a bit of a raw nerve there.

I waited until Tricia turned off toward the Kappa Phi house, then caught up with Holly, stretching my legs to match her longer stride.

"So what's the deal with the SAXis?" I asked. "I mean, every chapter has a kind of personality. The Kappa Phis take their cute pills every morning, and the Deltas cut me because they think my dad's a janitor. The Theta Nus are the brain trust and the Zetas are the cool club. The EZs are . . . well, you know."

"Right."

"But I can't get a handle on the SAXis. The only thing I've been able to pin down is they've got really great hair."

Holly folded her arms as if she were cold, despite the balmy evening. Her gaze stayed on the sidewalk, on the places where tree roots had pushed up the pavement into treacherous fault-line ridges.

"The SAXis," she said finally, "get what they want."

I wanted to ask her what she meant, but she lengthened her stride, and short of breaking into a run, I couldn't keep up.

✳ ✳ ✳

The Sigma Alpha Xis had transformed their chapter room into a Parisian sidewalk café. Little round tables covered with checked tablecloths—each with a tiny vase of delicate flowers—filled the room, and on the wall was a mural of the Eiffel Tower. A street artist painted at an easel, and a mime wandered through the crowd. Accordion music played softly, and I swear I smelled baking bread. The transformation was so complete that it must have been accomplished with a lot of money, if not by magic.

I admit, the idea occurred to me. But really, if you had the ability to do magic, would you squander it to impress a bunch of college freshmen?

"Welcome back, Maggie." I turned to see the president of Sigma Alpha Xi smiling at me. My brain supplied the name Kirby, which I remembered because it was like Furby, which was amusing only because she looked nothing like a gremlin toy. Except, maybe, that her smile didn't reach her eyes, which were all business. I'd seen that a lot at these parties.

Kirby gestured to the woman with her. "You remember Victoria Abbott, one of our chapter advisers."

"Good evening, Mrs. Abbott." She wore another classy suit tonight, a hunter green that looked amazing with her complexion.

"Please, call me Victoria." She smiled, and it did reach her eyes, just barely crinkling the corners. Her husband was quite young for a U.S. congressman—early forties—so his wife was probably about the same. She must moisturize like crazy, because she looked nowhere near that.

"Impressive, isn't it?"

"Excuse me?" I didn't think she meant her skincare routine or her designer suit.

She gestured to the room. "One of our alums is in graduate school for set design. She helped with the backdrops."

"Very nice," I said inadequately.

"And I believe you met Devon yesterday." A wave of a slim hand indicated the painter with the beret. "She's a fine art major."

"Cool." I was just full of brilliance tonight, but my brain was processing her knowledge of my social activities.

"I understand that you are an artist, too." I looked at her, my expression blank, and she gazed back expectantly. Finally she prompted, "You're a photographer?"

"Oh! Yeah." That was the problem with lying; you had to actually remember what you told people. "I was on the yearbook staff in high school."

Mrs. Abbott nodded. "I saw that on your Rush application. Are you thinking about continuing in photojournalism?"

Ah. Now I understood. She was feeling me out to see if I was the Phantom Rushee. At the other houses there had been a lot of questions about hobbies, but no one else had made the leap from yearbook photog to newspapers.

"I haven't decided yet," I told her, lying with the truth. My guard was up, but it was hard not to *look* as though I'd raised my defenses. "I'd like to take some pictures for the *Report*, see if I like it, but they don't let freshmen on the newspaper staff. My major is English right now."

"Oh? Are you a writer?"

The woman was like a terrier on a rat. My hole was getting deeper and she was digging in behind me. "I love literature. I've thought about being a professor, like my father."

"Ah, yes. Dr. Quinn. He was a TA when my husband was in college here."

I jumped on the opportunity to turn the subject away from me. "Did you meet at Bedivere?"

"Yes. We're both active alumni. Your sorority will be a vital part of your lives during college, and for the Sigmas, it remains so well after graduation. We're a special group."

Her hand touched my sleeve, and I felt a tingle, not on my arm, but in my brain. I stiffened, and I thought about my psychic exercises for dummies, about putting up a shield between us. Whether it worked or not, I wasn't sure, but there was no repeat of last night's voyeur-vision.

"Sigmas form a close bond, Maggie," Victoria continued seamlessly, as if she'd noticed nothing odd in my reaction. "You'll see what I mean, if you decide to join us."

Fortunately, she excused herself to introduce the skit, saving me from the most obvious response to that.

✳ ✳ ✳

" 'Resistance is futile.' " A fraternity guy, slumped in his desk in the back of the classroom, read aloud from the latest Phantom Rushee report while we waited for Dr. Hardcastle to arrive. " 'All will be assimilated. Come into the light, where all have shiny, shiny hair and many, many boy-friends.' " His buddies, all wearing some part of the Greek alphabet, laughed heartily. I wondered if they'd be so amused if the Phantom had been a guy rushing a fraternity.

He continued his recitation: " 'Unfortunately for the Sigma Alpha Xis, my mother always told me that if it looks too good to be true, it probably is.' "

The guy one seat down snatched the paper away. "She ragged on the SAXis? Man. This girl has balls."

Frat Man grabbed his newspaper back. "She's got to rag on them all, dipwad. It's like, equal time in the media or something."

"That's political campaigns, asshole."

Our class, by the way? Media and Communication. This is your brain on testosterone.

"I wonder if she's hot."

"She's probably some militant feminist lesbian."

"Lesbians are hot, dude."

Behold, the future broadcast executives of America.

$$* \quad * \quad *$$

My days had begun to bleed together. The last night of Rush was Preference Night, when the sororities invited only the girls they were prepared to give a bid. There were only two parties, so we—the rushees, I mean—had to narrow the choices, too.

Leaving Hardcastle's class, I'd glimpsed Cole as I passed the journalism lab, but as per our secret agent code, we did not make eye contact or acknowledge each other. I headed to the library to do some work and check my e-mail, and found a message waiting.

**From: cbauer@bedivereu.edu**
**To: mightyquinn@mailbox.net**
**Re: Secret Squirrel Retirement**

> I know we only made plans through Rush
> Week, but are you sure you don't want
> to keep going and pledge? Think of the
> book you could write. Look at this:
> www.newsnet.com/articles/greeksgowild

The link was to a news article about the seedy underbelly of Greek life—drinking, drugs, hazing, promiscuity—and the media blackout on the whole Greek system. How, unless an event got onto the police blotter, no one really knew about day-to-day life on Greek Row. This was what Ethan Douglas at the *Avalon Sentinel* had been talking about when he said my article lacked anything newsworthy.

The thing was, the longer the Phantom's opinions appeared in the *Report,* the greater the chance that I would be discovered. If I actually *pledged* a sorority—

My phone started vibrating across the table. I picked it up and leaned forward into the study carrel to whisper, "Hello?"

"It's Holly. Can you come to my room? We need to do an intervention."

"What?"

"The Deltas cut Tricia."

"I'll be right there." I'd jotted down her dorm and room number and closed my laptop before I realized that I was treating this like a real emergency—which was the other danger of continuing my undercover work. Perspective could be a slippery thing. How easy would it be to lose it?

*   *   *

"I don't understand!" Tricia sobbed as she sat between us on Holly's bed in Sutter Hall. Her hands were full of soggy Kleenex, and her eyes puffy and red. "I did everything right. I studied the house and I got my hair done and I bought new clothes and the right kind of purse."

"You did great," said Holly, rubbing her back in a soothing rhythm. I looked at Tricia's handbag, wondering what was so special. She'd dumped it onto the floor, along with her books, by the room's built-in double desk. "They're idiots. You're beautiful and sweet."

"Much too sweet for the Delta Delta Gammas," I told her.

"I should have dyed my hair." Miserably, she fingered one of her glossy brown curls. "That's what the consultant said, if I wanted to go DDG."

I had to speak up, because even undercover, there was only so long I could keep repressing my opinion. "If you ask me, you should be thanking your lucky stars that you aren't stuck for the next four years with a bunch of skinny clones, making yourself sick and miserable to be someone you're not."

"But what am I going to do?" She lifted her tissue-filled hands helplessly. "How will I get to know people? How will I get anywhere in life? When I called my mom, she said now I'll never find a husband!"

"Oh, for God's sake." My sympathy went a lot farther than my patience. Holly swiftly intervened before I could say something really unfortunate.

"Here." She went to her bureau drawer and brought back an airline-sized bottle of vodka, handing it to Tricia. "Drink this. Then you can lie down for a few minutes, and pull your-self together in time for the parties tonight. Those aren't the only Greeks in the sea."

Tricia made a brave face and unscrewed the cap. "You're right," she said, throwing back her shoulders and then throwing back the liquor, downing all three ounces in two deep swallows.

"Wow," I said.

She gave a coughing wheeze, a relaxed smile on her face. "I feel much better now."

Luckily, we were standing there to catch her when she slid off the bed and into careless oblivion.

✳ ✳ ✳

Holly and I managed to get Tricia back to her own dorm room; the major obstacle, once we got her upright, was to keep her from calling out "Screw the Delta Delta Gammas" to everyone we passed, especially after that one frat boy called back, "Been there, done that."

We put her to bed, made sure she was still breathing—snoring, actually—then grabbed a couple of hamburgers from the cafeteria before heading back to Holly's room in Sutter Hall.

I sat cross-legged on the extra bed, the Styrofoam to-go box in my lap. I'd assumed Holly had a roommate, but it turned out she was just schizophrenic. The decorating scheme was half Posh Spice, half David Beckham—designer sheets on the bed, soccer trophies on the shelf, all wrapped in a subtle scent of Prada perfume mixed with eau de athletic shoe.

"I don't get it," I said around a french fry. "My mom was

in a sorority, but she never made *me* feel like I had to join one to be a success."

"Was *her* mom Greek?"

"No, they were German." Holly rolled her eyes at the feeble joke. "But really. Come on. It's such a cliché, the carbon-copy girls and the MRS degree."

"Where do you think clichés come from?" She flipped her hair over her shoulder and took a bite of burger. For a lanky girl, she could pack away the cals. "You're going to pledge with me, right?"

"What?"

"SAXi." She swallowed her mouthful and looked at me levelly. "You're not going to make me go in alone, are you?"

There was nothing helpless about Holly—competent, confident, down to earth. But something about the way she said that . . . She munched on her burger as if we were discussing a trip to the mall, but something underneath that thrummed with the tension of checked emotion.

"What makes you think they're going to invite me?" I asked, resisting the pull of my crusader instincts.

"Only Sigmas know Sigma criteria." She turned her careful attention to tucking a tomato slice back into her burger. "But I've got a feeling."

I understood about feelings. My thoughts turned to Tricia, who was a little silly but not at all atypical of the girls going through Rush, hanging not just four years of hopes on the outcome of this week, but certain that their foreseeable futures hinged on what letters they pinned on their lapels. Bad enough that the Greeks considered themselves better than the rest of us. Normal, likable people seemed to think so, too. It seemed to me there was a pertinent, immediate need to puncture these pretensions.

"Okay," I said, decisively. "If they give me a bid, I'll pledge."

"I knew it." She grinned and wiped the mustard off her fingers. "We're going to be pledge sisters!"

She stuck out her hand and I clasped it, my guard completely down. Sight and taste and touch exploded like paparazzi flashbulbs in my brain: Holly in a private-school blazer and scratchy plaid skirt; on the soccer field, with no one in the stands to watch her; arguing with an elegant auburn-haired woman; then sneaking drinks in her room, amber in the glass, smooth and smoky on her tongue, the one oasis of color and warmth in her cold marble house.

It lasted the space of one caught breath. This time, my stomach stayed down; only my heart leapt, beat against my breastbone as I tried to get my bearings. Back in the dorm room, dizzy and befuddled.

Holly stared at me strangely. My hand still rested in hers. "Are you all right?"

"Yeah." I had to try again, with more confidence. "Yeah. I'm fine."

Only I wasn't. I was slipping a psychic gear, and no book could help this dummy now.

# 8

Gran took the teapot out of its cozy, poured a cup, and pushed the sugar bowl across the table to me. "Now, drink that and tell me again. Slowly this time."

The tea was almost the color of coffee. I like it strong and sweet when I'm in a panic. The first sip burned the roof of my mouth, but the pain was psychologically grounding.

"I don't know what else to say." The china cup barely rattled as I set it in the saucer. "I've never had vision things like that before. Not all flashy and . . . visiony." There were cookies, too, but even the rich chocolate smell wasn't enough to tempt my stomach out of its knot. "Maybe I've got a tumor."

Gran gave a dismissive snort and stirred her tea, the spoon clinking against china. "You don't have a tumor."

"All I know is that when this started happening to Cordelia on that show *Angel,* she went into a coma and died."

"Honestly, Maggie. Do you get all your psychic instruction from TV and movies?"

"No. I have a book, too."

She set her cup on the table. We were in the breakfast nook of her kitchen, as bright and cheery a place as I knew. Gran's house was all about tea and cookies and comfort. Though not always comfort in the way I envisioned. She had a limited tolerance for self-pity.

Folding her hands in her lap, she asked in a pointedly prim tone, "You consider a Dummies book the exhaustive source?"

I picked up my cup, but it was still too hot to drink. "It isn't like they have classes at the Y, Gran. You said I have to work it out my own way, and I'm trying."

"That's true." She softened, reached to cover my hand with hers. I tensed, waiting for the psychic shock treatment.

I did feel something. Love, which smelled just like Gran's face cream, the one she'd used when I was a kid; security, which tasted like Earl Grey tea.

My eyes sought hers. "Did you do that on purpose?"

"What do you think I did?" she asked, withdrawing her hand, her expression that of a patient teacher.

"Kept your baggage, I guess, from hitting me in the head."

She rose from her chair. "Come to the study."

I followed her through the living room into the second

bedroom, which had been in use as a study for as long as I could remember. When I stayed with Gran as a kid, she would put a soft pallet on the floor, and I would sleep among the books. When I got older, I stuffed my blanket into the crack beneath the door so that the light wouldn't show, and I could read all night.

Today, the blinds were drawn and the lamp that Gran switched on was golden and warm. She went to a corner and ran her fingers over the spines of a hodgepodge of new and old volumes.

"Does your book talk about using imagery to build up defenses?"

"I guess." There was a section about protecting yourself from negative energy. Naturally, I'd been pretty interested in that. "The guy talks about surrounding yourself with a halo of love and pixie dust and unicorns. Like that would last a second against some Hell-spawned demigod."

Gran paused to look over her shoulder, amused. "Well, pixie dust is sufficient for most people. What do *you* imagine?"

I fiddled with an incense burner, collapsing a spent cone of ash and releasing the scent of rosemary into the air. What was Gran trying to remember, I wondered. Maybe my grand-dad. I hadn't even known him, but I got a sense of him in this room, a big, ruddy-cheeked man who loved to sit in the arm-chair with a glass of scotch and a mystery novel.

Maybe this vision thing didn't have to be horrible scary.

Pulling a book from the shelf, Gran faced me, expectantly. What had she asked? What did I imagine when I thought about psychic protection.

"The *Millennium Falcon,*" I said. She laughed immediately, and then again as I explained. "You know when the TIE fighters are swarming in, and Han Solo is telling Chewbacca to raise the deflector shields?"

"Whatever works, I suppose." She laid a book in my hands. It was glossy but well used, a *Practical Guide to Meditation.* "Maybe you can add some of those to your exercises. I used that to"—she debated the right word—"insulate my 'baggage' from you. You could use the same thing to insulate yourself from things you brush up against."

"Thanks, Gran." I flipped through the pages of the book. It had big pictures and examples and step-by-step instructions. I liked it already. "So you don't think this is weird that I've suddenly got a new superpower?"

"No, because I don't think it's new." She straightened a picture, one of me and my parents at Disneyland. "You repressed your Sight for seventeen years. I think now it has to catch up with you. Naturally, you're going to have some growing pains."

She switched off the lamp and I followed her out into the living room. "Why was it so easy for you to accept *your* gift?"

"I suppose because I grew up in the old country." The lilt of her accent deepened when she talked about Ireland. "It was a simpler age. We didn't have a television, and I didn't even learn to drive until I came to America."

"Really?"

"You're very worldly and cynical here, and the need for *proof* blinds people to what may only be taken on faith."

I thought about that while I sat at the kitchen table, where my tea was now cool enough to drink. What she had said was true. My never-was-boyfriend studied the occult and my best friend was a witch. I'd had a demon stalker and lived to tell about it. But my first thought with the visions was that I must be going crazy.

It made me wonder how many things there were in the world that people just dismissed as coincidence or fluke, never realizing the extra layer of weird that overlay our mundanity, like a high-frequency radio station that most people's tuners never reached.

# 9

Rush, I wrote, sitting cross-legged on my bed, wearing my rattiest pajamas and stripped of the makeup and jewelry that Mom had insisted were compulsory for the final round of parties, *is like courting. First round is like speed dating. You rotate at the ding of a silent bell, learning more about someone from their dress and manner than from any rote list of banal questions. (What's your major, for example.)*

*The second round is the movie date. Can you agree on explosions vs. romance? Maybe a thriller for compromise. How will you spend your future time together?*

*Third round: dinner date. Your beau puts on the Ritz, shows off a little, and you learn if he makes an annoying smacking sound when he chews.*

*And finally, Preference Night: meet the parents. Not a proposal just yet, but a test run. A peek into the fold.*

I downed the last swig of my latte. It was stone cold, picked up on my way home from Greek Row, since I knew Cole would be waiting to slip my column into place, just in time to get Friday's edition of the *Report* to the printer. The school paper had a narrow window on the press—in between the *Sentinel* and the direct mail going out to advertise the weekend's sales.

Like my psychic education, my dating experience mostly came from the movies, too. But it wasn't hard to extrapolate. The two preference parties I'd gone to that night—the Zetas and the SAXis—had been intimate, one-on-one conversations. At each sorority a girl met me at the door and showed me around the house, including her own room. At the Zeta house, they'd found my mother's picture on the wall, and I laughed to see her hair teased up like a brunette Madonna, circa "Material Girl."

Kirby had met me at the SAXi house. I'd been hoping it would be Devon. Maybe I should have been flattered that the president escorted me room to room, but there was a probing intensity to her that put me on edge, and made me think about raising my deflector shields. She was full of questions. What were my ambitions, my goals? I wasn't sad when she pawned me off on a pre-med student named Alexa, and went to circulate among the tiny number of girls that were there.

It wasn't too late to back out, to renege on my word to

Holly. She didn't need me, and I wasn't going to change the world with my little commentary. The elite had always ruled and always would.

If I did bow out, my last article could be about taking the high ground, turning my back on the shallow inanity of sororities. But tonight, I was finishing this article for Tricia.

*And Rush can break your heart, just like dating. You can pin your hopes on a guy, change yourself for him, pretend to be something you're not, and if he doesn't love you back, you think it's the end of the world.*

*How much better would it be if women stopped judging their self-worth by somebody else's arbitrary standards. My mother always said, if he's worthy of you, he'll take you as is. This campus is full of organizations where the power of membership lies with the joiner.*

*And the world is full of guys who don't read Greek.*

I saved what I'd written and checked my watch. Just enough time to print it out and try to catch the most egregious typos. Unfolding myself from the bed, I carried the laptop to my desk and plugged it into the printer. Then I proofread, fiddled with the hook at the end, sent it to Cole via our supersecret system, and finally fell into bed.

✳   ✳   ✳

"Maggie!"

Dad's voice dragged me from the well of slumber. The dregs of a dream had come up with me, twisting my thoughts into dizzying patterns. I had to climb the shreds of reason and try to make sense of my room, which seemed fractured and reassembled in parts, like a cubist painting.

"Maggie! I know you have class this morning."

Downstairs. Dad was shouting up at me. I oriented on the familiar sound—it was far from the first time I'd been shouted awake—and the room came into familiar focus.

Unfortunately, the first thing I saw with any clarity was the clock on my bedside table.

"Crap." I rolled out of bed and went to the stairs to yell, "I'm up! I'm up!" Immediately I regretted it, and squeezed my pounding head between my hands.

Okay. Not a normal nightmare, then. I get these sometimes. Psychic hangovers, the aftermath of one of my real dreams, as opposed to the random firing of neurons that happens to nonfreaky people in their sleep.

Fortunately, I'd showered the night before, so I just had to find clean clothes and grab my homework and my laptop. When I woke up the screen with a tap on a key, I saw that I'd left a browser window open when I went to sleep. In it was the pop-up ad from the other night, the one with the strange, hypnotic pattern.

Without moving the cursor, I hit Control-P to print the screen. The window closed—and the browser crashed—as soon as I moved the cursor, but this time, I'd captured a hard copy. A spark of recognition gave me an idea. Wherever else I had seen that pattern, its most recent appearance had been on the back of my eyelids. And that, if anything, rated investigation.

✳  ✳  ✳

Dad handed me my travel mug of coffee when I reached the bottom of the stairs. "This isn't going to be a pattern, is it?"

"What?" I was still thinking about the pattern in my dream, which had somehow transferred into the waking world. Or vice versa.

He was in no mood for a sidebar. "If this sorority thing is going to interfere with your grades . . ."

Mom answered for me. "It won't." She was dressed for work, but she still looked green beneath her carefully applied makeup. The doctor had assured her that as she was out of her first trimester, the puking would stop any day now. He'd been saying that for two months.

"You won't let it get the best of you, will you, Magpie?" She kissed my cheek, her breath smelling of mint toothpaste and ginger ale. "I'm so proud of you. And if you want to continue in a sorority . . ."

"Really, Mom," I assured them both, "I'm not setting out to become a Stepford Greek. I have my reasons."

This earned me two sighs—one of dismay, and one of relief. "Oh, Maggie," said my mother. "Can't you, just once, do things like a normal girl?"

"Of course not, Laura." Dad grinned, his humor restored. "She's a Quinn."

I headed for the door, mug in hand. "Sorry, Mom. We can't all choose a destiny in accounting."

"You could choose a destiny outside of *The Twilight Zone*," I heard her grumble as I hurried on my way.

✳   ✳   ✳

Since I have biology lab only on Tuesdays, I used the open space in my schedule to visit Dr. Smyth in the chemistry department.

The earth science building was bustling, and redolent of an experiment gone wrong. Or so I assumed. Chemistry could be stinky, even when it goes right.

I tapped on the door to the professor's office, which was just off the lab. Because of the ventilation fans, the smell of burning tires was less pungent than in the hall. I loved the anachronism of the computers and modern equipment in the hundred-year-old space. It reminded me of *A Wrinkle in Time,* and how Dr. Murry had her electron microscope set up in the stillroom of their farmhouse.

"Dr. Smyth?" She looked up from her work, a frown of displacement on her face as she reoriented herself. "I'm Maggie Quinn. You helped me out with a chemistry question last spring."

"Oh yes!" Recognition swept away her confusion, and she waved me to a chair by her desk. "You were working on some kind of fantasy story the last time we talked. How did that turn out?"

I perched on the seat and set my satchel beside me. "Better than I thought it would." In that I was still alive.

"Why aren't you taking chemistry with me?" she chided.

"All the sections were closed. I'm in biology instead."

With an impatient wave, she dismissed the principles of our biological existence. "You should have called me. I would have opened one of the sections for you."

"I still have another science credit to earn. I'll be sure and take it with you." I wouldn't dare do anything different. Dr. Smyth was a force of nature, with flaming red hair and a vibrant personality to match. "I have another question for you."

"Excellent." She leaned her elbows on the desk. "What can I do for you?"

I pulled out the printout of the browser window. "This seems familiar to me. Maybe some kind of crystalline structure?"

She took the picture and immediately identified it. "This is a fractal design."

"A fractal! I couldn't place it." My moment of clarity was short. "But that's math, not chemistry."

"Well, it's both," she said. "You can create fractals by putting a solution of copper sulfate between two glass plates and applying voltage . . ."

I know my eyes must have glazed over. "And in non-geek?"

She started again. "Basically—and I'm really oversimplifying here—a fractal is a system of illustrating things that cannot be described with normal geometry. Tree branches and snowflakes and the stock market. Things that seem random, but if looked at in a mathematical way, aren't really."

"Like chaos theory."

"Right."

All I knew about chaos theory came from watching *Jurassic Park,* but I didn't mention that.

Dr. Smyth laid her hand on the printout. "Most people see fractals in computer graphics. Pretty pictures made out of irrational numbers."

"Irrational numbers," I echoed. "Like pi."

"And phi." She was into it now, like a kid showing off a favorite toy. "Phi—1.618—called the Golden Mean or sometimes the Divine Proportion. Grossly oversimplified, it means that the sum of $a$ plus $b$ is to $a$ as $a$ is to $b$."

"Um. I left my math brain in calculus. Can you translate?"

"All that's important is the proportion." She drew two equal squares touching, and then on top of it drew one rectangle that was equal in size to the two squares. Then she drew another rectangle that was equal in size to the first three put together. Then another, et cetera, until she had a diagram that looked like a stack of blocks.

"These rectangles are all in the 'divine' proportion," she said. "The Parthenon and the Great Pyramid at Giza were both built incorporating this ratio. It's been shown to be universally pleasing to the eye."

"Okay." I took her word for it, not least because it resonated in my memory.

"But watch this." She drew a curved line connecting all the corners of the progressively larger rectangles, until she had a spiral that looked familiar.

"That's a nautilus shell."

"And a cochlea." She tapped her ear, and I remembered that little shell thingy responsible for hearing from high school biology. "And even . . ." She drew a parallel spiral and connected the two with hastily drawn lines, like a ladder.

"DNA?"

"Subtly, but yes." She turned the paper back over and tapped the design from the computer. "Fractals. A pattern that repeats with self-symmetry to an infinitely small, or infinitely large scale."

I stared at her, a little helplessly. "You realize I have no idea what this means."

Dr. Smyth sat back in her chair. "It means that if you look at things from a certain perspective—in this case mathematically—there is nothing truly random in the universe."

"You couldn't have just said that?"

She grinned and handed me the paper. "What kind of educator would I be?"

I thanked her, promised she'd see me, eventually, for a class, and left. I wasn't sure I had any answers, but I definitely had more questions.

The first was why had this design popped up, twice, on my Internet browser.

And theoretically, if seemingly random events were mathematically not really random, then didn't it follow that if you changed the math of things, you could change the outcome?

I suddenly had a new appreciation for arithmetic. I guess I was going to have to start paying attention in calculus.

# 10

The campus of Bedivere U. is tree-shaded and quaint, full of redbrick colonial revival buildings on an unregimented layout. The buildings went up gradually over the last century, wherever was convenient or empty. It lent the campus a lot of charm, but made learning your way around, especially when you had back-to-back classes on opposite sides of the campus, a little challenging.

I'd grown up here, more or less. The two places I could find with my eyes closed were the library and Webster Hall, which housed the history department and archives. My father's office was on the third floor, and I headed there after my chat with Dr. Smyth. Dad was out of the office, and that suited me fine. I didn't need him, just a little privacy.

I cleared a space on his desk, made myself at home, and took out my laptop. It was new, acquired this summer after my old computer had gone up in a hail of brimstone. But what the heck. I needed one for college anyway.

Going into the application folder, I clicked on the SpyZilla icon. No red flags had popped up since I first saw that fractal screen, but that only meant that the software didn't find any cooties it recognized.

So I ran a manual search and found, without much effort, a suspicious script that the program didn't know how to identify. It wasn't known spyware or adware. It was just . . . spookyware.

*Destroy unknown script?* I clicked. "Hell yes."

"Dr. Quinn, did you see this—" Justin entered with a token knock on the open door, then drew up short when he saw me behind the desk. "Oh. Hey, Maggie."

"Hey." We stayed frozen for an awkward tick of the clock. I was trying to remind myself we were just friends. Whatever he was thinking, his brows were drawn into something approaching a scowl. I looked at what he had in his hands. "Something interesting in the paper?"

He held up the page with the Phantom Rushee article. "You're not really going through with this, are you?"

I glared, gesturing to the traffic in the hall. "I don't know what you're talking about."

"Oh, come on."

Closing my laptop—after making sure SpyZilla was done de-fractalfying my hard drive—I stood. "I'm working on something."

"In a sorority." Not a question. Just incredulous.

"Don't think I can pull it off?" I asked, slinging my satchel over my shoulder.

"I know you can. That's what worries me." He tapped the page. "It says right here: 'Resistance is futile.' These things—historically, sociologically—they suck people in."

"It's a sorority, not a cult, Justin. I'll be fine."

I swung out the door, already regretting the words. When would I learn not to tempt fate?

✳ ✳ ✳

Bid Day. The drama and angst of the whole week came down to this: The sororities submitted their choices—the list of girls to whom they would extend a bid. Meanwhile, the rushees listed their top three houses, in order of preference. There was a certain strategy in what you listed. You didn't have to list three, and some had only one pick, preferring to try again as sophomores rather than take a second choice. Others made sure they had at least one house on their list that they were assured of getting into. EZ, for example.

Then we all assembled in the Student Center ballroom to learn if we'd "matched." The doors were closed and no one was allowed in or out until we'd all received our envelopes.

Holly and I stayed together in line—Quinn and Russell are reasonably close alphabetically—an island of dispassion in a sea of drama. There were many tears—of disappointment, joy, or simple relief. Mostly there was hugging and squealing. Lots and lots of squealing. It bounced from the wainscoted walls and the parquet floor. The chandelier tinkled an echo. But the noise was nothing compared to the way the stratospheric emotion was scouring every psychic nerve in my body to a bloody, raw thread.

No story was worth a whole semester of this.

I had to do something; it figured it was desperation that made me put Gran's imagery book to practical use. Closing my eyes, I pictured deflector shields, like on the *Millennium Falcon*. I visualized the laser beams of angst bouncing off my defenses, ricocheting harmlessly back into the throng.

Holy cow. It actually worked. The muscles of my shoulders began to unclench and the knot in my stomach . . .

"Maggie! Holly!" Tricia threw herself at me, wrapping an arm around my neck and drawing Holly into the embrace. "It worked!"

"That's great, Trish!" Holly hugged her back.

*Something* had worked, until I'd completely lost concentration. The noise and emotion surged past my fallen defenses.

"Beta Pi totally wants me!" Holly had talked her into putting down her next highest choices after the Deltas. The Betas were brunette and bubbly, so we'd figured she'd be a fit.

Tricia bounced off to find other Betas; Holly bent down to frown critically at my face. "Are you feeling all right?"

Clearly, I looked as bad as I felt. "It's really hot in here." Someone squealed nearby and my eye twitched in reaction.

"We're almost done." This was relative. There was still a lot of alphabet in line behind us. Darn those Ss. The tradition was to release the rushees—now called pledges—all at once out into the quad, where our new sisterhood waited to greet us and escort us back to Greek Row.

I reached the front of the line; at least once I got my bid— I'd put down SAXi first, as I promised Holly, and the Zetas second, because I was assured of an invite, since I was a legacy—the matter would be settled, and I could find a seat in one of the chairs that ringed the room and observe from a small distance.

"Quinn," I told the Rho Gamma behind the table full of stationery boxes. "Maggie."

"Here you are." She held out a cream-colored envelope with a smile. "Good luck."

If I'd been thinking clearly, maybe I would have expected it. But my brain thrummed in my skull, as if I'd had about fifty espresso shots. As soon as my fingers closed on the invitation, a gray-white light blossomed on my retinas, like when you press on your closed eyelids and make a ghostly impression in the black. Only the brightness kept streaming in on my optic nerve, carrying impressions and images too rapid and bewildering to interpret, a moiré pattern splitting and repeating; infinite variety of waking dreams, pushed into my brain like water through a fire hose.

Consciousness tripped like a fuse, and everything went black.

✳   ✳   ✳

I woke up on the floor, with Jenna patting my hand and Holly leaning over me anxiously. "What happened?"

"You fainted," Holly said as I struggled to sit up.

Surely not. How . . . girly. "Really?"

"Don't worry about it," the Rho Gamma said, correctly interpreting my reddening face. "Too much emotion, girls forget to eat. Happens all the time."

"I never forget to eat." They helped me to my feet; my thighs trembled, but it was better than lying there with the Ss stepping over me to get their bids.

As if anyone would notice one more Drama Girl.

They walked with me to the chairs by the wall, and as I sat, Jenna turned to Holly. "There's some bottled water in the coolers behind the tables. Would you grab one for Maggie?"

"Really, I'm fine—" But Holly was already headed over to where the other Rho Gammas were handing out the bids.

Jenna sat beside me and put a comforting hand on my shoulder. "I know it's overwhelming."

I sunk my head into my hands, rubbing my pounding temples. "Tell me about it."

I didn't expect her to take me literally. "We Sigmas have a hard time in the middle of all this excitement, though some of us are more sensitive than others."

Her face conveyed nothing, and everything. She might have just been talking about a mundane sensitivity to emotional stress. But she met my gaze evenly, significantly. "I could tell you're one of the more sensitive ones."

"So . . ." I formed my next question carefully. "I'm not the only one?"

Jenna smiled, as if my ready acceptance pleased her. "Well, no one has ever fainted before."

"Oh." I had to wrap my head around that. Of all the things I thought I might hear today, that hadn't been it.

She laid her hand on my knee, pressing lightly to weight her words. "I think you're used to keeping your specialness a secret, Maggie, so I don't have to tell you that we Sigmas don't talk about this outside the house. You probably shouldn't talk about it much with your pledge class. Most of them have no idea of the latent potential inside them."

"I don't understand." I felt the way I had when Dr. Smyth explained fractal theory, as though there was some basic, fundamental thing here that my mental fingertips could brush, but not quite grasp.

"You don't need to understand it right now. That's what pledge class is for. To get you ready for initiation, when everything will be clear."

Holly returned and handed me a bottle, still dripping icy water from the cooler. I pressed it to the back of my neck, hoping the chill would shock my brain into motion. It also gave me an excuse to duck my head and let Holly and Jenna talk while I tried to align my scattered thoughts.

All this week, I'd taken secret pride in being what the sorority girls termed "Not One of Us." Now I had found out that actually, I *was* one of them. Or they were a lot of me. Or . . . something.

I sat with my head resting in one hand, shielding my face. A cold prickle of worry spread through me, and I didn't think it was just the icy water bottle, or the cracking of my illusion that I was special or unique.

The bid envelope lay in my lap. Opening it was a formality now, but I did it anyway:

SIGMA ALPHA XI
INVITES
MAGDALENA LORRAINE QUINN
TO JOIN OUR SACRED SISTERHOOD.

In the words of Han Solo, right before the *Millennium Falcon* got sucked into the Death Star: I had a *bad* feeling about this.

# II

I stood in the foyer of the Sigma Alpha Xi house with seven other girls. Other houses had thirty or forty new members—pledges, in the Greek vernacular. We had eight. No wonder SAXis had a reputation for being in a class of their own.

By their nature, the members of a house run together. They chose for type, and Sigma Alpha Xi did, too, if Jenna was to be believed—and I had no reason not to. Their criteria was definitely not physical similarity. At one end was lanky Holly, with her hair the color of autumn mums. At the other was me: short, too curvy on the bottom and not curvy enough on the top, with disobedient short dark hair. The other girls fell in the middle and had yet to differentiate themselves.

We, the pledge class, waited as a collective. Nervous, giggling, or silent, according to nature. The gigglers were Ashley, Kaylee, and Nikki. On the quiet, sober side were Holly, Alyssa, and Erica. A girl named Brittany had appointed herself pledge wrangler, and kept admonishing the gigglers to shut up and be serious.

The chapter room doors swung partially open and one of the Sigmas greeted us, wearing some kind of stole or wrap over her street clothes. We all shut up.

"Sigma Alpha Xi invites Ashley Adams to join our circle."

Ashley, a blond girl with a California tan, looked suddenly intimidated, and I wondered if she didn't have some Spidey Sense after all. She wiped her palms on her jeans, took the older girl's offered hand, and followed her into the room as another active member appeared in the doorway.

"Sigma Alpha Xi invites Kaylee Carson to join our circle." A dark-haired girl with a ballerina's build went in eagerly.

They continued alphabetically, until only Holly and I were left. Then Jenna appeared, a crimson stole hanging, Roman senator–fashion, over her elbows. "Sigma Alpha Xi invites Magdalena Quinn to join our circle."

My full name was on my school records, though I'd made it clear I preferred Maggie. We were too careless with names in modern culture, and I wasn't just talking about identity theft. Names have power, and calling things by their proper names can evoke it, or diminish it. Why else don't we call private body parts by their anatomical terms?

I followed Jenna into the chapter room, which had been transformed once again. The lights were dim; the air was cool, almost clammy on my bare arms. The rug had been rolled back, and inlaid on the hardwood floor was a spiral, like a nautilus shell or a galaxy.

*Nothing in the universe is truly random.*

Jenna led me inward along the loop, and I joined the ring of pledges in the center. Holly completed our group, and the doors closed.

At the north end of the room stood Victoria Abbott. Was it normal for an alumnae adviser to always be around? Something about her presence struck a wrong note with me.

In front of her was a cloth-covered table with several items on it: an oil lamp—think Aladdin and the genie—and an enormous book. Gutenberg Bible enormous, and possibly that old. A spiral of fragrant smoke rose from a small silver bowl—incense, exotic and spicy, making my head feel stuffy and strange.

Victoria spoke, in a soft but carrying voice. "We move through life in a series of patterns: family, friends, school classes and clubs."

One Sigma handed each pledge an unlit white candle as the alumna continued. "Today you will form the first of the new patterns in your life in Sigma Alpha Xi: your pledge class, a circle of sisterhood.

"Later you'll make new patterns as you get a big sister, find roommates, take offices. All of these will mean new roles, new positions in the design."

The actives moved into place along the spiral as Victoria lit a candle from the lamp. She handed it to Kirby, who stood beside her, a sober acolyte. "Like lightning, we branch out into the world, but no matter how far we get from the beginning, here is where the flame is begun."

The chapter president passed on the flame. Each girl in turn touched tapers with those next to her, and flickering lights spread inward along the spiral, toward the pledges in the center. Someone beside me sniffled, and I fought the urge to squirm at the seriousness of it all.

Then the flames reached us, and we passed them among our candles. The circle closed like a circuit, and I felt a rush of electricity along my skin. It flowed—a tangible energy potential—outward along the spiral, humming like a magnetic field in the room.

Whoa.

Eight of the girls handed off their candles and moved toward the center, making eddies and currents in the energy field, like turbulence in water. Jenna stopped in front of me with a small smile of encouragement.

"Our pledge emblem is the North Star," said Victoria. "The guide of adventurers and explorers."

Jenna held up a small, lacquered gold pin, like a tiny brooch. "This is mine," she whispered, opening the clasp. "And my big sister's, and her big sister's. So I hope you keep better track of it than you did your name tag."

She held the point to the flame of my candle, only for a few seconds. Around the circle, others did the same. Jenna reached for my hand and, stupid me, I thought she was going to place the pin in my palm. Instead she pricked my finger, and I hissed in pain and some alarm. A tingle raced up my arm, settled at the base of my skull, then dissipated.

A small drop of blood glimmered garnet on the sharp tip. After Jenna carefully fastened it on my shirt, I reached up and touched the warm gold. Images, quick and fast: Jenna, on the Panhellenic Council; a woman in her early twenties, rising star of real estate in Houston; an assistant DA in Chicago, on the board of governors of the school. All of them had worn this pin.

No fuzziness followed the vision this time. As quickly as the images came, I was able to mentally catch them, instead of feeling assaulted by each. The song the Sigmas had been singing—I hadn't heard them start—ended, hanging resonant in the room, like a chant in a cathedral.

Into the charged air, Victoria spoke. "The compass marks the path to our destination."

From directly opposite her, Kirby said, "The flame is knowledge and power shared."

A quarter of the way around the circle from the president, Jenna spoke. "Indigo for depth of feeling and depth of passion."

And across from her, Devon, the girl from the second night of Rush. "Crimson for blood, for inspiration, and creation of things special and rare."

*And one ring to rule them all.*

It occurred to me that I might be in *way* over my head.

# 12

The SAXis' powder room, like everything else in the house, was decorated in dark red and blue. Excuse me—crimson and indigo. That hadn't seemed ominous during Rush, but now I was seeing patterns everywhere.

I had Justin's number dialed almost before I locked the door, and turned on the water to hide the sound of my voice. No answer. I hung up without leaving a message and paced in the tiny space, irrationally angry with him. Forget my petty, girly worries over the status of our relationship. How could he be in class when I needed him?

A pledge had to go through a learning period before being initiated as an active member of the chapter. I had never intended to go through with initiation. Even if they were only quasi-faux-sacred sorority vows, I wasn't comfortable taking them under false pretenses. Since the pledge period was sort of probationary anyway, I'd been able to justify a little finger crossing.

But I hadn't expected this. Ritual with a capital R. Jenna's little sensitivity bomb was nothing compared to this.

A knock on the door made me jump. "Just a minute!" I called, then splashed my flushed face and wiped the smudged mascara with my fingers before I opened the door.

Jenna stood in the hall. "Hey. There's food in the dining room. We had barbecue catered in."

"Great," I said.

She looked at me closely. "You okay? You're not freaking out because of what I said earlier?"

"No." What I needed here was not so much deflector shields as a cloaking device, because she didn't look convinced. "Okay," I admitted. "I've never met anyone else like me. I'm a little freaked."

Taking my arm, she said, "Don't think about it too much. It just connects us more closely."

We had to go through the front hall to get to the dining room. I didn't expect to see Cole Bauer standing there.

He didn't expect to see me, either, and his face went slack in surprise. Then he looked past me, and turned the expression into one of pleasure. I glanced over my shoulder and saw Devon, the art major with the flippy hair, whom I'd talked to the second night, coming down the stairs.

She looked from Cole to me to Jenna as she walked over to us. "Hi," she said, a slight strain in her voice.

"Going out?" asked Jenna.

"Yes." She looked a little nervous and slightly defiant, which might have had something to do with her next statement. "Victoria knows I'm going, now that the official stuff is done."

Jenna held up her hands. "I didn't say anything."

Devon joined her date—because it was obvious he was—and said, "Hey, Cole. This is one of our new pledges, Maggie Quinn."

"We've met, actually." I was thinking fast, covering his slip of recognition. "In the journalism lab, when Hardcastle crushed my dreams of being the first freshman staff photographer."

"Oh yeah." He nodded. "That's too bad. Are you taking photography with Goldsmith?"

"Yeah."

Devon slipped her hand through his arm. "Well, we'll see you guys. Later, Jenna."

They left, and I became aware of someone standing on the stairs, looking down at the casual little scene. "Is she still with him?" It was Kirby, coming down the steps. She didn't look happy.

"She hasn't seen him all summer," Jenna said, clearly making an excuse. Then she grabbed my arm again. "Let's go eat."

∗   ∗   ∗

They were talking about me when I reached the dining room. Well, not about Maggie Quinn, überpledge, but the Phantom Rushee, undercover reporter.

One of the actives said, "Is it wrong that I thought she was kind of funny? She did have the chapters all pegged. The EZs and the Theta Moos." I choked on my Coke at that.

"And what were we supposed to be? Some kind of fembots with shiny hair?"

"That would have to be the Kappa Phis," said another.

Nikki, one of the pledges, asked, "Is it true they make all their members get boob jobs if they're not a C-cup?"

Another pledge, Brittany, directed a loud question to President Kirby and Jenna, the ex-RG. "So *nobody* knows who she is? Not Panhellenic, or the Rho Gammas or *anyone*?"

"Not a clue." Jenna munched on a chip. "But I think the Delta Delta Gammas have a hit out on her."

"Couldn't Devon make Cole tell her?" asked Melissa (I think). I was already regretting the absence of name tags.

"She wouldn't." All the actives looked at the speaker, in a beat filled with surprise, and a tension I didn't understand. The girl lifted her hands in a shrug. "That's what her big sis told me."

The curious eyes turned to Kirby, but her attention was on her plate. I knew I was missing something significant, and wondered if it was as simple as disapproval of Devon's relationship—her choosing a boy over her sisters—or something else.

✳  ✳  ✳

By the time I pulled into my driveway it was late, and I felt as if someone had stirred my brain with a spoon. The stairs to my room seemed steeper than usual; I practically had to drag myself up by the banister.

The upstairs loft is arranged so that the stairway opens into the sitting/study area, and a pair of French doors close off my bedroom. Hanging on the left side was what, in the dark, looked like a Christmas wreath.

September had flown by fast, but this was ridiculous.

I flipped on the light; the wreath was made of crimson and blue fabric, thickly braided. Stuck on, quite artistically, were several ornaments: a lamp, a star, a compass, and what looked like an octopus. Oh yes, and the letters ΣΑΞ.

On the right side was a whiteboard framed in SAXi colors, also with the letters, with a dry-erase marker hanging from a string. Someone had written a note: "Maggie— Welcome to the Sigmas! This door decoration is to help you study for your pledge exam! You'll learn what all of these things mean soon. ΣΑΞ ♥ U!"

Underneath was another note, in handwriting I knew. "Congrats, Magpie! Your new friends seem so nice! Love, Mom." Thankfully, she wrote out love instead of drawing a little heart.

I wondered if I would feel less creeped out if this were hanging on a dorm-room door rather than actually inside my home. It seemed like something I maybe should be worried about under the circumstances, but I was so tired. I parked the thought in a corner of my brain to examine in the morning.

Stripping off my clothes, I fell into bed, relieved that the next day was the weekend, and I didn't have to speak Greek again until Monday.

✳   ✳   ✳

I woke late, even for a Saturday. My head felt furry on the inside, and the sunlight that streamed through the sheer curtains hammered against my eyes. All the signs of a psychic hangover.

With a groan, I sat on the edge of my bed and rubbed my hands through my hair. I hadn't dreamed, so it must have been the residual from yesterday's drama queen rally. A lot had happened, so much that my brain felt full, unable to process it all. I had pledged a sorority last night, yet there were no accompanying signs of imminent apocalypse.

I padded downstairs in an ancient Bedivere T-shirt, sweatpants, and socks. The living room was deserted, but Dad sat at the kitchen table with his laptop, papers spread around him.

"Good morning, sleepyhead."

With a grunt of reply, I headed to the coffee, which was tepid in the pot. Desperate, I filled a mug and put it in the microwave.

"How did it go last night?" he asked.

"Okay." I stood with my hand on the microwave and thought about that. The details were fuzzy, as if I was viewing them through a dirty window. Interesting. High emotion could make an unreliable witness. But I wondered if there was some kind of protection inherent in the pledging ceremony.

Or maybe I just needed caffeine. The microwave beeped and I took out the mug, stirred in sugar and a lot of milk. "I found out my editor is dating one of the sisters. I wonder if he'll still want me to continue the articles."

Dad rose to get some orange juice out of the fridge. "I wouldn't be sorry if he didn't. You might get home before midnight once in a while."

"It'll be better now that Rush is over."

"Hardly. Now it will be meetings and parties. . . ."

"God, what a chore. How I suffer."

Glass in hand, he looked at me in that knowing way

parents have. "So, how long are you going to keep up this Phantom Rushee business?"

"Cole and I agreed on an article a week up until initiation. Then I'm out."

"Not going to write your name in blood, huh?"

"Uh, no." Not when it might be literal. I rubbed my punctured finger and thought about symbolism. Blood brothers, candle-lighting, colors and ciphers. "Hey, Dad. Put on your historian hat for a sec. What's the evolution of fraternities and sororities? Despite all the Greek letters and stuff, they don't have roots that far back, do they?"

He considered the question, rubbing the Saturday stubble on his jaw. "Well, secret societies do. Think about the Templars, the Masons. But the first fraternity was Phi Beta Kappa in 1776, and it was more of a literary organization. Social fraternities didn't come along until the nineteenth century."

"The way they carry on about ritual and tradition, you'd think they'd been around since the dawn of time."

"They took Greek letters as their names to give that air of tradition and ritual. It's human nature. Being in on a secret makes a group feel superior to the ignorant masses."

That made sense; there was certainly no lack of superiority complexes on Greek Row. "But you don't think it really makes a difference in future success, do you?"

"Networking is a powerful tool." He shrugged. "All other things being equal, it could be an advantage later on."

"But does any one chapter strike you as more successful? At least on our campus?"

He shook his head. "I'm afraid I've never given much

thought to the Greeks on campus, unless a student's grades slip. Even then, the individual house doesn't mean much to me."

"Okay. What do you know about Congressman Abbott?"

"Just what I read in the papers." He looked at me curiously. "What does he have to do with the Sigma Alpha Xis?"

"Well, his wife is one. She's the chapter adviser."

What *could* it have to do with the SAXis? Probably nothing. But it was a place to start, when I didn't have much to go on.

It was time for a little old-fashioned, completely mundane detective work. Mumbling an excuse to my father, I rose and headed for the stairs.

"You forgot your coffee," he called.

The stale smell of nuked coffee was too much, even for me. "I'll get some on the way to the paper."

"Maggie?" I turned at the concerned note in his voice. "What are you up to?"

"Just getting my Nancy Drew on, Dad."

He met my innocent look with one of narrow-eyed doubt. "There isn't any . . ." He glanced to check that Mom wasn't in the living room. ". . . you know. Any weird stuff going on, is there?"

"Don't tell Mom," I whispered. "But all Greek stuff is weird to me."

He let out a pent-up breath. "I can't tell you how relieved I am to hear that."

I hated to lie to my dad, even by omission. But really. There just wasn't a way to introduce the subject of sorcerous sororities without getting into a much more involved discussion than I could handle before lunchtime.

*    *    *

Upstairs I found a message from Justin on my voicemail. "Hi, Maggie. Saw that you called last night. The reception in the old library is awful. Since you didn't leave a message, I figured you were okay. Call me if you want."

Of course I wanted. Didn't I make that clear?

But *should* I? In the security of my room, I felt a little silly for freaking out yesterday. And I knew I shouldn't always rely on Justin. The fact that I wanted to run to him, to play the damsel-in-distress card and get his attention, made me that much more determined to do this without him.

Resolved, I deleted the message.

# 13

A couple of decades ago, the town had passed a bond to restore downtown Avalon to its original redbrick streets and Victorian faux-gaslight glory. The courthouse was in the center of the town square; the surrounding blocks were dotted with long-standing businesses, like the *Sentinel*, interspersed with new stores, mostly antique and quilt shops. Froth and Java was on the corner, and I left the Jeep parked in the lot there rather than trying to find street parking.

Latte in hand, right on the threshold of the newspaper office, I suddenly remembered what else was on Main Street: the offices of Congressman Peter Abbott.

The skin on the back of my neck tingled, like a cold wind had blown across my nape, and I knew I'd been spotted. Frozen with my hand on the door, I raised my deflector shields, but of course they did nothing against a perfectly good pair of eyes and the ability to put two and two together.

"Maggie Quinn, isn't it?" Victoria Abbott's voice came as no surprise, but I flinched anyway.

Caught. How *stupid* could I be?

I turned, brushed my hair from my face. The buildings made a wind tunnel and turned the mild day brisk in their shade. "Hello, Mrs. Abbott."

She was dressed casually today, like a Ralph Lauren ad instead of a *Vogue* spread. If not for the dread curdling the cream in my coffee, I would have really coveted the leather bag she had slung over her shoulder. Her eyes looked me up and down, canted over to the words *Avalon Sentinel* on the office window, and came back to my face.

"Perhaps we should talk."

"Um. Sure." Perhaps I wouldn't just die on the spot. Victoria Abbott was intimidating on a mundane level—even without the memories of last night's ritual flooding back to me when I saw her. How could I have forgotten?

I expected her to lead me back to the congressman's office, but maybe she didn't want my body discovered there. Instead, she headed toward Froth and Java; gesturing to an outside table, she asked, "Would you like a refill?"

"No." I remembered my manners. "No, thank you."

She sat, crossed her legs, and waited.

Cops use that technique: Keep quiet and let the suspect hang himself. There's a need to fill silence, and when you're guilty, it becomes a compulsion. I had to bite the inside of my lip to keep from blurting out . . . everything.

She was strong, but I was stubborn. I looked at the puffy clouds blowing across the sky, the Saturday antique shoppers, the clock on the courthouse—anything but Victoria.

Finally, she said, "I know what you're up to."

I powered up my psychic force field. "All I'm up to is research. I need the *Sentinel's* archives for a school paper."

All technically truthful.

She lifted a perfectly sculpted brow. "Then you're not the Phantom?"

I started to speak, but no sound came out. No lie, no truth. Nothing. Victoria leaned forward and said under the cover of traffic noise, "There's no point in lying. I'm good at seeing through things. Just like you, I think."

She held my gaze, watching while I considered and rejected excuses and lies, one after another. Finally, I decided to be direct. "Are you going to kick me out?"

She rolled her eyes, and the atmosphere became almost normal. "You really think I care about a pissant school paper?"

Well . . . *I* cared.

"I see great things for you, Maggie Quinn." She tapped the table with manicured fingernails. "But let's establish some ground rules. The Phantom can mock the Greek system as she pleases. The hypocrisy, pretension . . . I don't care."

That not only sounded as though she wasn't going to kick me out; maybe she wouldn't turn me into a frog, either.

"But not one word," Queen Victoria continued, "about

specific Sigma members, business, or rituals. Everything that happens in that house is off the record."

Relief turned to suspicion. "But . . . why?"

"You are a Sigma, and Sigmas excel in their careers. This is the start of yours, so why should I hold you back?"

"I . . ." Words failed me.

She set her folded arms on the table. "I don't believe in coincidence. However you came to join us, I think you're meant to be a Sigma."

"Look, it's not that I don't appreciate the second chance. But I'm not—"

"Maggie, don't be coy." She gave me a cut-the-crap stare. "Jenna told me she talked to you about the special qualities we seek in Sigmas. I need you to be a leader."

"But I'm not." The argument was pointless, but I made it anyway. I wasn't a follower, either.

Victoria's mouth turned up in an enigmatic smile. "You have ability and ambition. You could go far, Maggie, if you open yourself to the possibilities that Sigma can offer. I can put in a word for you at a real paper. A big newspaper."

Moments like this rock my world, shake my faith in my own freakitude. Was that all there was to the SAXi success ratio? Was it really just networking?

While I sat reeling, she gathered her bag from the back of her chair. "I'll let you think about it. If you come to your pledge meeting on Monday, I'll know we have an understanding."

"That might be awkward," I said. "The other houses—heck, the other Sigmas—want my guts for garters."

Rising, she smoothed any wrinkles from her khaki

trousers. "Kirby and the other officers do not know you're the Phantom, and we'll keep it that way. Our little secret."

She laid her hand on my shoulder. I'd been visualizing my psychic force field the whole time—which was one reason I hadn't managed many multisyllable answers. I *so* did not want to see into this woman's psyche, almost as much as I didn't want her to see into mine.

I got nothing but an impression of locked and barred doors. Of course. *Her* deflector shields.

She left, and I sat on the café patio for a long moment, getting my mental feet back under me after being knocked on my metaphorical ass. Victoria had a lot of confidence, not only that I'd stay with the Sigmas, but also that I wouldn't report this whole conversation.

Like anyone would believe me.

✳   ✳   ✳

The city newspaper offices were technically closed, but of course there were people working. Fact-checking had been one of my intern duties, so I knew my way to the archives. They called it the tomb—a basement room, musty and dimly lit. You didn't need a lot of light to stare into the microfiche reader.

What, specifically, I was looking for, I had no idea, but the conversation with Mrs. Congressman Abbott had given me a starting point, out of perversity if nothing else.

I started with Peter Abbott's official bio. His first office had been that of president of Gamma Phi Epsilon, here at Bedivere. He'd left for law school, but returned to Avalon to practice. Went to Congress by special appointment when the seat opened by the death of its occupant. Two years later, he won it in his own right. The guy had been flagged as a wunderkind who spoke eloquently to promote his innovative ideas.

Victoria had a marketing degree, and ran Abbott's campaign. Funny career choice, being a politician's wife, after what she'd told me about Sigmas excelling in their fields.

I'd been there awhile—judging by the crick in my neck—when a tap at the door heralded Ethan Douglas, editor-in-chief of the *Sentinel*.

"Heard there was a phantom in the basement." He grinned as he leaned against the doorframe.

"Hardy-har-har."

"Working on something new?" He nodded to the microfiche.

I turned the chair to face him, stretching my arms over my head to de-kink my back. Forties office furniture wasn't exactly ergonomic. "I'm sort of following a thread. Still on this Greek thing." Clearly he'd guessed my Secret Squirrel project. "How about you? Were you in a fraternity?"

"Yeah. Pi Kappa Iota back at Plains State University."

"Do you think it made a difference in your career?"

His freckled, boyish face twisted ruefully. "You mean, did it help me get the job as editor-in-chief of a small-town newspaper a hundred miles from any major metropolis?"

"Er . . ." I would never win awards for my tact.

He let me off the hook. "Don't go cross-eyed at that machine. What are you looking for that you can't find in the online archives?"

"Old stuff." I didn't want to go into why I was avoiding the Internet. Fractal spyware was a little hard to explain.

He turned to go, then paused, catching a hand on the doorframe. "Hey, Maggie. Your Phantom column is good stuff. Not news, but good. Can I call you if I need something covered at the university?"

I blinked, since I'd figured that ship had sailed. "Sure. Of course."

"Great." Flashing a grin, he took off, leaving me in the tomb all alone.

Okay, I had to wonder if Victoria had been busy. But, no offense to Ethan, she'd said a *big* paper.

I rewound the film and went to put it back in its box. Then I flipped through the index, free-associating a bit, the way I do when I want my logical brain to stop trying to outshout my subconscious. Bedivere University. My fingers trailed through the subheadings until I saw Fraternities and Sororities. I found the oldest dated articles and pulled the film.

The Greeks came to BU in the 1940s, about fifty years after the university was founded. Despite some opposition, the first three fraternities and two sororities formed chapters without incident. They moved into houses at the north end of campus, converted to living spaces for the boys and girls.

Sigma Alpha Xi showed up in the fifties, followed shortly by their "brother" fraternity, Gamma Phi Epsilon. Their arrival firmly established the current Greek Row, and a line drawing from a 1957 article showed the area, labeling each house.

I printed the page and carried it to a desk lamp. Greek Row was actually two streets which dead-ended in the park that bordered campus. Some ground had been lost to parking lots, but essentially the layout was unchanged. It had a certain proportion that resonated. Grabbing a pencil, I traced a curved line through the houses—sorority and fraternity both.

What I had on the page when I was done bore an undeniable similarity to the phi diagram that Dr. Smyth had drawn, the same logarithmic spiral inlaid in the floor of the Sigma Alpha Xi house—which lay directly in the center of the coil, like a spider sitting in the middle of her web.

# 14

Professor Hardcastle had the personality of a piece of dry Wonder Bread—capable of holding the contents of an information sandwich, but completely without flavor or texture. Media and Communication was an entry-level class, so it wasn't a very interesting sandwich on any level. On a Monday morning, it was hell.

At the end of the hour, I roused myself from my stupor and gathered my books. Hardcastle stopped me as I walked down the steps of the lecture hall. "Miss Quinn."

I stopped, warily. "Yes, sir?" There were enough Greeks in the class to make me nervous at being singled out.

"Were you serious about working on the newspaper?"

"Yes, sir." Honestly. Was I serious about breathing?

"Bauer needs some help with layout, and I thought about you, since you seemed so fired up to work."

"Sure." I contained my glee, which of course had *nothing* to do with Hardcastle having to eat his "No freshmen" words. "When should I come in?"

"Bauer asked me to send you to the journalism lab now, unless you've got another class."

"Not for a couple hours. I'll go on down."

I assumed that this was a ruse because Cole wanted to discuss something. I'd written the week's Phantom Pledge column over the weekend, covering the trauma of Bid Day, and I'd justified leaving out all details of the Sigmas' ritual in several ways. One: the most interesting thing, i.e., the hoodoo I'd felt, was so unbelievable that I was beginning to doubt it myself. Two: most of the stuff—candles, recitation, circles—was common to at least one other house. I knew this because I called Tricia, who, per usual, was happy to tell me anything that went through her head.

And three: I kind of liked being the Phantom Pledge. And I really liked having a weekly column in the pissant school paper.

I followed my nose—ink and toner and film developer— to the journalism lab, a large room where rows of computers lined one wall and filled the middle desks. Several of them were occupied, but I didn't see Cole, so I wandered to a big whiteboard showing the progress of the current issue. There was a Linotype machine, too, one of the old ones that used heated lead to print type on long rolls, which were then cut and pasted onto the layout. How medieval.

"Maggie?" I turned to see Cole Bauer in a second doorway. He looked like five miles of bad road—worn and rough.

"Hi, Cole." I peered closer. I didn't think it was just the fluorescent lights. "Are you feeling all right?"

"Great. I'm feeling great." I had to admit that, despite his haggard appearance, he seemed very . . . bright, somehow, like a headlamp set on high beam. My eyes and my Sight were getting two different messages.

"You wanted to see me?" I asked.

He waved me over. "Come in here."

The office might have once been a closet, but it was on par with most grad student digs. He closed the door and gestured for me to take the desk chair. "I read through the clippings you gave Hardcastle with your application. Your pictures are good, too. And you've had editing experience, right?"

"Yeah. I edited the AHS paper for a semester." I had a weird feeling about this conversation; my skin prickled with unease. "But it was just a weekly, not a daily." Or almost daily, in this case. The *Ranger Report* came out Tuesday through Friday.

"Great." He laid his hand on a stack of articles beside the computer. "These all need fact-checking and copyediting. We'll start there."

"All of these?" It was a pretty big pile. "For which edition?"

"I put them in order. There are only three or so for tomorrow."

"Um. Okay." Good thing I had a long break until my afternoon classes. "Should I give them to you when I'm done?"

"The first couple. I'll be around, but I'm working on a project of my own. I appreciate your help."

"Sure." There was definitely something off about Cole today. "Are you really okay?"

Cole smiled. "I'm fine. Just . . ." He weighed his words, then shrugged. "I don't know. Maybe you'd understand. I'm writing a book."

"Oh, really." I tried to sound impressed, but honestly. I'm a communication major. Nearly everyone I'd met was writing a book.

"I've got this idea. A fully formed, like Athena from the forehead of Zeus, kind of idea." He ran his hand through his hair, which fell lankly around his thin face. "It's wonderful and terrifying both, and I just feel that if I don't write it now, quickly, the inspiration will desert me."

"Ohh-kay." His intensity was certainly terrifying—I agreed with that much. "Is that why you look like you haven't slept in days?"

"I don't want to waste writing time."

"You're not doing drugs or anything?"

He laughed in surprise. The ambush question also gave me his uncensored reaction. He was clean. In fact, he seemed to find the idea absurd. "No. I don't need drugs."

"I get it. Writing is your antidrug."

"Exactly."

I gazed at the pile of copy and sighed. "Fine. But only because you're my sorority brother-in-law."

He kissed my cheek. "I knew I liked you. I'll put you in the acknowledgments."

"Great." He left me to work on his computer. I touched my skin where his lips had brushed. No vision this time, just heat, as if he were truly burning with inspiration.

# 15

I don't consider myself a Faust so much as a cat—consumed by curiosity. But both meet a bad end, metaphorically, so maybe it doesn't matter, except to explain why I showed up at the Sigma Alpha Xi house for the pledge class that afternoon. I wasn't buying what Victoria Abbott had to offer; I just couldn't let the mystery lie.

The other seven pledges and I met with the active designated to teach us what we needed to know, congregating in the TV room of the SAXi house. Besides Holly and myself, there were Brittany, Ashley, Nikki, Kaylee, Alyssa, and Erica.

Tara, the pledge trainer, had a pleasantly curvy figure

and long, honey-colored hair that she wore parted in the middle, hippie-style. She handed us each a thick booklet. "These are your Sigma Alpha Xi handbooks. You will have to learn everything in here for the test, but don't worry. We'll help you."

I flipped through the pages. There were sections on the meaning of the colors, the symbols, the mascot. No chapter, however, on "How to Win Friends and Influence Fate."

"First we'll go over the rules," said Tara, settling into an armchair with a big, worn binder in her lap. The rest of us were on the sofa or the other chairs, forming a loose circle.

For an hour, Tara read out of the handbook about what Sigmas could and couldn't do. To summarize:

Sigmas keep their grades up. (Self-explanatory.)

Sigmas don't dress inappropriately. (Some ambiguity here, but the gist was that "provocative" wasn't nearly as big an issue as "tacky.")

Sigmas don't drink alcohol. (Completely ignored in practice, until someone got caught by the authorities.)

Sigmas don't have sex. (See above re: get caught, comma, don't.)

Sigmas don't talk about chapter business outside the chapter. (The first rule of Greek Club is don't talk about Greek Club.)

There was a Standards Board to enforce these rules, made up of the chapter officers, an alumnae adviser, and, if serious enough, a representative from the national office.

Next there were rules specific to pledges:

Stand up when an active enters the room.

Do everything an active tells you, unless it's hazing, but of course, hazing is against SAXi national policy.

Pledges do not have serious boyfriends.

At the general murmurs from the eight pledges, our trainer looked up from the binder. "We're serious about this one," Tara said. "Pledgeship is only ten weeks. You can hold out that long."

Brittany raised her hand, clearly appointing herself spokeswoman. "When you say hold out, you mean . . ."

Tara leveled an unequivocal stare. "No sex." The pledges giggled, maybe figuring the rule was as meaningful as the one for the actives, but she nixed that idea. "I'm totally serious this time. All your focus should be on learning about your sisters and your sorority. Sex will only get in the way of that. If you get caught, you'll be brought before Standards."

Nikki raised her hand, her face bright red. "So when you say 'no sex,' you mean, like, *nothing*?"

Tara rolled her eyes. "Do I have to draw you a diagram?"

Brittany had a prim know-it-all tone at odds with the subject. "There's a *lot* of room between the neck and the knees."

"And it doesn't seem fair," Ashley followed, "that the pledges from the other chapters will have a head start getting to know all the guys."

Tara's earth-mother patience was slipping. "You can get to know them, you just can't screw them."

"So making out is okay?" Brittany again. "I'm just trying to make sure we *all* understand the rules."

"Above the waist only? Or everything but . . . you know." In case we didn't, Nikki made a circle with two fingers and demonstrated with another one.

"Eww!" Ashley screwed up her face. "Gross, Nikki!"

"Oh, like you haven't."

"Look, people," Holly snapped. "Tab A, slot B. Don't do it. How hard is that?"

I started to laugh. What else could I do?

Tara tried to get control of the group again, and steer them back on track. "You guys are *way* overthinking this."

Brittany got huffy; with her high, clipped voice, she sounded like Minnie Mouse in a snit. "I'm just saying, we all went through Rush because we wanted to meet guys."

"You should have done fraternity Rush then," Holly said.

Tara jumped in to prevent a catfight. "I know what you mean, Brittany. But trust me. Sigmas have their pick of the guys."

"Sigmas are hard to get but worth the trouble." I didn't realize I'd spoken aloud until they all looked at me. "That's our reputation," I explained, paraphrasing what I'd read on a chat board while working on my next Phantom article. "It does seem better than 'Their pledges put out.' "

Tara gave me a studying look, and I wished I'd remained under the radar. I'd spent Sunday reading Gran's book and working on my deflector shields, but I ought to practice keeping my mouth shut.

"What's a sorority girl's mating call?" Holly asked, earning Tara's glare. " 'I'm so wasted!' "

"That's not funny!" Brittany said, outraged. If she'd been standing, I think she'd have stamped her foot. Possibly the girls laughed at her as much as Holly's awful joke. I know I did.

Tara took the opportunity to move things along, and

turned the page in her book. "We've spent so much time on this that we didn't discuss officers. Any nominations for pledge class president?"

"I nominate Brittany," said Nikki, and Ashley seconded. That seemed to be Ashley's major function, seconding things.

"Anyone else?" Tara looked around the small circle, and her gaze rested on me. "Maggie? Victoria told me you might be interested in being pledge president."

After a shocked silence, of which a lot of the shock came from me, Brittany protested. "But Maggie never contributes anything to the discussion."

"That's got my vote," Holly drawled. "I nominate Maggie."

I shook off my frozen surprise. "I can't be pledge president."

"She's right. She doesn't know anything about Greek tradition," said Brittany. I suddenly realized who she reminded me of: Tracy Flick in *Election*. She even had the Reese Witherspoon haircut.

"I second Maggie!" said Kaylee, clearly in favor of anything that didn't involve Brittany ordering us around.

"I decline." But no one was listening to me except Brittany, who echoed, "She declines!"

Tara looked at her watch. "Great. Next week we'll vote for either Maggie or Brittany as president."

"But I don't want to run."

"Line up outside the chapter room in ten minutes, girls." She dismissed us, and the group scattered. I marched toward Tara, but Holly strong-armed me out of the room.

"You can*not* stick us with Brittany for ten weeks, Maggie."

"Why don't *you* run?"

She headed downstairs. "Because my mother wants me to."

"Of course." We joined the steady trickle of girls on the central stairway that connected the three floors. "I don't know why Victoria told Tara that I wanted to do it."

Holly glanced back, the steps putting us eye to eye. "Because *she* wants you to run. You're obviously on the short track to the inner circle. Lucky you."

I would have felt a lot better about that if Holly had seemed at all jealous of my special treatment. Because the inner circle that came to my mind was the one in Dante's *Inferno,* and that wasn't anywhere I wanted to be.

# 16

Tuesday morning I woke up with an uneasy knot in my stomach. I sat up, rubbed my eyes, and gazed around the room. All was normal in the bedroom—morning light diffused through blue and green pastel curtains, and the disorder was minimal, at least in the bedroom half of the room. The French doors were open to the study, which looked like a tornado had hit and dropped the contents of a library. Situation normal.

I hadn't dreamed, so that couldn't be what was bugging me. Climbing out of bed, I shuffled to the bathroom, pulled the shower curtain closed, and turned on the water. Eight o'clock class today, but a hot shower always helped me think. Standing under the spray, I did an inventory. Calculus homework, check. Biology lab report, check.

I *had* dreamed. The realization hit while my hair was full of shampoo. It wasn't simply that I couldn't remember. There was an absence in my mind, a hole where the dream had been, as if it had been excised like my wisdom teeth. It didn't hurt, but I couldn't help mentally poking at it.

Weird. I rinsed off and thought about calling Gran, but as soon as I went into the bedroom and saw the clock, that impulse disappeared. I had just enough time to find some jeans that didn't make my butt look too big, and get on my way.

Downstairs, Mom was dressed for work, wolfing down a bowl of bran flakes. "It must be a good stomach day," I said, making a beeline for the coffee pot.

"So far." She swallowed the last bite and rinsed out the bowl, putting it in the dishwasher. "Lisa called last night."

I stopped, midpour. "The home phone?"

"She said she tried your cell."

"I must have turned it off for the meeting."

"Anyway," said Mom. "She wanted to make sure you were okay. Something about the last time you talked." Mom was busily gathering her purse and briefcase, making sure she had her saltines, just in case. "You didn't have a fight, did you?"

Spooning sugar into my travel mug, I tried to remember. When was the last time we'd talked? Was it the fight?

"Time to go," Mom said. "You'd better scoot, too."

I looked at the clock and said a word that made Mom protest. It was going to be a long, busy day. I'd find time to call Lisa tonight. And Gran, I reminded myself. Don't forget.

✳   ✳   ✳

After calculus, I put in an hour at the editor's desk, hurried to the science building, dissected an earthworm, then came back to work straight through the afternoon. I didn't mind skipping lunch, because frankly the only thing grosser than the outside of an earthworm is the inside of one.

By the time I had to leave for history class, I'd entered all the corrections for the next day's edition and uploaded them to the server. Cole was hard at work at his own computer when I stopped by to tell him I was leaving.

"Thanks, Mags." He didn't look up from the screen.

"Hey, Cole." I waited until he made eye contact, and I knew I had his attention. His face had always been long and thin, but there were dusky shadows under his eyes, and furrows of fatigue around his mouth. "Don't forget to sleep occasionally, okay?"

"Sure thing." He said it absently, and went back to work. I turned to go, but stopped when he said, "Hey."

"Yeah?"

He picked up the day's edition of the *Report*. "Good job today."

I smiled and one knot of my tension slipped loose. "Thanks."

Handing me the paper, he waved me off. "Now go to class."

I dashed out the door, into the brisk September air. The leaves were starting to turn, mottling the green with yellow, and I hurried to the history building. It should be an intramural event: the cross-campus sprint.

The only thing I cared about was beating Dad there, and I managed that. I burst into the lecture hall, red-faced and

127

puffing like a steam engine, but I'd made it five minutes before the hour.

"Maggie!"

I scanned the tiers of desks and saw Ashley pointing to an empty seat beside her. Great. As if the Sigmas weren't encroaching on my life enough already.

Unfortunately, everyone else had figured out to come early, so it was the closest empty seat. It was also surrounded by Greeks. I slid down the row and dropped into the desk, pulling out my notebook. A lot of the students took notes on their laptops, but I was a traditionalist. I also knew shorthand.

"I saved you a seat," said Ashley, unnecessarily, since I was already occupying it. "Will was just reading today's Phantom Pledge report."

"The phantom is a pledge now?" I asked, not ingenuous at all.

"Seems so," said the guy I assumed was Will. He was wearing the fraternity uniform—cargo khakis, letter jersey, beat-up athletic shoes—and slouched so far down in his chair that his butt was almost hanging off. Not that I was looking at his butt or anything.

"Listen to this: 'As I reached out to take my own envelope,'" Will quoted, "'stark fear took over, welling up from my nonconformist heart. When I took that bid I would be subsumed, assimilated. Resistance was futile, but my real terror came from knowing that part of me didn't want to resist.

"'What is more potent than the temptation of belonging? It's a Faustian lure—acceptance, superiority. All you have to do is hand over the soul of your individuality.

" 'Any sane person would end the experiment here. Yet here I go, into the social jungle, upriver to the heart of darkness. My reports from this point on may be few, carried out by pontoon boat. Wish me luck. I love the smell of beer keg in the morning.' "

Victoria might yet turn me into a frog.

I thought they might laugh, but the clump of fraternity guys was quiet, contemplative. It was Ashley who spoke first. "Well, that's a little harsh."

"Not really," said a shaggy-haired boy in a purple shirt. He sat beside the reader, Will, on the row above us. "You girls are *scary* when you get your Rush game on." The guys laughed, breaking the pensive tension. "I can totally see you going all Francis Ford Coppola."

"Come on," she protested, twisting in her seat to glare at him.

I took the paper from Will and had a surreal moment, talking about myself in the third person. "Do you think she'll go native, like Martin Sheen?"

"Whatever makes a better story," said Purple Shirt. "It's all a gimmick anyway."

"You think so?" Will looked right at me, making me nervous. "I think she got it at least a *little* right. I mean, I admit that part of the reason I pledged was to feel like a big deal on campus."

A snort from Purple Shirt. "Dude. You're Gamma Phi Epsilon. You guys are the big swinging dick on campus."

Since Will didn't hit him, I figured this was a term of respect. Guys are gross.

"Eww," said Ashley, and faced forward. Will exchanged a

grin with me before I did the same. Just in time—in walked my dad.

"Hey," whispered Ashley while Dad settled in at the front of the hall. "I think Will is totally into you."

"How can you tell?" I hissed back. "We talked for five seconds."

"That personal admission to encourage intimacy . . . he was looking straight at you." She nodded decisively. "Totally into you. You should go for him."

"Um . . ."

"And he's a Gamma Phi Ep! Perfect."

"Why's that?" The name was familiar. SAXi's brother fraternity—a redundant term.

"Because *all* Sigmas date G Phi Eps. It's tradition."

At least as far back as Victoria and Peter Abbott. I jotted a note in the margin of my paper: "Things to check out."

"Literally all, or figuratively all?" I asked, keeping an eye on Dad's progress plugging in his laptop and getting the projector going.

"Well," Ashley hedged, "everyone I've interviewed for my pledge book."

Now she had my attention. "Your what?"

She showed me the front of a binder, which was decorated with stickers and had "$\Sigma A \Xi = \blacktriangledown$" written on it in paint pen. "Brittany said we'd better start doing our interviews of the actives now, so we're not stuck doing all fifty right before Hell Week."

"Hell Week?"

"The week before initiation. That's when we have our pledge test, and have to turn in our pledge book with all the interviews complete. Weren't you listening in class?"

If Brittany had been talking, then chances were not.

"We're supposed to say Sisterhood Week," Ashley continued. "There's usually some fun quests and assignments and stuff to bond us all together."

"Sounds like a blast."

"I can't wait," she said, missing my irony entirely.

$$* \quad * \quad *$$

The rest of the week progressed the same way: class, paper, class, sisterhood, homework, fall into bed exhausted. I stopped worrying about my lack of dreams; my neurons had nothing left at the end of the day. Not only were the normal brain cells getting a workout, but the freakazoid ones, too. I didn't get sick with them anymore—my deflector shields were becoming second nature to me now—but I still got flashes sometimes, still saw things in people's expressions that I wasn't sure anyone else could see. Maybe it was a trade-off—more waking weirdness for less nightmares. I couldn't say I didn't like it.

Saturday I slept and caught up on my reading for history. Dad tended to call on me whenever he asked the class a question and got nothing but cricket-filled silence, so there was no slacking off with his assignments.

Tara, the pledge trainer, had moved our class to Sunday evening so that we wouldn't have the time constraint of the chapter meeting immediately following. I picked up Holly at her dorm; on the way to the Sigma house, she grumbled that this meant Brittany could talk as much as she wanted, and then realized that "when" I was president, I could shut her up. Which I had to admit was more tempting than anything Victoria Abbott had mentioned.

We settled in the TV room, and Tara—looking more hippie than usual in a long bohemian skirt—started the meeting.

"From now on, the president will call the class to order. So we need to decide who that's going to be. Nominated, we have Brittany and Maggie. All those in favor of Maggie?"

Holly raised her hand. So did Kaylee and Alyssa. I did not, even when my pledge sister kicked me in the ankle. "Ow! I'm abstaining."

"You can't abstain," said Tara.

"I have a conflict of interest." My tone was as unshakable as I could make it. "So I courteously decline to vote."

Her mouth turned down. "Fine. Those for Brittany." Ashley, Erica, Nikki, and of course, the girl herself raised their hands.

"Brittany should abstain, too," Holly protested.

"She doesn't have to." Tara's voice was deep with disapproval, not of my opponent, but of me. "Brittany wins."

To halfhearted applause, Brittany beamed, put her hand on her heart, and made a face of embarrassed gratitude. "Thank you all for your support. I really appreciate the trust you've placed in me."

"Okay," said Tara, opening her binder. "Let's—"

But Brittany wasn't done. "I actually have some ideas for our class. Is it okay to do this now, Tara?"

She blinked, her earth-mother calm taking a hit. "Actually . . ."

"Thanks. It'll only take a sec." She whipped out a long, *long* checklist from the front of her own notebook. "First of all, everyone"—she glared at me—"should make a real effort to try and hang around the house more. Second, I think we should have mandatory checks of our pledge books at every meeting. We don't want *some people*"—why didn't she just say Maggie?—"waiting until the last minute."

Holly shot me the death eye, and I had to admit, I was really regretting my abstention just then.

"Are you two listening to me? This is important stuff. Now. On to Homecoming. I expect everyone to really pitch in and show the actives what we can do. . . ."

✳  ✳  ✳

On Tuesday after history, someone called my name just as I was about to duck into Dad's office. "Hey, Maggie! Wait up!"

Will, the Gamma Phi Epsilon from class, loped down the hall toward me. I'd only seen him slumped in his desk, and he was taller than I'd realized. I had to tilt my head back to look at him as the rest of the class went on by. Including Ashley, who gave me a wink of great significance.

"Maggie, right?" he asked.

"That's a good guess, since I'm the only one that stopped when you bellowed it down the hall."

He laughed. "I was just starting conversation. But I've been sitting behind you for weeks, and we haven't been properly introduced. I'm Will." He stuck out his hand. I had gotten into the habit of steeling my defenses before shaking hands. Sometimes I felt like that guy in *The Dead Zone,* and look how crappy things had turned out for him.

A slight tingle, as if I'd hit my funny bone, but no voyeur vision. I breathed in relief and surreptitiously brushed my palm on my jeans as he released it.

"Are you going to be there Friday?"

I drew a blank. "Friday?"

"You know. At the Underground. Sigmas and Gamma Phi Eps are getting together for a mixer."

"Oh yeah. They talked about that in the chapter meeting on Monday. I thought it was a type of drink."

He laughed. "You're cute."

"Uh. Thanks?" I assumed this was a compliment, but since I'd slipped into a parallel dimension where fraternity guys even talked to me, I couldn't be sure.

"Are you going to be there?"

"I don't know." The Phantom Pledge would need material, I guess. "Maybe."

"You should go." Will grinned, and it was cheeky and charming, darn it. "If you make up your mind, I'll see you there."

"Great." I smiled, a little too brightly.

"See ya then."

"Yeah. See ya."

He jogged off. I watched him go, mentally composing the opening line for next week's column: *Would this guy even notice me if I was wearing my Darth Vader T-shirt instead of Greek letters?*

I swung into Dad's office, then stopped, because Justin occupied a small desk in the corner, diligently typing notes into a laptop. He looked very industrious; maybe a little too much so. Justin couldn't lie with silence, either. Had he heard my conversation with Will? Did I care? Of course I did. No point in lying to anyone about that, least of all myself.

"Hey." He looked good; he'd gotten a haircut, neatly trimmed, short enough on the top to stand up when he ran his hand through it, something he'd apparently done recently. It suited the clean-cut lines of his face. I hadn't seen him since . . . when? My weeks were running together.

He glanced up as if I'd surprised him. "Oh. Hi, Maggie."

Terrible liar. "What are you doing here?" I asked.

His attention returned to the screen and his fingers to the keys. "I'm your dad's teaching assistant. Didn't you wonder why I'm always hanging around?"

"Just figured I was lucky." I wondered if Dad had mentioned this fact. "I knew he was your academic adviser."

"Well, now he's my boss, too." He went back to typing.

"Ah." I watched, taking in the taut set of his shoulders, the clipped ends of his words. "You might as well say it."

"Say what?"

"Whatever has got you wound tighter than a Swiss watch."

"I don't know what you're talking about."

"Fine." I turned to go, but his question stopped me.

"Don't you think you're enjoying this a little too much?" He'd finally looked up, turned in his chair to give me his full attention.

"Enjoying what?"

He made a vague, encompassing gesture. "The whole Greek thing."

Casting a glance out the door to the crowded hallway, I lowered my voice. "You know why I'm doing this."

He rose, closed the distance, kept his voice at the same soft intensity. "I know why you *think* you're doing this."

"What's that supposed to mean?"

"Come on, Maggie. You were flirting. With a fraternity guy."

My mouth worked in silent indignation. So he *had* heard me. Spied on me, even. "I was not!"

"You thought a mixer was a kind of drink? Come on. The real Maggie wouldn't give a guy like him the time of day."

"What do you know about the real Maggie? You seem to think I'm so high-maintenance that a relationship with me would suck up all your study time."

His jaw clenched. "That's not what I said."

"That's what you meant."

"I think I know better than you what I meant."

"You think so?"

A cough from the doorway jolted me back to our surroundings, and I whirled toward the sound. Dad stood there, looking stern. "Should I come back later?"

"No, sir." Justin's face had turned scarlet.

"I have to get to my next class," I muttered, certain my burning cheeks matched his. Ducking past him, I escaped into the hall.

# 17

I'd been assigned a desk in the journalism lab. I shared it with two sophomores, but still. As I entered the last of the edits to an article about the downtown Harvest Days festival, Mike, the senior who served as the sports editor, called across the room in a harried voice.

"Hey, Quinn!"

"Yeah?"

"Bauer says you take decent sports pictures."

What was I supposed to say to that? "Well, *I* think so."

"I've got an article about how critical defense is going to be to Saturday's football game, and no current pictures of the defense. Can you run down and snap something usable?"

"Sure thing." Somehow I managed not to jump up and down and shout "Photo credit! Score!" I still had to get something he considered "usable."

I uploaded the current article to the server, grabbed my stuff, and headed to the practice field.

∗　∗　∗

For a girl allergic to exercise, I do know my way around a football field. Two years of photographing our high school games had at least taught me defense from offense.

"Twenty-three, thirty-two, *hike!*"

I pressed the shutter button and caught the snap. My digital camera—a graduation gift from Gran—made a vintage film sound. Click, whir, snap! Click, whir, slam! Click whir, oof!

A padded player walked into my shot; at my glare, he mumbled an unimpressed "Sorry" and continued to the bench, cup of Gatorade in hand.

Getting creative, I took some pictures of the guys lined up on the bench, shoulder to tank-sized shoulder, knees sprawled wide, forest green helmets between their feet. And then someone walked into my shot again.

This guy wore a T-shirt and track pants, which he filled out nicely without any padding. "Sorry about that."

"I'll live," I said with an exaggerated sigh.

He looked at the badge I'd clipped to my shirt. The Bedivere Rangers weren't exactly big conference football, but they didn't let just anyone wander onto the sidelines and take pictures of drills. "Are you taking over for John?"

John was the usual sports guy. I thumbed backward through the shots I'd taken so far. "Nah. Just filling in."

"Too bad."

I looked up, squinting in the afternoon light. The sun was behind him, and I couldn't see his face. Please tell me a coach hadn't just hit on a freshman. "Uh. Okay."

He took a step to the side, and I could see that he wasn't so creepy after all. "I'm one of the trainers for the offensive unit. If you need anything for an article. Or anything."

Okay, that explained it. I'd had people suck up to me when I was on the Avalon High staff, mostly to get their pictures in the yearbook or a quote in the paper.

"Just here to snap a few pics to go with John's article," I said, lifting my camera in what I hoped was a hint.

"Sure. You're a Sigma Alpha Xi pledge?"

I looked down at my shirt and feigned surprise. "Wow. I guess I am."

The guy laughed in a want-to-make-points way. "I'm AD Phi. I think we have a mixer with you guys coming up soon."

So he was sucking up because I was a SAXi? Interesting.

"So, maybe I'll see you around."

"Sure," I said, and started to turn away, my attention already back to my camera's view screen. Then I thought of something he could help me with, and glanced back over my shoulder. "Actually . . ."

Mr. Offensive Trainer snapped his eyes up to my face. "Yeah?"

Holy crap. He'd been checking out my butt.

"I, um . . ." I actually blathered, a blush heating my face. "Er . . . Can you point me to the defensive coordinator?"

He blinked, as if he'd expected something different. "Sure. Over there. Tall, skinny guy."

"Great." I was reluctant to leave until he did. Just in case the checking out hadn't been positive. "See you around."

"Yeah." A smile this time, and he turned away.

Okay. Maybe I did check him out just a little bit. Fair is fair, after all.

✳ ✳ ✳

I showed off my photo in the paper at lunch on Friday. Holly and I were falling into a Monday-Wednesday-Friday habit, and often Jenna and Devon joined us. Brittany and Ashley did, too, which was less pleasant. Ashley, I'd discovered, was fine on her own, but tended to take on the other girl's most annoying characteristics when they were together.

"With your name under it and everything." Holly stopped devouring her chicken salad sandwich long enough to grin at me. "Awesome."

"I don't see what's the big deal," said Brittany, peering at the newspaper spread out on the table. "It's on the back page."

Devon came to my defense. "Anywhere on the outside of the paper is better than the inside."

Art majors often took a layout class, which overlapped with print journalism majors. I wondered if that was where she met Cole.

"Not only that," I said, "Mike said I could take pictures of the game this weekend."

"Maggie, that's huge!" Devon hugged me, nearly pulling me out of my chair. "And you're only a freshman!"

"Cool," said Brittany, finally impressed. "Football players are hot."

"No, they're not." Ashley did not defer to her on the subject of hotness. "They're all fat and stuff."

"That's the padding."

"I know the difference between padding and *padding*." She grabbed a nonexistent beer belly.

"Okay," Brittany conceded. "But the quarterback and the running guys are hot, especially in those white pants."

I stared at them in bemusement. Moments like this, I wondered if I had imagined the vibe I'd gotten from Victoria. No way were *these* girls tapped into some kind of sorcerous contract for power and world domination.

"Are you coming out with us tonight, Maggie?" Jenna had obviously decided to ignore the other pledges.

"No. I have a family thing."

"On a Friday?"

"Yeah." I didn't want to tell them that my thing involved parking my brain in neutral and watching the Sci-Fi Channel with Dad. I seriously needed some downtime. It was hard juggling homework, undercover investigating, *and* doing your editor's job for him, too.

"Come on," Holly said, with a glint of mischief. "Tell them it's a required activity."

"I'm saving that for when it actually is."

"Speaking of," said Jenna, "are you two keeping up with your pledge books and things?"

"Well, *I* am," said Brittany, even though Jenna hadn't really been talking to her. "I have to set an example, since I'm pledge president." She hadn't reminded us of that yet today.

"I'm good," Holly said between potato chips.

Jenna uncapped her Snapple. "Homecoming is in a couple

of weeks, and we've got to work on the float. You really need to make time for that, Maggie."

"Me?" I already felt like I was spending all my time with the Sigmas.

"Yes. We hardly ever see you at the house, except for pledge class and meetings."

"Blame Devon," I said breezily. "She asked Cole if there was a place for me on the *Report* staff. How's his book coming, by the way?"

I'd only meant to change the subject, but the two actives reacted as if I'd asked about the thermonuclear bomb Cole was building in the basement. Jenna gave her sorority sister a look of blistering intensity and Devon paled, the blood draining from her face, leaving her freckles standing out like raisins in a bowl of oatmeal.

"I don't know what you mean, Maggie. Cole isn't writing a book."

"Oh. My mistake." I brazened it out the best I could. "I must have misunderstood."

What was the big deal about the man's literary ambitions? He was already a journalist. How big a stretch could it be? Yet I could feel waves of sick worry coming off Devon.

I glanced at Jenna and found her watching not her sister, but me, and I wondered what I had given away.

# 18

"I don't know why you're so surprised, Mags." I hadn't given Jenna's roommate permission to call me Mags—only Lisa was allowed to do that—but she was driving the car, and I didn't want to correct her. "You'd be cute even if you weren't a SAXi."

"Gee, thanks." I was in the backseat, keeping my eyes on the road so that I wouldn't get carsick. Jenna had called shotgun, and Holly was beside me laughing just a little too loudly at that. Not because she was mean, but because she'd started the party early—I could smell it on her breath.

"I'm so glad you decided to come," she told me. "You can sleep when you're dead."

"Great. Something to look forward to."

Alexa found an empty spot down the street from the Underground and I tried not to flash the world as I climbed out of the BMW. When I'd shown up at the SAXi house to get a ride with the other girls, Jenna and Alexa had pronounced my jeans and cutest T-shirt unacceptable, then proceeded to go up and down the halls until they'd found an outfit that wouldn't shame the Sigma Alpha Xis' reputation for hotness.

"Stop that." Jenna slapped my hand as I tugged down the skirt. "It covers everything. Do you think we don't know the difference between hot and tacky?"

I had no doubt they did. My eye was less trained, and had widened at the amount of leg showing in the mirror.

"Here." She handed me a Maryland driver's license. "Tonight you're Mavis Bucknell. At least long enough to get in the door."

"I don't need this. It's an eighteen-and-up club, right?"

She wouldn't take the card back. "Just in case you want to have a drink."

Mavis and I looked nothing alike. At least I hoped we didn't. "This is never going to pass for me."

"Just trust me."

The music grew louder as we neared the club. When we reached the door, I could feel the bass beat against my sternum like an extra heart. An enormous guy, his bald head as shiny as an egg, sat on a stool outside. Elbowed by Jenna, I handed him Mavis's license. He stared at it, stared at me, then handed it back, along with a wristband that identified me as legal.

"It worked!" I shouted this at Jenna once we were inside,

where the lights throbbed against my retinas the way the music did against my ears.

"Of course it did!" She winked at me. "Like a charm."

Lisa and I had come here this summer, shortly after my birthday. We'd danced, guys had flirted with me to get introduced to my friend, and I'd had a good time—not everyone could dance with Lisa at the same time, so I had plenty of partners. But techno-pop wasn't my thing.

The dance floor was writhing with college kids. I didn't see anyone who looked even close to thirty—though with the strobes and dim light, it was hard to tell.

I looked around, but didn't see Jenna until she appeared in front of me and pushed a drink into my hand. "Here."

"What is this?" I took a wary sip. The drink was sweet and fruity and didn't taste like alcohol at all. The club was hot with pulsating music and sweaty bodies, and I took a deeper gulp.

"Sex on the beach." Jenna laughed at my grimace. "You're such a prude."

"It's not that." It was because even I knew it was a total sorority-girl drink. I was standing in a club, dressed in a trendy hot outfit, and drinking a sex on the beach. I had become what I most feared: a cliché.

"Hey!" someone yelled in my ear, the only way to get sufficient decibels over the music. I looked up and saw Will from history class. "You decided to come."

"Yeah!" He bent down so that he could hear me. "Jenna talked me into it."

"Excellent!" He pointed to the dance floor, his lips moving, but no sound reaching me through the din.

"Sure!" I looked around for Jenna, to get her to hold my drink, but she had disappeared again. I finished the last sip and stuck it on a passing waiter's tray.

Will grabbed my hand and we threaded through the gyrating bodies until a space opened up. The pulse of the music filled my head, drove out spare thoughts, criticism, and commentary. In the small pocket of air, we danced close together, and I didn't worry about looking like a dork, or if my legs were so pale they glowed in the blacklight. No talking, just motion and instinct.

The beat was primal, spoke to parts of me that weren't used to being included in the conversation. One song bled into another. I glimpsed the other SAXis on the dance floor. In groups and pairs, we came together for one song, then back into the mix and out the other side for the next.

I lost track of partners, until suddenly I was facing Will again. He grinned down, and I smiled up in answer. My skin was damp and hot, and when Will put his hands on my waist the temperature spiked again. Add friction and stir. His jeans brushed my bare legs, my chest brushed his shirt. He smelled of a subtle, spicy cologne and sweat; this was good. But it wasn't right.

I stepped back, bumped into the girl behind me. "I need some air."

"Sure." He blinked, seemed disoriented by the abrupt shift in mood, but let one hand fall from my waist. The other stayed there and steered me through the overheated crowd. The bouncer didn't give us a second glance as we emerged into the cold night and relative quiet.

The clean air swept through my brain and I felt immediately better. Leaning against the wall, I could feel the music pounding, muted, through my back and hips, and I closed my eyes.

"You okay?" asked Will. "You're not going to hurl or anything, are you?"

"From one drink? God, no." At least, I hoped not. My main exposure to alcohol up to this point was wine with Christmas dinner and a mostly-soda-and-not-much-whiskey Dad had let me try from his birthday bottle of Glenlivet.

"Tell me something about yourself," he said, leaning a shoulder against the wall.

I turned my head, brows knitting in confusion. "Like what?"

"I don't know." He shrugged a shoulder, looked at me with that charming smile. "Anything."

"I think the second *Aliens* movie, the James Cameron one, may be my favorite movie ever. Definite top five." Not sure why *that* was the "anything" that popped out. Maybe it was a test.

"Is that the one with the space marines?" I nodded, and he grinned. "You're a geek, but at least you like kick-ass movies."

I'm not sure if that qualified as a pass or not. While I was thinking about it, he bent his head and kissed me.

Deflector shields! I put up my mental defenses as quickly as I could. I didn't want any *Dead Zone* flashes now, while my head was fuzzy from drinking and dancing. And I didn't want him to know that, as nice a kiss as it was . . . I really, really wished he was someone else.

# 19

When I dragged myself home after the game on Saturday, Mom and Dad were on the couch watching a movie. "Look, dear," said my mother, elbowing Dad in the ribs and pointing at me. "Doesn't that girl look like our daughter?"

"I couldn't say, Laura. It's been so long since I've seen her."

"Very funny." I slumped in the recliner, too tired to even put up the leg rest. "And untrue. I saw you on Thursday in class."

"Was that you? I didn't recognize you, sitting in the group of Greeks."

I groaned. "Not you, too. Justin gave me grief about that already, so no need to add to it."

"Is that what you two were arguing about?" Dad asked.

"We weren't arguing. Just sort of . . . discussing in really intense voices. Why don't you guys realize, I'm just doing it for the paper."

"Ah." He used his *Father Knows Best* voice. "And it has nothing to do with Mr. Alphabet sitting behind you?"

"Wait." Mom grabbed the remote and paused the movie. "I thought you and Justin were just friends now. And what's this about a cute guy? Why don't I know about this?"

"Possibly because you have more important things to think about than my quasi-social life?"

"I'm feeling great." She laid a hand on her belly, where the bump seemed to have grown substantially all of a sudden. Just how long had it been since we'd done more than pass each other in the kitchen?

"When am I going to find out if I'm getting a brother or a sister?" I asked.

"Maybe you can read my palm and tell me."

I looked at her sharply. For Mom to even refer to my ability was huge. I guess she figured that if she didn't acknowledge it, the weirdness would somehow just go back to being science fiction. So this was Mount Rushmore big.

"Do you really want to know?" I spoke cautiously, afraid to break the fragile moment.

She seemed tentative, but intrigued. Dad, too, had picked up on the change, and he glanced between us. "You've always said you couldn't see the future."

"It's not the future. XX or XY—it's already set." Mom and

Dad exchanged a look, and I picked up the DVD rental box, pretending I didn't care what they decided. "I probably couldn't tell anything anyway."

"What the heck." Mom gave an embarrassed laugh. "Give it a try."

Grinning, I moved to the couch, nervous and excited—like a kind of stage fright. This was the first time I'd used my new superpower on purpose, but I'd been studying Gran's meditation book diligently. Mostly I'd been concerned with keeping up my defenses, but there were other chapters, too. Breathing deeply, I visualized my deflector shields powering down. After weeks of putting them up, it felt weird and naked.

Mom gave an anxious laugh, almost a giggle, and I shushed her sternly. "You are blocking the flow of positive energy."

"Really?"

"No, not really. You're just making me nervous."

I placed my hand on Mom's gently rounded stomach. A flutter, not under my fingers, but in my heart.

What a strange feeling—alone in the dark, but surrounded, buoyed, and loved. Our pulses meshed—Mom's slow, the rhythm of the universe; mine, the steady pulse of a star; the baby's quick, the turn of a day. A perfect ratio, divinely in proportion—infinitely big, and infinitely small.

Something splashed against my skin, and I opened my eyes. My parents stared at me as I wiped tears from my face, too enthralled to be embarrassed.

"Don't paint her room pink, okay? It only reinforces gender stereotypes."

Mom laughed, and pulled me into a hug. I blinked away a

strange dual vision, as if the connection between my sister and me still resonated. Dad wrapped us all up in his arms and right then, I couldn't feel worried about anything—my professional good fortune, my sudden sex appeal, the Sigma Alpha Xis, or any of it. I felt just like my sister—surrounded, buoyed, and loved.

# 20

On Monday morning, the chill in the air caught me off guard. Flame-colored leaves chased each other across the ground. Fall had snuck up on me somehow. Midterms and Homecoming were closing in fast. September had slipped away, and October was hurrying on its heels.

Ordinarily, I love autumn, but the obvious passage of time disturbed me; it fueled a nagging unease, as if I'd forgotten something important. The more I tried to grasp it, the more quickly it floated away, elusive as a dream.

The thought brought me to an abrupt halt on the sidewalk between the communication building and the science hall, forcing a clump of Kappa Phis to break apart and go around me.

The brisk air seemed to briefly blow a fog from my mind. How many times had I woken with the feeling that I *had* dreamed, but couldn't recall any of it? I'd been dismissing this for—God, it must be weeks now.

I pressed my fingers to my forehead. When was the last dream I could remember? It had to be over a month ago, during Rush maybe. That had to be significant. Didn't it?

A hand touched my shoulder and I whirled around with a shout. Cole stepped back, raising his hands in the universal sign for "Don't beat my head in."

"Sorry! I just wanted to see if you were okay."

"Yeah." I put a hand over my thudding heart, to make sure it wasn't actually coming out of my chest. And then I looked at him again, to make sure he wasn't wearing a Halloween costume. He looked like a zombie. The shadows under his eyes were greenish purple, as if he hadn't slept in a week.

"Are *you* all right?" I didn't mince words. "You look like crap."

He laughed and shrugged. "What can I say. The muse is a real bitch sometimes."

"Yeah, but . . ."

"Don't worry about it, Maggie." He started walking toward the communication building, and I fell in beside him. "Mike loved the pictures from the game on Saturday, by the way."

"Great. Thanks for the assignment."

"I had nothing to do with it."

I glanced up at him; he'd said it honestly. "But I'm just a

freshman. I figured you were throwing me a bone because I don't get a byline on the column."

"A column that I loved, by the way." I'd written about my suddenly elevated attraction, thanks to my Greek status. We climbed the steps to the building and Cole held the door for me. "But you shouldn't sell yourself short, Maggie. I'm a GDI and I would totally go for you, if I were any less nuts about Devon."

GDI was how non-Greeks proudly referred to themselves. I think it started as an insult, but the "God Damn Independents" had adopted it like a banner.

"Thanks," I said, not mentioning that Devon was a Sigma, too, so he hadn't exactly proven his point.

"Anyway," Cole continued as we headed for the journalism floor, "Mike thinks you're his early Christmas present. Said you always seem to have your camera pointed at the right place at exactly the right moment. That takes some serious talent. Or luck."

With a grin, he waved and turned into his classroom. For the second time that morning, I was rooted to the spot by a thought hitting me like a slap across the face.

Was I lucky? Or was something else at work, making things fall into place? Sigmas are successful, Victoria had said. Things would go my way if I took what SAXi had to offer.

I'd been slacking. Nancy Drew would never lose track of time like this. And since I had to start somewhere, I'd start with the mystery of Devon and Cole.

✳  ✳  ✳

*Spying* was such an ugly word. But if you want to get technical, that was what I was doing outside Devon's door. I'd brought my interview book to give me an excuse to talk to her, but she was not alone.

"We *know,* Devon," said Kirby. I'd always thought of her as Victoria Jr., but the edge in her voice was more overt. Mrs. Abbott was velvet-gloved steel. Kirby had less finesse, or wasn't bothering with it now. "Did you think you could keep it a secret?"

"No." Devon sounded as though she was crying. "I just didn't think it would matter so much."

I heard Jenna's voice next, soothing and kind, good cop to Kirby's bully. "I'm so sorry, sweetie. But you have to give him up."

Kirby spoke without pity. "We told you that Cole wasn't right for you. No, I will not shush, Jenna. We told her! There are rules to how this works, and she ignored them."

"But I met him before initiation. I didn't know," Devon sobbed. "And by then I'd already fallen in love with him."

"I know, honey." Jenna's voice, full of sympathy. "But that's why you have to let him go, now. It'll only hurt him more if you wait."

"What if you're wrong?" Devon had found some defiance. "You don't know everything."

"I know enough not to break Victoria's rules."

A tiny pause, enough for a horrified gulp. "Victoria knows?"

"Not yet." Kirby's voice was heavy with implied threat.

"And she doesn't have to," Jenna said, offering a way out.

There was a longer silence now, then Devon spoke firmly. "I'll give back my pin. I'll quit the Sigmas."

Kirby's laugh had razor edges. "Sure you will. Before or after that show in the university art gallery this December? Don't act so holy, Dev. You want that showing as much as you want Cole."

The doorknob rattled, covering any answer to that.

Maybe Devon didn't have one. With no time to retreat, I raised my hand as if I'd just arrived and was about to knock. The door swung open, and I nearly hit Kirby in the forehead.

"Oh!" I jerked my hand back. "I . . . Gosh, I'm sorry. I was looking for Devon to . . ." I held up my pledge book—an unadorned binder full of loose-leaf paper. ". . . you know. For my book."

Jenna brushed past Kirby and grabbed my arm, turning me away from the room and the president's dagger stare. "Not right now, Maggie." She sounded harried, maybe worried. "Maybe after chapter meeting."

I didn't bother to pretend I didn't know something was wrong. "What's going on?"

"Nothing. Boyfriend troubles."

"You really are serious about that no-sex thing, huh?"

"For pledges, yes." We'd reached the top of the stairs. "For actives . . . well, it depends. You have to be very selective, Maggie. That's why we don't want pledges to get too involved with anyone before they know the rules."

"Of what? Who passes the test?"

"Yeah."

"And Devon's boyfriend doesn't? Because he's not Greek?"

She gave me a gentle push toward the stairs. "It's complicated and it's none of your business. Go to the TV room. There are a bunch of actives to interview there."

I could tell I'd reached the limit, pushed as far as I could under the guise of In Everyone's Business Girl. With a last look over my shoulder, I headed down the stairs. Jenna returned to Devon's room, where Kirby stood in the doorway, watching me leave.

*　*　*

Holly had forgotten she was angry with me, until Brittany came into the TV room and started trying to organize the pledges for a slumber party. Then she remembered, and left me to go on to the meeting by myself.

Following the others down, I stopped on the bottom stair when I saw Victoria and Kirby talking in the lobby. The chapter president saw me first, and the alumna turned a moment later. "Maggie!" Victoria smiled and gestured me closer. "Come tell me how it's going with you."

Obediently, I closed the distance. She linked her arm with mine and drew me into the empty chapter room, which had been set up for the evening's meeting—table for the officers at one end, chairs arranged in rows facing it.

"I saw the photo you took in the *Report*. And your classes are going well? Are you finding some time to socialize?"

Everything about her said that she knew—or at least had a very good idea—that things had been going stellar for me. "Yes, ma'am. A blast."

"Good. I'm glad you're enjoying the benefits of being a Sigma Alpha Xi." Her tone was a study in ambiguity. She could have been talking about purely social benefits, but I didn't think so.

"I am a little disappointed," she continued, "that you weren't elected pledge president. It would have been yours if you hadn't abstained."

I picked my answer carefully. "I didn't feel that I could in good conscience vote either way."

She looked at me. I can't read thoughts, but I didn't have any trouble interpreting hers: *A conscience. How quaint.*

Aloud she told me, "You're already off to a great start, Maggie. Being a pledge officer could have been part of that."

I chose to misinterpret her. "Actually, at the *Report*—"

She turned to me, a layer of her mask falling away. "How do you think you got your position at the paper, Maggie? Do you think they'd keep you on for a moment if you were unable to continue that column?"

The chapter room seemed suddenly empty and isolated, the air stuffy and thick. Carpet covered the design on the floor, but I seemed to feel it pulsing with life beneath the soles of my feet, like a hibernating animal.

What the Hell?

No, wait. Let me rephrase that. Something a lot like fear gripped my chest, made it hard to breathe.

How had I forgotten this?

Victoria took a maternal tone, which seemed even scarier with the stifling power trapped inside the room with us. "We discussed this, Maggie. I see potential in you. But you must assert your position over the others early. Every class has a leader, and it is important you take that role."

"Brittany seems to have her stuff together."

Victoria dismissed her with an irritated wave of her hand. "She's not an alpha wolf, just a yapping bitch cub."

The velvet gloves were off. I could keep playing stupid; I could run away, forget about the Sigmas and whatever the Hell they had under the carpet; or I could man up. Get my Forces of Good game on.

I visualized power flowing into my deflector shields, hiding my purpose. "Here's the thing, Victoria. I'm not a front-of-the-pack sort of girl. I'd rather let Brittany be president than have her fighting me at every turn."

She considered me for a moment, then surprised me by laughing, shaking her head. The atmosphere immediately cleared, as though she'd released a spell. I'd fooled her, or she was pretending I had, and I couldn't tell which.

"I like you, Maggie." Her hand rested gently on my shoulder. "You're good for this group precisely because you have a mind of your own." Her fingers tightened, not painfully, but in firm affection. "That you are at initiation is what matters."

"I can hardly wait."

"In the meantime, you do need to be more of a presence. Spend time with your sisters, go to the mixers. Have fun."

"Yes, ma'am."

"You'll be working on the Homecoming float with the Gamma Phi Epsilons." She put her arm around me as we walked toward the door, where girls were queuing up for the meeting. "Gamma Phi Eps and SAXis make very good matches. Ask Jenna and Kirby."

"I thought we weren't supposed to have boyfriends as pledges."

"Maggie, those rules are for the girls with no understanding of what's going on here."

"That would be me, Victoria." That much was honest.

She smiled. "You know to trust me, and your officers. As long as you let us guide you, you'll have a good head start when initiation comes around."

Initiation. It all came down to that. I don't know what worried me more—that I had to play the game until then, or that the longer I played it, the easier it got.

# 21

I left the SAXi house immediately after the meeting, explaining that I had a midterm paper due, which was not a lie. After waking up to the chill of autumn that morning and working on Homecoming articles all day at the paper—not to mention my audience with Queen Victoria—I had a tense awareness that time was slipping away. My Spidey Sense usually kept me very goal-directed, but for some reason I'd been spinning my wheels for weeks, and now I had to make up lost ground.

The university library had two distinct halves. The west side was a century old; the shiny "new" section was built twenty years ago. They didn't match up exactly, so getting from one side to the other involved stairs and doglegs, making me sometimes feel like a hamster in a Habitrail.

I preferred the old half, which had a strong sense of continuity in the musty smell of old paper, in the cramped stacks and scarred wooden tables. I followed the bread crumbs of the Dewey decimal system to the shelves I wanted, then stood staring at the spines, waiting for something to shout "Pick me! I'll answer all your questions, even the ones you're too clueless to ask."

Regrettably, the books remained silent, so I grabbed some useful looking titles, more or less at random. Staggering out of the stacks under the weight of eight fat tomes, I had to wonder why the more abstruse the subject, the more impressively massive the book had to be.

I set them on the nearest table and paused to catch my breath. Somehow I was not surprised to see Justin emerge from between another set of shelves, carrying a large book of his own.

He stopped when he saw me, and we stood that way for a moment. I had a weird feeling in my stomach, sort of like déjà vu but not quite. His hair was messy, his jeans and sweater rumpled, and I missed him more than ever.

"Are you stalking me?" I asked.

His mouth curved in a lopsided smile and he pointed to the next table over, covered from one end to the other in paper and books. "I live here. Maybe *you're* stalking *me.*"

My inner voice hummed in a contented *See, I do know what I'm doing* kind of way. I sighed. "Nothing in the universe is entirely random."

"What's that?" he asked, bemused.

I shook my head. "Nothing."

He cast me a curious look, but let it go. I remembered that we'd argued—well, discussed intensely—the last time we spoke. It seemed as though he might say something about that, or at least something personal. Instead he set down his own book and picked up one of mine.

"*The Encyclopedia of Earth Magic.*" He glanced at me, then warily picked up the next two. "*Sacred Geometry. Finding the Goddess Within.*" Until he read them aloud, it hadn't occurred to me to wonder if we had a particularly esoteric library at Bedivere.

"Taking up some new hobbies?" he asked.

"No." I retrieved the books and neatened the pile self-consciously. "I'm working on a project."

"What kind of project?"

Crap. *Now* my skills at subterfuge chose to fail me?

When I didn't give him an answer, he laid his hand on the stack of books, as if he was going to keep them from me. "Like your friend Lisa? *That* kind of extracurricular project?"

"God, no." I tucked my hair behind my ears and explained . . . sort of. "It's an angle for the column. Origin of symbols, female power. That kind of thing."

He looked at me, hard, then relented. After all, I wasn't exactly lying. "What do you want to know? Anthropology of occult folklore is *my* deal. Why didn't you just call me?"

What a stupid question. Because I was stubborn, and he'd hurt my feelings, of course. It occurred to me that because Justin was older—definitely more knowledgeable and probably more sensible—I'd more than once put him on a pedestal. But really, guys could be so obtuse sometimes.

Instead of pointing this out, I asked, "Don't you ever think you're crazy to believe this is real? Even in the face of experience?"

"Of course," he answered quickly. "Faith isn't absence of doubt. It's belief without proof, not without question."

He spoke as if he would know, which I found interesting. Justin's character was so clearly defined: forthright, gallant, conscientious. But for such a straightforward person, he was still a mystery in some ways. He'd never given me much detail on what had formed him, or set him on this unusual course of study.

The silence lengthened, and he answered my unvoiced question. "I guess that's why I'm here, trying to bridge the gap between faith and science."

I let myself smile at that. "Not enough windmills to tilt at?"

He smiled, too, and the distance between us—from Avalon to Ireland, from Greek Row to the Bedivere library—seemed to shrink for a moment.

But only for a moment. "Hey, Maggie." Will appeared from around one of the shelves. "I thought I heard your voice."

I stifled a sigh, and greeted Will with a wave. He ambled over, a couple of books tucked under his arm, and gave Justin a friendly nod. "How's it going?" Then to me, in a teasing voice, "No fair getting help from the TA on your term paper."

Casually, I turned the stack of books to hide their titles. "If I really need help in history, I *can* get it at home."

Will shook his head sadly, but his eyes were laughing. "I just knew you were going to throw off the curve."

"Professor Quinn doesn't grade on a curve." Justin was trying to be nonchalant, and wasn't entirely successful.

If he noticed, Will amiably pretended not to. "All on me, then." He gestured to the stack of books. "You checking those out? I can carry them down for you."

"Um . . ." He wasn't a Sigma, but I didn't know how much the Gamma Phi Eps were in bed with them—metaphorically speaking—and the titles of the books were unusual to say the least.

"They're mine," said Justin. "This one is yours, Maggie." He handed me the book he'd been carrying, a history of the Knights Templar. Which, in addition to being a secret society, was also part of our history assignment. No coincidences.

"And," he added, "there's nothing wrong with calling me for help. That's my job."

Not the most flattering way to make that offer, especially given my bent pride. "I'll keep it in mind." I left it at that, since Will was rather obviously waiting to walk me out.

Would it completely have blown my cover to stay? Maybe the library wasn't the best place to talk about the weird stuff. The shelves made it too easy for someone to eavesdrop, and I knew I wasn't the only Sigma with deflector shields.

But that wasn't the real point. Would it have killed Justin to give me some hint that he wanted me to stay?

"I wasn't interrupting anything there, was I?" Will asked as we wound down the stairs to the circulation desk.

"No." That didn't sound entirely convincing, so I added, "We were talking about school."

He nodded, and we checked out our books. On the way out, he asked, "Did you eat yet?"

My stomach growled as soon as he mentioned food. "I was going to grab some McNuggets on the way home."

He held the door, and coaxed me with a smile. "I'll spring for a Happy Meal."

What the hell. I could placate Victoria, learn about fraternities for my column, and eat at the same time. It wasn't a date, it was multitasking.

$*$ $*$ $*$

It was only fast food, but by the time I got home and dragged myself up the stairs to my room, the long day had crashed down on me, and I still had calculus homework. I set the Templar book on the desk and wrote myself a note on a Post-it. "What is the deal with the Sigmas and the Gamma Eps?" Further investigation would have to wait until the next day.

Later, post–math homework, I lay in bed thinking about how silent my warning system had been the last month or more. What were the odds that, as much time as I had spent with these girls, there hadn't been one eating disorder, chemical dependency, or boyfriend crisis to trip my switch?

And then there was the no-dream thing, which distressed and frustrated me. Because those were basic. That was how my freakiness had first shown up.

According to Gran's book, you could psych yourself into meaningful dreams by relaxing, inviting the dream to visit your sleep. Or you could meditate, or pray if that was your thing.

Before graduation, I hadn't been to Mass in years. But

facing Evil with a capital *E* makes a convincing argument that somewhere, in some shape or form, there was Good with a capital *G*, too, and I wanted no mistake about which side I was on.

I'm not saying Team Father, Son, and Holy Ghost is the only team in the *G* league, but it's what I defaulted to when I needed to get my spiritual ducks in a row. Even so, I'm not exactly what you call a reverent traditionalist.

"Okay, God." I stared up at the dark ceiling. "Maybe you could throw me a bone here. I'm going in circles and could really use a signpost." I paused, trying to sound at least a little supplicant. "So . . . anytime you're ready, that would be great."

I didn't really expect an immediate answer, but the silence in my head disappointed me anyway. My fingers had crept up to the small gold cross that I always wore—a confirmation present from my gran. I usually forgot I had it on, which was a fairly obvious sign that while I was committed to the capital *G*, I was a little lax on the protocol.

With a sigh, I dropped the pendant. Then I rolled over, burrowed into the covers, and closed my eyes.

*God, we both know I suck at praying. But please . . . just show me what to do.*

✳ ✳ ✳

I woke in darkness, heart pounding. Fumbling for the lamp, I switched it on. My eyes darted around the room for what had awakened me, but found nothing. I *sensed* nothing.

Throwing on my robe, I padded downstairs without bothering to turn on a light. Unconcerned about the parents' privacy, I went to their bedroom and opened the door a crack, held my breath until I heard two sets of soft, even snores. They were fine, and something deep inside me unknotted.

Gran's picture was on the piano in the living room. Walking carefully in the dim glow of the hall nightlight, I picked up the framed photo. A slumbering sense of her floated into my brain, like the clean lavender soap smell of her sheets. Fine.

Why could I sense my grandmother through her photo, but from the Sigmas I got nothing? No dreams and no clear sense of their nature. That was important.

But how? Time was running out. Initiation was six weeks off, and then the window of opportunity would close.

I set the photo down and climbed the stairs, feeling like I was wrapped in wool—sweaty and hot. Why couldn't I think? I was a fast thinker, intuitively leaping tall quandaries in a single bound. What had changed?

Falling onto my sofa, I picked up my cell phone to see what time it was, whether I could get any more sleep that night. I had a text message from Justin. *Call me. Please.*

What had I said? Show me what to do.

Flipping open the phone, I dialed. He didn't pick up until the fourth ring, and sounded still asleep. "Hullo?"

Swallowed pride doesn't always go down easily. I couldn't seem to talk around mine. Alert now, he said, "Maggie?"

"I . . ." It wasn't just the stubbornness. The wet wool feeling was invading my head, seeping in through my skull, making my tongue thick and heavy. "I need help."

"Are you home?" I heard the sound of rustling fabric, as if he was getting dressed. "I'll be right there."

"No, don't. The parents—" God, my head. The more I tried to tell him there was something wrong, the more it ached. "I'll meet you somewhere."

"Not in the middle of the night you won't." Keys jingled and a door opened, then shut again. "I'll come get you. Meet me outside."

He hung up before I could protest again.

# 22

I think purgatory must be like an IHOP at two in the morning. The fluorescent lights ward off the dark, but give no warmth. The people who come and go look tired, like they'd rather be somewhere else but aren't. You can get food and coffee, but it's not very good.

Justin took his coffee black. He poured us both a cup from the blue plastic carafe before he even let me speak. His brown eyes were bloodshot, his hair sticking straight up. He had sleep creases on his cheek. But he was there.

"Now. Tell me about the Sigma Alpha Xis."

I did. Everything I remembered, and the things I didn't,

I told him about that, too. I told him about Victoria and the paper, and how tempted I was. I told him how I kept writing notes to myself to check things out, and then forgetting them.

He listened to all of it, then said, "That's everything?"

No, it wasn't. I was certain I was leaving something out, but I couldn't think what. The wool-headed feeling had lifted while I waited for Justin outside in the brisk air, and the headache with it. But I still had the sense I was forgetting something.

"It's everything I can recall," I said.

"So you think . . . what, exactly?"

"That's just it." Why wasn't I able to find the right thing to say to make this make some kind of twisted sense? "There's something wrong, something off. It's all feelings, no evidence." I sank my head into my hands. "I don't know."

The coffee cup scraped on the Formica as he pushed it aside, making room for his elbows. "Hey. Let's be organized. Tell me what you do know."

I looked up. He had his arms resting on the table, his head at my level, his gaze searching mine. "You'll figure it out, Maggie. What *do* you know?"

"Okay." I ordered my thoughts. They'd all poured out randomly before. "One. Victoria told me the Sigmas always succeed. Everyone else acts that way, too. Things just go right for them. Even my pictures for the paper—I always seem to have my camera pointed at the right place at the right moment."

"But you've been doing sports photography for a while, right? You might just have a knack."

"Not in *every* shot."

He conceded the point. "Okay, that's a start. What's next?"

"Two. They're freaked out about Devon dating an independent." That made Justin laugh. "I know. Not that strange, either. All sororities want status, success, and guys, not necessarily in that order. See why I doubt myself?"

"Don't start that." He poured another cup of coffee. "Your feelings are evidence enough for me. The fact that you're not remembering things . . . maybe that's because you're on the inside. It's affecting your radar somehow."

This was the first hopeful, useful thing I'd heard in weeks. "You think so?"

He shrugged slightly. "Have they given you anything? The BU bookstore is full of Greek stuff. Anything like that?"

"No." Then I frowned, trying to remember. "Maybe. A T-shirt, the pledge pin . . ."

"It would be something you might keep on you all the time, or maybe by your bed."

I shook my head, not quite in denial, but in frustration. "You see? This is what happens."

Justin leaned in again, lowering his voice and catching my gaze. "Have you considered that there may be some greater power at work here? You joke about Faustian bargains, but maybe that's not a coincidental analogy."

"Sorority girls from Hell? Isn't that like saying French people from France?"

"I'm serious, Maggie."

"I know you are, Justin." He was talking capital *E* stuff, much more than just *Mean Girls* meets *The Craft*. "But if it is—and I'm not saying I think that—and I'm in a position to do something about it, I can't just run away."

He sighed. "No, you can't. I'm just worried that because you've made friends there—"

"What?" I demanded. "You think I'm enjoying myself too much? That the attention and success are going to my head?"

"No." He said it simply, taking the indignant wind out of my sails. "Because you've been wrong before."

I stared into my coffee cup. "This isn't like Lisa."

"Yes, it is." His tone was firm, but tempered with regret. "Your friendship, once you give it, is hard to lose. It's one of my favorite things about you."

I didn't want to look at him. Didn't want to hope. But, jeez, talk about mixed signals lately.

A shadow fell on the table and I looked up, thinking it was the waitress. I was surprised to see Cole standing there, hands shoved in the pockets of his jacket.

"What are you doing here?" I asked.

"Can't sleep." He indicated the laptop case slung on his shoulder. "Trying to work. Thought maybe a change of location . . ."

"You're not having writer's block, are you?"

"No," he growled, in a way that meant yes. "Don't you have an eight o'clock class in the morning?"

Justin, who had been watching this curiously, finally spoke. "You have an eight o'clock class?"

"What is this? Maggie has two dads? I'm a big girl." Cole was scowling at Justin, as if he were to blame for my being out so late. I made introductions. "Justin, this is the editor of the *Ranger Report*. Cole, this is my friend, who was helping me with a project."

"Great. I'm glad someone's getting some work done." He started to grump off, then turned back. "While you're working on that Homecoming float with the SAXis, see if you can take some pictures we can use."

"Sure." I wasn't about to disagree with him in this mood.

"And Hardcastle says you're putting in too many hours at the *Report*. So don't come in until the afternoon."

He left, taking a spot in a corner booth and dragging out his laptop. I watched him go, then turned back to Justin, who looked questioningly back at me. "He's not usually like that," I said.

"I hope not."

"Yeah." But if Cole was miserable, then I'll bet Devon was miserable, too. And miserable people like to talk about what's at the root of their problems.

Justin climbed out of the booth. "Come on. Let's see if I can get you home without your father shooting me."

"That would be a shame. To get the punishment with none of the sin."

I hadn't meant to flirt, but he looked down at me with raised eyebrows anyway. "I wouldn't know anything about that."

"Punishment or sin?" I asked as we waited to pay the cashier.

He shook his head, holding out. "I don't think I can answer that without incriminating myself."

I had out my wallet, but Justin glared until I put it back in my bag. "I'll bet you were the model student when you were in college," I said. "All studious, and home by ten when you had an early class."

"I'm still *in* college."

"I mean, when you were a normal freshman, before you decided to become a weird academic."

"Actually." His mouth turned up in rueful memory. "My friend Henry and I almost got kicked out of school."

"For what?"

He paid for our coffees with a five and waved off the change. "Nothing that I'm going to admit to you."

"Come on," I cajoled. "I know almost nothing about you before we met."

"It's safer that way."

"For who?"

"For me," he said with a grin, and held open the door.

✳ ✳ ✳

I used my extra time between morning classes to go over to the Sigma house. The first floor was the foyer, chapter room, dining hall, and kitchen. The floors above that were bedrooms, with two wings running out from the central hub of the staircase. The banister and balustrades were dark polished wood, the stairs creaky underfoot. The hallways were carpeted and wainscoted, like a stately home.

Devon was on the second floor. I didn't know her schedule, but her door was ajar. I tapped on it and poked my head in. She was alone, lying on her bed, a thick art history book on her chest. "Got a minute?"

She laid the book aside and sat up. "Sure."

I noticed that her eyes were puffy and her hair was less flippy than usual. "I'm working on my pledge book, and I was wondering if you had time to answer a few questions."

"Sure," she said again, and patted the end of the bed. "Have a seat."

I couldn't help staring at the walls of her tiny room. They'd been painted with a mural of the seaside, complete with sunbathing women checking out a buff lifeguard. "Nice," I said.

"Thanks. Gotta do something with all the extra energy."

Not sure what she meant by that—not sure I wanted to know—I let it go and pulled out a pen and my book. "Our pledge president has been riding us about these."

"We all thought you were going to be pledge prez." She folded her legs, Indian-style. "When Tara told us in board meeting you weren't . . . Well, I thought smoke was going to come out of Victoria's nostrils."

"That wouldn't have surprised me at all." I poised my pen. "So you're on the board?"

"Yeah. I'm the house committee liaison. I coordinate with the alumnae house board, tell them that the exterminator didn't show up or the toilets are blocked again. Real glamorous, huh?"

I grinned. "Very sexy."

"It's a thankless job. And a pain, because I have a master key to all the locks, so somehow I'm always the one that gets called whenever someone needs to get in the initiation closet."

"The initiation closet?" I chewed my pen and didn't have to work very hard at looking nervous. "They don't, um, lock pledges in there or anything, do they? I've heard stories about putting girls in coffins and stuff like that."

"Lord, no." She made a face. "The closet is just where we store all the ceremonial stuff. And the Christmas decorations.

But there's never enough storage in the rooms, so people are always wanting to stick their crap in there."

And Justin wondered why I doubt there's big bad magic here. They kept their cauldron in the broom closet.

She shifted on the bed; with her freckles and wan face, she looked young and vulnerable. "Don't tell Kirby that I blabbed anything about initiation, okay?"

"No problem." Whatever was up with her, Devon's distress had appealed to my do-gooder nature, and I was firmly on her side. I looked down at the blank page of my book, and tried to think of a decent question. "So, where are you from?"

"Alabama."

"If you were a flavor of ice cream, what would you be?"

She laughed. "Pistachio."

I made up some more questions, something to fill up the page. What I really wanted to know, though, I saved until I closed the binder and capped my pen. "Can I ask you one more thing? Off the record?"

Her gaze turned wary, but she didn't decline. "Okay."

"Why are the other sisters—Kirby and Jenna, at least—so set against Cole?"

She hung her head in her hands, elbows on her knees. "Oh, Maggie. You're just a pledge. You'll understand soon."

"Is it because he's not a Greek?"

"No."

"Because he's not a Gamma Phi Epsilon?"

"No. Not exactly." She folded her arms tightly. "I can't talk about it with you, Maggie. Please believe me."

"Then at least tell me why it was a secret that he's writing a book?"

Her face crumpled, tears welling and slipping down her cheeks. "Because I'm his muse." At least, that's what I thought she said. It was a little hard to tell through the sniffling.

"Why is that bad? Is the book about you? The Sigmas?"

"No." She dashed at her tears and struggled for calm.

"Okay." I let it go, waited until she got herself together, then asked, as gently as I could, "Did you break up?"

She nodded, biting her lip. Then shook her head. "We're on a break. I'm giving him some space."

"He doesn't look like he wants it."

Devon nodded and stared at her interlaced fingers. "We need it."

I didn't bother to ask her to explain. "Can I do anything to help?"

Raising her head, she gave me a miserable smile. "No. Thank you. Cole told me you were helping him at the paper. You're a good person, Maggie."

"No." I shook my head. "Not really. I'm just a sucker for star-crossed love."

# 23

On Thursday, Will took the seat next to me in history class. Dad raised his eyebrows when he saw the new arrangement, and called on me several times during the discussion to make sure I was paying attention, especially since Ashley, on my other side, kept giggling like we were in junior high.

After dismissal, while everyone gathered their books and tromped down the steps to the door, Will turned to me with a smile. "So, I'll see you tonight?"

"What's tonight?" No wonder I'd never had a social life; I couldn't keep track of it all.

"Working on the Homecoming float." The *Of course* was implied.

"Oh yeah. I'll be there. Mandatory for pledges."

"Great." He gestured for me to go ahead of him. I'm not sure how far he planned to accompany me, but I stopped by the front desk, making it clear I intended to linger. Dad nodded to Will, who said, "Professor" courteously back to him, then "See ya" to me before he left.

Dad did the eyebrow thing and I ignored it. Again. "Hey, Dad."

"Greetings, offspring." He closed his laptop and disconnected it from the video port on the podium.

I helped him gather the rest of his things. "Ironic that I stayed home to be with you guys while Mom experiences the miracle of childbirth, and I'm never home."

Dad gave me a fond look. "I know perfectly well why you stayed home, Magpie. So does your mother."

"Yes, well . . ." I blushed, because staying home was one of those things I knew I had to do if I wanted to be able to live with myself, but I wasn't always gracious about it. "I have to go. See you tonight."

"Will you be home for dinner?"

"When am I ever?"

"What is it tonight? Mr. Alphabet?" Meaning Will.

"Homecoming float." I rolled my eyes to show my school spirit.

"Ah." He put his hands over his heart. "Your mother would be so proud."

✳   ✳   ✳

The float construction took place by the detached garage between the Sigma Alpha Xi and Gamma Phi Epsilon houses. Convenient. The place had once been a carriage house shared by the two homes, but now it was owned by the Gamma Phi

Eps, and they stored, among things that did not bear investigating, the flatbed trailer that would serve as the base for the float.

A cold front had blown in. The guys worked on the float with their breath making clouds around their red faces. The girls stood in the shelter of the garage, wrapped in scarves, hands tucked in pockets.

The theme for the parade was "Ahead to the Future." All the clubs on campus put forward an entry, except maybe the Young Republicans, but only because they were afraid of potshots. Each sorority teamed with a fraternity, and since it was a measure of social ranking, the pairings were vitally important. Except for the Sigmas and Gamma Phi Eps, who were always first in status, and always matched with each other.

Not that they always won the school prize. That was irrelevant. The real prize was intangible—the jealousy of your peers.

This year's float, in keeping with the theme, was a spaceship. I was sure no one else would think of that.

"Well, ours will be better than everyone else's," said Brittany when I pointed this out. She was all over the place, directing the builders and chastising the observers. The rest of the Sigmas were happy to drink hot chocolate and let sexism work for them.

I had brought my pledge book, and put my time to good use. Four more pages filled before the boys had gotten the first of the framework put up.

"That's cheating," said Brittany. "You can't do two mandatory things at once."

Holly drawled, "You're just jealous you didn't think of it."

"Am not." Her hands went to her hips. "And I did think of it, I just decided it would be *cheating*."

"Here." Jenna shoved a mug of hot chocolate at her. "Have a drink."

"Please," said Holly. "Put something in her mouth to shut her up."

"I volunteer," called one of the Gamma Phi Eps. Brittany's cheeks darkened and she flounced off, finally robbed of speech.

Jenna laughed and handed the mug to me instead. The drink was steaming hot and tasted like it had peppermint mixed in. The warmth went straight to my toes.

"So," she asked, "who's the guy from the library?"

I didn't quite choke. "The who?"

She gave me a don't-be-coy look. "Will told David, who told me, that you were talking to someone in the library."

"Is it normal for fraternity guys to gossip like old women?"

Her shoulder lifted in a shrug that didn't deny the point. "Will likes you. He thinks this guy is why you've been playing hard to get."

"Hand to God," I swore with complete honesty. "Library Guy and I are just friends."

"Good." The wind pinked her cheeks; in her knit hat she looked like an impish five-year-old. "Because David also told me that Will *really* likes you."

"Gosh! Did he pass you a note in gym class?"

She laughed. "Don't you take anything seriously?"

"It's part of my charm."

Jenna glanced around, then gestured to the lowered tail-gate of someone's pickup. "Let's sit over there."

I followed her over, past where Devon was painting very realistic comets and nebulae on the panels that would go around the bottom, representing space, the final frontier. The hot chocolate—and whatever was in it—was making me mellow, so I settled beside her on the tailgate, the metal cold even through my jeans.

We watched the guys for a bit; I saw Will over by Jenna's boyfriend, David, the yenta of Gamma Phi Epsilon, horsing around with their electric screwdrivers—which sounds like a metaphor for something, but it's not. When Brittany told them to stop goofing off, they saluted her and went back to work.

"Gamma Phi Eps"—Jenna picked up where she had left off, and her tone was *significant*—"are good matches for Sigmas."

"You mean they're . . ." I tapped my forehead. I could mean psychic, or I could mean crazy. Or both, which is how I felt lately. "Like us?"

Jenna shook her head. "Not any more than any other random population of people."

Dead end on that question. "Well, that's a relief. I was worried there was a conspiracy."

She looked at me sharply. "A what?"

"To breed a master race of television psychics."

Jenna folded her arms and didn't laugh, but looked as if she wanted to. "You have no idea how special you are, do you? Even among us. That's why Kirby pushed for Brittany to be pledge prez. You could run laps around her when it comes to . . ."

"What?" I asked, when she didn't go on.

"You'll find out when the time is right."

I let my irritation show. "I hate being in the dark."

"I know." She sounded honestly sympathetic. "But you shouldn't be thinking about it so much. It'll give you a headache." Her hand squeezed mine where it rested on the tailgate, and her fingers were almost as cold as the metal. "Just wait until initiation. You'll understand everything then."

Initiation again. All roads led there, where I *so* did not want to go.

# 24

Two weeks slipped away in a circular blur of class, newspaper, homework, Homecoming, and Sigma Alpha Xi activities. I overheard two actives saying that since losing the election for pledge president, I really seemed to have discovered my Sigma spirit.

Whatever.

Ethan Douglas, editor of the *Avalon Sentinel,* called and asked me to do an article on the student art show in the campus gallery, and Will asked me to Homecoming. The more time I spent with the Sigmas, the more things went well.

Except, of course, that I didn't want to go with *Will* to Homecoming.

I saw Justin on Tuesdays and Thursdays, but since Will walked with me from history to the arts building, we didn't speak more than "Hey" and "How are you." Which, as I had nothing to report, was enough. Theoretically.

On Thursday before the parade, I tried my best to corral the SAXis and Gamma Phi Eps into a picture with the not-quite-finished float. I'd gone around Greek Row to interview the other houses and had the same problem; getting them all to behave long enough to get a workable photo was like herding cats.

"Come on, guys! Squish in." I framed the shot for my third attempt. "This is for the school paper, so maybe you could hide the liquor bottles this time?"

They did, *finally,* and when I was done, Devon, Holly, and Jenna crowded in to look at the camera's view screen. "Can I have a copy of that?" Jenna asked.

"Sure. I can print you one after I upload them." I checked my watch. "Which I need to do if there's a hope of this running in tomorrow's paper."

"Can you use my computer, Maggie?" Devon asked. She was looking more like her perky self, so I suspected her "break" was over. "Cole has sent stuff in from there."

"Probably. Do you mind?"

"I wouldn't have offered otherwise." She waved for me to follow her. "Come on."

Since the front door of the sorority house required a key—only Sigmas and their pledges had one—a lot of the girls didn't lock their rooms, especially if they were just going downstairs. Devon was one of them.

"Here you go." She woke the desktop computer with a jiggle of the mouse. "We're on the school network, like a dorm."

"Thanks." I pulled the USB cable out of my camera bag and started hooking up.

"Do you need me? Otherwise I'll go back outside."

"I'm good. I'll close the door when I leave."

She took off, and I uploaded the photos, first to the computer and then through the Internet to the *Report* server. While I waited for them to finish loading, I browsed the bulletin board on Devon's wall. It was full of pictures—of her and her pledge sisters, of Cole, of parties and vacations.

A set of keys hung from a hook. The fob was a woodcut cartoon octopus with indigo SAXi letters. Not the most convenient thing to tuck in your pocket on the way to class.

No way was it that easy. Keeping an eye on the open door, I plucked the ring from the hook. I got a muddled sense of a series of girls who had held them, but overwhelmingly, these belonged to the house. When I concentrated, I could distinguish each one: front door, chapter room, outside storage shed, and finally a musty, stuffy dark place. The closet.

I checked the hall: Grand Central Station. The whole chapter was here, mostly out working on the float, but also in and out of rooms to get coats and drinks, up and down the stairs. Okay, maybe not that easy.

Grabbing my own key ring from my camera bag, I flipped through it until I found one of the same standard industrial-shaped keys as the one for the closet. It was to my family's rented storage unit, so hopefully if Devon did touch the ring, she wouldn't sense anything out of the ordinary. The worry would be moot if she tried to actually *use* it, but the whole thing was a gamble in the first place.

*Things work out for Sigmas.* I said it over and over in my mind, like a mantra. *I'm a Sigma. I might as well put it to use.*

# 25

"I think I can get into the closet where they keep their supersecret stuff."

Justin stared at me, his sandwich frozen halfway to his mouth. We were eating lunch in Dad's office; he wouldn't notice any extra crumbs and—privilege of tenure—he usually left at noon on Fridays anyway.

The sandwich went back down onto the wrapper. "How are you planning to do that?"

"There's this big mandatory party tonight at the Abbotts' place for all the alums who are coming for Homecoming. I'm going to slip out, go back to the Sigma house."

"They just leave their supersecret stuff lying around?"

"Well, not exactly."

He eyed me sternly. "So you're going to break in."

"Of course not. I have a key." I took a bite of chicken salad, chewed, and swallowed, all under his inscrutable stare. "But there actually is something you can help me with."

✳ ✳ ✳

Once again I had done my shopping at the fine establishment of Grandmother's Closet. Tonight's ensemble was very *Breakfast at Tiffany's*—black cocktail dress, pearls, and ballet flats. I'd learned my lesson on footwear: you never knew when you'd be facing down hordes of ravenous demon spawn, and kitten heels could be a real encumbrance.

The Abbotts' Victorian mansion was brightly lit, inside and out. The doors and windows opened to the veranda for guests to wander. Which they did, squealing with delight when they saw a sister, or clasping hands and slapping backs with a brother.

The Gamma Phi Epsilon alumni were there, too. Lawyers, CEOs, bestselling novelists. I knew these weren't *all* the university's notable alumni, but being in the room with them, it seemed that way.

The student members were encouraged to circulate and schmooze. There was an open bar for those old enough to drink, and the pledges took well-orchestrated shifts carrying trays of punch and canapés around. I was bringing an empty tray to the kitchen and checking my watch when Holly came up and wrapped her arm around mine.

"My mother wants to meet you."

"Your mother's here?" I set the tray on a console table in the hall, since I was obviously not going to get back to the kitchen. "You didn't say she was coming."

"I was hoping her plane would crash."

Holly had been hitting the sauce. The only thing that gave her away, though, was the brightness of her eyes and redness of the tip of her nose. Well, and the looseness of her tongue.

I knew Holly drank, but since her underwear-drawer stash consisted of little airplane bottles, I hadn't been too concerned. Now I wondered.

"Should I be worried?" I asked.

"Only if you're allergic to brimstone."

If she only knew.

Still clinging to my arm, she pulled me to a corner of the room, where a gorgeous auburn-haired woman in a three-thousand-dollar suit held court in the midst of a bunch of Gamma Phi Eps. They were, man and boy, practically tripping over their lolling tongues.

It wasn't simply that the woman was beautiful. She radiated charisma. Once you were in her sphere, it was hard to look away. The power was palpable, raising the hair on my arms. Holly had told me her mother was a lawyer; if she stood in a courtroom and told me the moon was made of green cheese, I would believe her.

"Holly!" She beckoned her daughter through the entourage. "Is this your new friend?"

"Mom, this is Maggie Quinn. Maggie, this is my mother, Juliana Baker-Russell-Hattendorf-Hughes."

Riiiight. No passive aggression there.

The multinamed lady shot Holly the briefest of glares, then extended her manicured hand to me with a smile. "A pleasure, Maggie. Holly has spoken of you often."

I braced before taking her hand, shields at full power. That battle station was fully operational. "Nice to meet you, Ms. . . ." No way could I remember all those names.

"Hughes is fine. Or Juliana, since we're sisters, after all." She released my fingers and I resisted the impulse to shake my hand the way a dog shakes off water. "I hear you're trying to decide between English and photojournalism."

"Well, the journalism seems to be out in front at the moment."

"Make sure you stay in touch, then. I have some contacts with the news services."

"Too bad Jane and Ted got divorced," Holly said. "She and Mom are like *that*." She held up her crossed fingers.

"Great!" I grabbed my friend's arm firmly. "Nice to meet you, Ms. Hughes!" Chirruping too brightly, I dragged Holly away before her mother the Death Star could blow up Planet Freshman with her laser eye beams.

"Very nice," I drawled when we were out of earshot. "Thank you *so* much for introducing me."

"You're welcome." Once we reached the kitchen, she pulled her hand from mine and sagged against the counter, making the busy catering staff reroute around her. "God, why did I wear high heels? I'm six feet tall already. Trade shoes with me, Maggie."

"I don't think they'd fit." I glanced at my watch. I had to make up an excuse and get out of there to rendez-vous with Justin.

"I hate my mother."

The caterers were eyeing us with less annoyance and more curiosity now. I patted Holly's shoulder, hoping to coax her to use, as my mother said, an inside voice. "She'll be going back home after the weekend."

"Doesn't matter." She pulled off the offending shoes and tossed them on the floor. I fetched them before they could trip an innocent food service worker; Holly grabbed an open bottle of champagne, poured a generous helping into a punch glass, and downed it before I could stop her.

"She killed my father, you know."

I stared at Holly, mouth agape, but she went on, oblivious to the dead stop in the kitchen. "He had a heart attack in the middle of fucking her. How's that for a cliché?"

"Peachy." I reached for her arm, intending to lead her to a more private place, or at least relieve her of the bottle. But she easily avoided my grasp.

"Maybe I'll just go in there and tell all those boys about *that*." She stepped in the direction of the party and yelled, "Stay away from her, boys! She's a black widow, that one!"

This was getting serious. There was a room full of alumnae witches in there, and I didn't know how far sister- *or* motherhood would protect Holly if she really made them mad.

"Come on." I tugged her insistently toward the back door. "Let's go get some fresh air."

"Why?" She looked down at me belligerently. "Because I shouldn't embarrass my darling mother?"

"Because you shouldn't piss her off!"

A flash of sobering fear entered her eyes. "No. I shouldn't. Let's go."

Ignoring the staring caterers, I led her onto the back porch, where the bracing air ruffled our dresses and, I hope, cleared her brain. She tilted her head back and stared at the bright stars whirling through the spiral arm barely discernible on the inky fabric of space.

"Sorry," she finally said.

"It's all right. Nothing like airing family laundry to make a party special."

She smiled slightly. "That's not the half of it. Steven divorced her because she was sleeping around, and this new guy doesn't even care, as long as he gets his first."

"Nice."

"She's a succubus. I don't want to be anything like her, yet here I am. At her alma mater. In her sorority."

Something struck me about that choice of word. "Succubus?"

"A demon that sleeps with men to steal their souls."

"Yeah. I know. But you mean that figuratively, right?"

She laughed. "How else would I mean it?"

Well, I'd learned not to take these things for granted. And when I say I got a feeling of power off Juliana Baker-Russell-Hattendorf-Hughes, I mean some *serious* power.

"Do you have somewhere to be?"

I looked at her, startled, probably a lot guilty. "What?"

"You keep glancing at your watch."

Some spy I am. "Oh. No." Gosh, that didn't sound guilty at all. "Well, yes. I have to—I need to—"

She raised her brows expectantly. I made one last-ditch effort at a save. "I'm meeting someone."

Her eyebrows shot up even farther. "*You* are meeting someone?"

The disbelief in her tone was a little insulting. "Yes. Why is that so incredible?"

"Because you're so . . . Gidget." She laughed at my offended expression. "Okay. Maybe not. You're too snarky."

"Aren't you going to tell me I shouldn't date an independent, or all Sigmas date Gammas, or whatever?"

"No. I'm rebelling vicariously."

I stepped off the porch, then turned back, whispering, "Aren't you going to tell me not to have sex while I'm a pledge?"

Laughter in her eyes, she asked, "Would it make you feel better if I did?"

"Yes."

"Okay. Don't do anything I wouldn't do. How's that?"

"You either. Seriously." I sobered to warn her. "Stay away from the booze and stay away from your mother."

"Deal."

# 26

"You're late." Justin put the car in drive and headed the few blocks to Greek Row. "I was about to go in and get you."

"Like Orpheus in the underworld?" I grabbed my jeans from the backseat and pulled them on under my dress. "That's sweet."

"You joke about those things, and I never know how serious you are. Is it any wonder I worry about you?"

"I know. I get it. I'm high-maintenance. So you've said."

"We're not having that argument again. What really bothers me is—God, Maggie! Do you have to do that?"

I had unzipped my dress and extracted my arms so that I

could pull on a black cat-burglar sweater. "What? Don't be such a prude, Justin." All the same, I yanked the turtleneck over my head and squirmed into it quickly.

He cruised past the SAXi house, which was quiet and dark, and looked for a spot to park a few doors down. "What really bothers me is that you keep picking crusades that I can't help you with. High school, now a sorority. You're going to a convent next, I know it."

"Why is my chastity such a big issue with everyone lately?"

"What?"

"Nothing." He parked the car and got out. I buttoned my jeans and wiggled the dress down my legs, stepping out of it as Justin opened my door. Grabbing my camera bag from the floorboard, I climbed out and tugged down my sweater.

"At least let me go in with you," he said.

The SAXi and Gamma Phi Ep houses were quiet, but there was plenty of activity on the street as the other chapters worked on their floats for the morning's parade.

"Then who'd keep a lookout?" I checked that I had the right keys. "Distribution of manpower."

Shaking his head in frustration, he rested a hand on the roof of the car. "I cannot believe I am so whipped," he grumbled, "and we're not even dating."

I looked up at him in irritation. One, he was blocking my way. Two, "If you're looking for sympathy, you're talking to the wrong person, *pal.*"

A rapid series of emotions moved across his face, and he opened his mouth to say something, then snapped it closed. "Later," he said, and stepped out of my way. I shouldered my bag and headed for the house, walking as though I had every right to be there.

Technically I wasn't breaking and entering since, as a Sigma, I had a key to the front door. Maybe, if I got caught, a judge would see things my way. If I ever made it to see a judge. I guess the Sigmas could decide to simply sacrifice me at the next meeting and save the court's trouble.

Justin was right. I really had to stop joking about things like that.

Still, I couldn't help feeling conspicuous as I entered the foyer, hyperaware of the chapter room to my right. Too easy to picture something lurking behind the closed door, like a monster in the closet. And the more I pictured it, the more powerful and gruesome it became, until it seethed in my mind with reason-killing ferocity.

*Get a grip, Maggie. You're not five years old anymore.*

But I hurried past all the same.

The stairs sighed softly under my feet as I climbed to the second floor, holding my camera bag against my side to keep it from swinging. The upstairs hallways ran north and south, with the bathrooms at one end. The storage closets were opposite, so I turned left at the top of the first flight of steps.

I crept, cat-footed, past the bedrooms, even though I'd done a mental check of all the residents while at the party. The hall seemed endless, but finally I reached the closet and contemplated the solid wood door and the deadbolt.

Not worried about fingerprints as much as I was psyche-prints, I filled my mind with images of octopi and compasses and indigo auras before I inserted the key and turned the knob. I expected an atmospheric creak as I pulled open the door, but the hinges glided smoothly, without a sound.

The closet was pitch dark and a little musty, but underneath the smell of old plaster and carpet glue was something spicy, and a little earthy, with a tangy metallic thread: the incense from that first night. I'd found the right place.

I flipped the light switch with my elbow and stared at the perfectly mundane storage room, maybe ten feet by twenty. Industrial shelves against the walls. Boxes marked "Xmas Lights" and "Skit Night" and a rolled canvas backdrop on the floor. Lightbulbs and Sam's Club–sized packages of toilet paper. In the corner was a large water heater, and beside it a neat stack of luggage, stored for the semester. No sign of anything the least bit mysterious.

Poking around, I found a box of white candles like we'd used in the pledging ceremony, and the crimson stoles, folded neatly. Finally I found a few boxes labeled "Initiation," and inside were a lot of white togas, several skeins of silken cord, and more candles—indigo and crimson.

With a derisive snort, I pushed the box back onto the shelf. I'd expected something a little more exciting than inventory from the Wiccan Gift Shop.

About to give up, I made one last turn around the tiny room, this time using all my senses. Nothing leaped out and snagged my attention.

And by that I mean an actual nothingness; there was a *hole* in the back corner.

Everything, even lightbulbs and Christmas decorations, feels like something, even if it's just the psychic equivalent of white noise. The dead space reminded me of the strange blankness in my head when I woke with the aftereffects of a dream, but no memory of it.

I walked to the corner, and saw a cabinet. Plain, industrial.

Locked. I pulled a Nancy Drew: taking the barrette from my hair, I reshaped the wire clasp until I could slip it between the double doors, catch the latch, and pull it up.

The monster wasn't downstairs. It lived in this box.

A dank smell, like old, wet leaves, rolled out of the cabinet, and with it a feeling of ancient power. I'd felt something like it once before when I'd touched an artifact forged millennia ago for arcane purposes. This tangible energy was not as old, but just as icky. There was a baseness to it; death and sex and blood—the earthy, metallic smell beneath the spicy sweetness of the incense.

I saw the censer on the top shelf, the burnished metal looking warm even in the incandescent light of the bare bulb. A bowl the size of a candy dish, it had a lid with holes for the smoke to emerge. Turning on my camera, I took pictures of the censer and of the symbols etched in the brass.

The lamp sat next to it; they looked like a matched set. I took down a plastic bottle, unscrewed the top, and sniffed. Oil, with a pungent smell. I soaked one of my lens-cleaning cloths with a little of it, and tucked it in one of the pockets of my camera bag. Tucked behind the censer was a Tupperware container that held the incense, and I took a sample of that as well. Who knew all those *CSI* reruns would come in so handy?

On the bottom of the two shelves was the book, lying by itself. I wiped suddenly damp palms on my jeans. The feeling of danger and power was so strong, I would have rather put my hand in a vat of earthworms than pick up that heavy volume.

And that's about what it felt like: when my fingers made contact with the leather binding, my skin tried to crawl up my arm and away from the Evil—capital *E*—that I sensed inside.

With a deep breath, I pulled the tome from the cabinet, holding it away from my body. It was heavy: big like a coffee table book, and fat like a dictionary. The leather of the cover was pale and smooth, darker where generations of hands had touched it, and worn at the corners and edges.

No lettering or symbols marked the outside. Gingerly, I set it on top of a box of toilet paper and opened it, letting the thick pages fall where they pleased.

Calligraphy script, illuminated diagrams, and a lot of text I didn't understand and wasn't going to grasp in the short time I had. I snapped pictures of as many pages as I dared then, hoping that was good enough, I closed the book and with great relief slid it back onto its shelf.

My phone vibrated in my pocket, startling me. I fumbled it open without looking at the caller ID.

Holly's voice, tight and quiet. "Victoria and my mother just shot out of here like a pair of greyhounds after a rabbit."

"What?"

"Maggie, I don't know what you're doing, what you're *really* doing. But *they* know. And wherever you are, they're going there now."

I didn't have to be told twice. I shut the cabinet doors, using my impromptu jimmy to hook the latch back in place. The dreadful wrongness disappeared, the blankness coming back down like a curtain.

Grabbing my camera bag, I dashed out of the closet, locking it behind me, then sprinted down the hallway to Devon's room. *Please don't let this be the one day she locked her door. . . .*

It wasn't. As I fumbled the closet key onto its proper ring, my phone vibrated again: Justin, warning me they were outside. House keys returned to normal, I shoved my own into my pocket and started back out.

Too late. I heard the creak of footsteps on the stairs and ducked back into the room. What the hell was I supposed to do now? There was a fire escape, but it was on the far side of the staircase.

The women's voices came closer, becoming distinct as they neared Devon's door. I pressed myself to the wall and visualized becoming one with the house. *Deflector shields, don't fail me now.*

"You can't really think it's her."

"What I think, Victoria, is that you need that girl, so you are blind to the fact that she's playing you for a fool."

"I have the situation under control."

"Oh, you are *all* about control." Juliana's voice was derisive. "Control and playing it safe."

Victoria answered tightly. "Not everyone is about using people up and throwing them out. I'm making a long-term investment."

"So am I."

"In yourself, you mean."

"Do *not* fuck with me, Victoria." Frost rimed the woman's voice. They must have stopped directly outside. I could feel the icy power through the door, sense the dominance shifting between the women like weather patterns. "Never forget who started this. You would never have had the guts to do what I did. And if I hadn't, where would you be? Married to a city councilman with two mortgages and a minivan in the garage."

But Victoria wasn't done. "Don't threaten me, Juliana. Where would *you* be if I hadn't kept this house going the last twenty years? You need us. You need *me.*"

"Not as much as you think," she purred, clearly a threat. "But my daughter does. Now open the door and let's see if someone has put their hand in the cookie jar."

I'd been careful to put everything back, not just where it looked right, but where it *felt* right. But I worried that my fear and revulsion might be the psychic equivalent of a neon sign.

Hurrying to the window, I raised the sash and looked out. Only one floor up, but my heart pounded as if it were a dozen. Looping my bag bandolier-style, I sat on the ledge and swung out one leg, then the other, turning so that I hung out the window, then lowering myself until my dangling feet found the ledge below.

How did a girl as unathletic as me keep getting into these predicaments? And why was it *always* heights?

Clinging white-knuckled to the brick overhang, I managed to lower the window sash, which is tricky from the outside. Then I realized I was going to have to let my feet go, hang from my fingertips, and drop to the ground. Let's see— sprained or broken ankle versus the Witch Queens of Endor.

I'd take my chances on crutches.

Luckily it was autumn, and that meant rain. The ground yielded, absorbed my weight, then dumped me onto my butt, where I have the most padding. I'm telling you: Things work out for Sigmas.

# 27

"Drive," I wheezed, diving into the backseat of Justin's car after my sprint from the SAXi house. "I have to beat them back to the Abbotts'."

Justin stepped on the gas and the little Honda sped down the street while he fired questions at me. "What the hell were you doing in there? How did you get out? And what do you mean you're going back to the Abbott house?"

I pulled off my sweater, yanked the black dress over my head, struggled out of my jeans. "Holly will cover for me, say I've been there the whole time."

"How do you know that?"

"Because she hates her mother." I contorted in the back-seat, wrestling with my zipper. If it were a dream instead of a nightmare, the car would be parked and Justin would be back there with me. God had a real sense of humor sometimes.

"You're determined to give me a heart attack," he grumbled, taking another turn at full speed and throwing me against the car door. "I'm going to be gray by the time I'm twenty-five."

"You know I can hear you, right?"

Letting him grouse, I pulled my phone from my jeans and called Holly to tell her I was on the way back, and what I needed from her. When I hung up, Justin asked, "Are you at least going to tell me what you found?"

"I took pictures of everything." Searching the floorboard, I came up with my right shoe. "I'll show you after I put in an appearance at Victoria's house."

"How long?"

The left shoe was harder to find. "I just have to be there when they get back."

When he stopped the car in the street beside the Abbotts' house, Holly was coming down the back steps. "You really trust this girl?" Justin asked, twisting in his seat so that he could look me in the eye.

I didn't think too hard, just went with my gut. "Right now, yes."

"More than you trusted Lisa?"

Low blow. I shot him a glare as I stuck my cell phone into my purse. "Less than I trust Lisa, if my life is at stake."

"Maggie." He caught my hand before I could climb out of the car. "You took pictures of what was there. We can figure out what is going on from outside. You don't have to go back in."

His eyes were almost black in the faint light of the dashboard, fathomless with worry for me. I wanted so much to take that away. Not that I wasn't scared; since I'd touched that book, all my flippancy, my ambivalence, was gone. This wasn't just some sorority girls with supernaturally shiny hair, tweaking the probabilities in their favor. This was the capital *E*. I'd be an idiot not to be scared.

But I'd be worse than a coward if I didn't do everything I could to stop it. And right now, everything meant going into Victoria's house and preserving my place within the Sigmas.

"If things were the other way around," I asked, "would *you* retreat to a safe distance?"

"That's not the point."

I smiled, even though there was no time for it. "I love that you're such a chauvinist."

He didn't bother to deny it. He didn't really have a chance, because the car door opened and Holly said, "Just kiss already. We've got to get going."

Justin glared at her, then at me. "If you're not at my place in thirty minutes, I'm coming back here . . . with crosses and holy water if necessary."

"Okay." I looked him in the eye as I said it, making it a promise. "Thirty minutes."

I climbed out of the car and straightened my dress. Holly grabbed my arm and we hurried to the back porch. I cast one last look back to make sure Justin was leaving. Did that make me Orpheus or Eurydice? Things didn't turn out well for either of them.

\*   \*   \*

I entered the kitchen on Holly's heels. The catering staff continued packing up their stuff, casting curious glances our way, but mostly ignoring us the way Holly ignored them. "I have been hiding out back here, avoiding Mommie Dearest. We'll just say that you've been helping me while I've been . . ."

"Drunk off your ass?"

"Don't diss the drunk that saved your butt." She peered out the window as a car pulled into the drive behind the house. Justin's taillights had barely disappeared.

"Come on." She pulled me down the hall to a small bedroom with an attached bath. Holly went into the bathroom and sat on the side of the tub. I stared, bemused, until she pointed to the stack of finger towels by the sink. Catching a clue, I ran some water and soaked a cloth, ready to pretend I'd been tending to her for some time.

The back door slammed, then footsteps rang in the hall. "Holly?" I knew Juliana's voice now. Her telling Victoria to eff off had made a big impression. "The waitstaff said . . ."

She appeared in the doorway to find Holly looking wan, while I mopped her brow and her damp red hair.

"Oh, *Holly.*" Her expression was a mixture of disgust and disdain. "Are you determined to humiliate me? You couldn't be drunk at one of your *own* parties?"

"What fun would that be?" Holly asked, convincingly inebriated and belligerent.

Juliana eyed me next, and I felt the full weight of it in my stomach. "And you. What have you been up to, Maggie?"

"She's been with me, Mom."

"Holly wasn't feeling very well," I said, lies on top of lies, all smoke screen. "I thought I'd better stay with her."

Victoria appeared behind the other woman and took in the scene. "Oh. Holly, really."

Juliana turned her attention to spin control. "Fortunately, Holly had the good sense to take herself out of public view."

The currents of power shifted again, and Victoria now had the upper hand. "Do you realize how serious this is? At the very least, she should be brought up before Standards."

"Oh, really. You want it to come out that a minor got drunk at your house?"

Victoria didn't blink. "She'd nevertheless be out of the sorority."

To my surprise, Juliana backed down. She might have the edge where mojo was concerned, but Victoria had boxed her in. Her eyes flashed at the knowledge, and her mouth went white at the corners, making her look much closer to her real age.

"I won't forget this, Victoria." She turned to go, calling her daughter to heel. "Come on, Holly."

"Can't I just go back to the dorm?"

"Now." In her anger, all semblance of shielding dropped away, and she stood before us, a mass of fury and frustration. Holly rose, jaw jutting but silent, to face her.

I felt a protective spark in my chest, wanting to shield the girl who, screwed up as she was, had helped me. But Victoria's tiny head shake silenced me; I would only make things worse for Holly by speaking up for her.

Instead I just offered her a hand up, and steadied her once she was on her feet. "Will you be okay?" I whispered.

"You say that like I've never done this before." She gave me a tipsy salute and trailed after her fuming mother.

When they left, the chapter sponsor folded her arms and

leaned against the doorframe, studying me, reminding me I wasn't off the hook yet.

"You two have become rather good friends, haven't you?"

"We hit it off during Rush."

"Her mother expected her to be the head of her pledge class. Holly lacks your ability and ambition, but don't let your friendship bring down your guard."

"No, ma'am."

"Even among wolves, there are alphas and there are betas."

"I understand." In the other room, I'd thrown my purse onto the bed, and it began to buzz in time to my vibrating phone. Had it been thirty minutes already?

"Go ahead." Victoria stepped aside to let me pass.

I answered as soon as I fumbled the cell free from my bag. "Hi, Mom."

"Are you on your way?" Justin's voice brooked no argument.

"Just about. Let me ask." I closed my eyes for the briefest moment, hoping my cloaking device would last just a little longer, then turned to face Victoria. "My mom's not feeling well. Wants to know if I can come home."

"Of course," she said. "You have to take care of your family."

I smiled a humble thank-you and she accepted it with a regal nod. "On my way now," I said into the phone.

"You'd better be," he said, before I closed the phone and picked up my purse.

"Thank you for hosting the party," I told Victoria, falling back on good manners to get me out the door.

"I'm happy to do it," she answered, in the same polite tone. "Now, go home and take care of your mother. She's in a delicate condition, after all."

"Thanks," I said again, and made my exit through the back door to where my Jeep was parked down the street.

It wasn't until later that I thought to wonder when I'd told her that Mom was pregnant.

# 28

Justin lived in an efficiency apartment, part of off-campus housing, not far from Greek Row. I'd never been to his place before. Actually, I'd never been to any guy's apartment before, so I had no idea how his compared.

Mostly, he had books. There was a futon, a milk-crate side table, a large desk with neatly organized work stacked beside a closed laptop, and some cinder-block-and-plank shelves that held CDs, a small TV, and a smaller stereo. But mostly books.

"It's not much," Justin said as he gestured me in. "But make yourself at home."

"Sure." Small, but obviously his space. Posters on the wall; a distinctive quilt covering the back of the futon. Two enormous bulletin boards over the desk were filled with notes and pictures of green, wet places and weathered Gaelic faces.

A framed picture on the bookshelf showed a formally posed couple. The man stood behind the woman, his hand on her shoulder, her fingers covering his. They smiled at the camera, but there seemed to be a connection solely between them. They could only be Justin's parents. He looked just like his dad, but he had his mother's friendly brown eyes.

Another photo showed Justin looking about fifteen or sixteen and very gangly, laughing with another boy who had him in a headlock. They wore khakis, oxford shirts, blazers with a crest on the pocket. The other boy was bigger, with shoulders like a linebacker, black hair, and startling blue eyes.

I picked up the picture. Images welled in my head, incomplete and indistinct: classrooms and chapel, roughhousing after school, fights and reconciliation.

"We look like a couple of dorks in those uniforms." I hadn't heard Justin come up behind me. "That's Henry," he said, nodding at the photo.

"The one who almost got kicked out of school with you?"

"Yeah. We'd planned to go to the same college. Man, was I mad at him when he went to seminary instead."

"You don't think he'll make a good priest?"

"It's a little hard to reconcile that with the guy who used to sneak *Playboys* into our dormitory." He set the photo back on the shelf. "Are you hungry?"

My stomach growled at the thought of food. Aside from a few canapés, I hadn't eaten. "It feels later than nine o'clock."

"I'll order a pizza while you upload the pictures."

He'd brought in my camera case, and I'd had my laptop in the trunk of the Jeep. I set up on the end of his desk and rolled the chair over, careful not to catch the skirt of my dress in the wheels.

Justin hung up with the pizza place and joined me. "Okay. Let's see what you've got."

I opened the pictures on the laptop screen. "This is the incense burner from the pledging ceremony. The lamp was there, too."

Propping one hand on the desk and the other on the back of my chair, he leaned over my shoulder. "Can you zoom in on the symbols?" I did, and he made a thinking noise.

"They look like astrological signs," I said.

"Or alchemical, which borrowed a lot from astrology. Go to the lamp." He leaned in closer to look. "Yeah. Those are definitely hermetic."

"What's that?" I asked, trying not to breathe too deeply, because he smelled so good.

Fortunately—or not—he went to the bookcase and pulled down a hefty tome. "Hermeticism is an occult tradition, based on the writings or teachings of the god Hermes Trismegistus."

"Like the Greek god Hermes?"

"Sort of. Hermes rolled up with the Egyptian god Thoth. Both were bringers of knowledge to their cultures." He set the book in front of me, pointing to a bunch of symbols that looked like the ones on the chapter's brassware.

"Except that the only thing fraternities have to do with real Greeks is their letters." I looked up at him. "So what's this got to do with the Sigma Wicca Phis?"

He flipped a few pages, to a grainy picture of a guy dressed in a strange robe holding a staff of some kind. "Hermetic occultism had a renaissance in the nineteenth century. This guy, Aleister Crowley, formed a group called the Hermetic Order of the Golden Dawn. Huge influence on twentieth-century mysticism. Their ritual drew from everybody: Kabbalah, hermeticism, Egyptian paganism, alchemy, astrology . . ." He made an "and so on" gesture. "Some people think hermeticism also inspired the Illuminati, Freemasons, groups like that."

"More secret societies," I said, half to myself.

"Right." He scanned the thumbnails of the rest of the pictures, and pointed to one of the book. "What's this?"

"That"—I tried to keep my voice even—"feels like bad news." I clicked and brought the image up front. Foreign words and strange symbols crawled across the screen, and I shuddered.

He leaned closer than before, peering over my shoulder. "Oh my God." Reaching around me, he took over the trackpad and clicked through the first few pages.

"What is it?" I asked, knowing I wouldn't like the answer.

"It's a . . . Well, it *looks* like a grimoire." I could feel the tension in him, despite his attempt to keep his tone academic.

"A grimoire is like a spell book, right?"

"More or less." He pushed away from the desk, paced a little, came back to look again. "You said this thing was old?"

"Really old. And very creepy."

"Authentic grimoires were written in medieval times as

213

kind of magical primers. Some contain astrological corre-
spondences, recipes for mixing medicine, instructions for
making talismans . . ."

"That doesn't sound too bad." It was a feeble attempt at
hope; I knew it couldn't be that simple.

"Others have instructions for spells and potions, information on angels and demons, and directions on how to
summon them."

The bottom dropped out of my stomach. "Oh."

"Very." He stared back at me, past traumas looming large
and dark in our shared history. The air thickened with
dreadful possibilities.

Someone pounded on the door. Justin jumped, and so
did I, with a girly squeal to make it worse. He gave a shaky
laugh, breaking the tension. "Pizza's here."

While he paid the driver, I turned back to the computer
screen. I couldn't make anything of the book pages. I recognized the Latin, but even the diagrams were esoteric and
uninterpretable.

I drummed my fingers on the desk, thinking about rituals and artifacts. I tried not to think about summoning
demons. But that was like saying "Don't think of a purple
elephant." So I thought of a purple elephant, and picked up
my phone.

Justin came out of the kitchen with a plate full of more
pizza than even I could eat. "Who are you calling?"

"Lisa. We need a witch on our side."

"No." He took the phone from me. "We don't."

I stood, followed his retreat. "Maybe she can figure out
what this stuff is supposed to do."

"I can figure it out." He held the plate in one hand, and the phone easily out of my reach.

"When?" I set my hands on my hips. "I haven't forgotten about your thesis, and class, and teaching assistant job. You think I have no consideration, but—"

"Would you stop?" He faced me, mirrored my belligerence. "I never said you asked anything that I don't *want* to give. Time, resources . . . driving your getaway car."

"You *said* you were whipped."

"Well, I'm not. I'm perfectly able to say no to you, Maggie." He held up the phone. "As in 'No, we are not calling your demon-summoning friend.' "

I folded my arms. "You know what, Justin? Even if you *were* my boyfriend, I would only take that under advisement."

He stared at me for a long moment, at the stubborn set of my chin and the fight in my stance. Then, with a sigh he handed me the cell and the plate of pizza.

"Thank you." I caught his eye, making sure he knew I meant it.

He sat on the single barstool and pulled over the pizza box. "You'd just call her when you got home, so you might as well do it where I can hear."

At the desk, I put the phone on speaker so that I could eat and type while I talked. Lisa answered on the third ring. "Maggie?"

"Hi, Lisa. I need your help with something."

"Fine, thank you," she said pointedly. "And how are you?"

"Are you busy?"

"It's ten o'clock on a Friday night. Why would I be busy?"

"Great." I saved the photos and attached them to an e-mail. "I'm sending you some pretty big picture files."

Silence. "Are we ignoring the fact that you haven't returned my phone calls for the last two months?"

I felt the blood rush out of my head and pool in my stomach. "Two months? It hasn't been that long."

"Yes. It has."

Oh my God. I had a vague memory of Mom telling me she'd called. Once. Was it like the Post-it notes—written then forgotten?

"Lisa . . . something's been going on."

She sighed. Loudly. "Let me go to my computer." I heard the squeak of a chair and the slide and click of a mouse. I took a few bites of pizza while I waited. "What am I looking at?" she asked.

"It's a long story. There's an incense burner, a lamp, and a . . ."

"I know what this is." Another pause, another mouse click. A worried sigh. "Magdalena Quinn. How do you get into these things?"

"So, do you understand it?"

Her voice turned droll. "My Latin is a little rusty to translate on the fly."

"But you could interpret what this is supposed to do?"

This time the pause was loaded. "Why are you asking me to do this? Where's the square?"

"Um, the square is right here," I said without turning around.

A beat of realization. "I'm on speakerphone, aren't I."

Justin called from across the tiny room. "Hello, Lisa."

I did glare at him then and picked up the phone, turning off the speaker. "Now it's just you and I."

"Why, Maggie? You said I shouldn't be studying this stuff."

"And *you* said the whole reason you were doing it was to counter it." I let that rest between us a moment. "Are you going to put your money where your mouth is?"

"Is that what this is? A test?"

"No. It's strategic outsourcing."

That made her laugh, once, and softly. "Okay. It's going to take me a few days. I'm just a dilettante."

"I'm relieved to hear that."

"What are you doing with a boy in your room at ten—no, ten-thirty at night?"

"He's not in my room. I'm in his."

"God, Maggie. There's hope for you yet."

"Good-*bye*, Lisa."

Shutting the phone, I let my shoulders sag. I didn't realize how tense I'd been until I felt Justin's hands on my arms. My dress was sleeveless, and his fingers were warm on my skin as he gently turned me to face him.

I stared at the top button of his shirt, the hollow at the base of his throat, shy but expectant. Giving in to my hopes, I raised my head and closed my eyes, waiting. He let go of my shoulders, and reached for . . .

My pledge pin.

He unfastened the clasp from my dress without so much as brushing anything important. Then he went to the kitchen counter and dropped it into a glass of cloudy water—salt water, for spell-breaking. Of course.

He glanced at me curiously. "Feel anything?"

Oh, the irony. It burns us, my precious.

"No." I folded my arms over my chest. I felt plenty, but didn't think that was what he meant.

"Huh." His brows knit in disappointment. "I thought maybe that was the source of the spell."

"What spell?"

"The one where you keep forgetting that you're supposed to be investigating the Sigmas."

Now I felt something. Incredibly stupid. I dropped onto the futon, pressing my fingers to my forehead. "It isn't that I forget. It's that I keep losing focus. Losing time."

Justin fished the pin out of the glass and sat beside me. "There must be something else. You've got to search your room, Maggie. Anything Sigma-related . . ."

"I know." I held out my hand and he dropped the gold pin into my palm. "This was too obvious. That's why I didn't think of it."

"Sure," he said, leaving *If that makes you feel better* unspoken.

There are two ways to sit on a futon: perched on the edge, or half-reclining. So we reclined, side by side, half friends and half something else.

"What's next?" His baritone voice rumbled in my ear.

*You realize we're meant to be together, or I accept that we're not.* But I wasn't making the mistake—again—of assuming we were in the same headspace.

"I have to be with the Sigmas on the parade route at six a.m. to help put the finishing touches on the float. I don't have to ride on it, thank God, because I'm taking pictures for the *Sentinel.*"

He turned his head to look at me. "The Avalon paper? Not the *Report*?"

"Yeah." I gazed at the ceiling, ignoring his gaze on my profile. "The guy who was covering the Homecoming festivities came down with strep throat. Ethan Douglas called this morning and asked if I'd do it."

"Okay." His tone was condemningly neutral.

"I *know*!" I thumped the cushion with a frustrated fist. "But how could I leave him in a jam? Curse this SAXi luck!" Justin laughed and I sat up, thinking about the problem while I could, before I lost focus again. "It's a karma engine or something. The probabilities always go in their favor. It's like they're manipulating chaos theory."

"Nothing is without a price, especially where magic is concerned. So, what's the trade off? Something has to be powering this magic."

"That's what I'll work on." I flopped back down, turned my head to look at him. "You'll remind me when I forget, right?"

His hand covered mine. "If you promise to be careful." He looked me in the eye, weighting his words. "They're not really your friends, Maggie. Their goals are not your goals. You can't trust anyone."

That was the thing. Even knowing that this blanket of complacency was false, was laid on me somehow, it was hard to remember. Trust no one. Not even, it seemed, myself.

# 29

I woke slowly on Sunday morning, enjoying the warm light on my eyelids, floating on the surface of sleep like a leaf on a lake, suspended between awareness above and the knowledge below. The shreds of a dream were close this time, the closest they'd been in months, but as soon as I tried to grasp them they skittered away, blown by a wind that stank of old bones. I stretched my thoughts like fingers, but the images dissolved and sank out of reach.

"Dammit!"

"Magdalena Lorraine." Mom's voice popped my eyes open. She stood at the open French doors, her arms full of folded jeans that I must have left in the dryer. "That's a hell of a word for Sunday morning."

I groaned and sat up, pushing my hair out of my face. The only thing worse than no dream was psychic hangover with no dream. "What time is it?"

"Ten." She stayed on the study side, viewing my bedroom with extreme displeasure. "What on earth happened in here? It looks like a tornado touched down."

And it did. Shoes spilled out of the closet, drawers vomited out their contents. "I was looking for something."

"Well, clean it up before tomorrow. You don't want to start the week like this." She used the "My house, my rules" voice, and I didn't argue. "Did you have a good time at the game?"

"It was work. I took pictures for the *Report*."

She found a place to set the jeans. "You were out late."

"The game went late. Overtime. We weren't supposed to win, but we did, with this crazy play." Even *I* knew it was awesome, and I didn't even like football.

"I noticed that Justin drove you home. And you sat talking in the car for quite some time."

"Jeez, Mom. At least it was the front seat and not the back." I wondered if I would have been so cranky if Justin and I had done anything other than talk about the Sigmas.

"Okay, okay." Raising her hands in surrender, she turned toward the stairs. "Hurry up and get dressed. Dad said he'd take us to brunch before your pledge meeting."

Pledge meeting. Speak of the devil.

✳ ✳ ✳

When I walked into the Sigma house and saw Kirby and Victoria in the foyer, I thought for sure they were on to me. I mean, on to me in a way they could prove. I froze in the doorway, ready to flee, but then I saw Holly behind them giving me the thumbs-up.

"I'm afraid we have some bad news," said Victoria, a great disparity between her sober expression and her satisfied, even gleeful, mood. I didn't know which Sight to trust.

Kirby, on the other hand, was all displeasure. "Brittany was brought before Standards this afternoon, and asked to leave Sigma Alpha Xi."

Behind them both, Holly was almost doing a happy dance. I let the front door close. "But, what happened? She was such an . . . enthusiastic pledge."

"A little too enthusiastic." The chapter president looked ready to spit nails; it wasn't aimed at me in particular, but the white-hot frustration held tightly in check made me question Brittany's safety.

"That's not important," said Victoria, taking my arm and guiding me toward the chapter room. "She broke the rules, she is out, and now you, as vice president, must take her place."

I pulled away from her grasp. "What?"

She regarded me calmly, never considering I'd refuse her. "It's time to step up, Maggie. Your sisters are relying on you."

Placing a hand on my shoulder, she urged me through the inner doors. The temperature in the chapter room was so cold, I thought someone had left the window open. But then I saw Juliana seated in the armchair, and realized the icicles were metaphorical. Maybe that was why Victoria was so smug. I wondered if she'd convinced the other alum to help her get Brittany out of the way, on the pretext that Holly would move up.

The other pledges were sitting in a loose semicircle, very straight-backed and uneasy. I didn't think it would take any superpowers to pick up on the atmosphere. Tara stood between the girls and Juliana, as if she were defending her chicks.

Jenna met me at the door with a hug. "It's all right," she whispered. "Brittany's all right, and you're going to be where you ought to be, so don't worry about Kirby or Juliana."

"Um . . . okay." I could tell she believed it, whether it was true or not. Her protective assurance seeped in through her embrace, and lulled my judicious fears.

Kirby had gone to the head table; Victoria positioned herself opposite Juliana, as if to counterbalance the weight of her anger. The carpet covered the floor, but I guessed the spiral's arm encompassed us all.

"Let's get this thing going," said Kirby, all steel, no glove. "I am very sad to announce that Brittany has decided to resign from Sigma Alpha Xi."

No murmur of surprise or outrage; no one called the chapter president on this blatant lie either.

"According to the chapter bylaws, we will now install the new pledge president. Maggie?"

Jenna placed a hand on my back, and, feeling like I was climbing to the guillotine—Juliana's glare was sharp enough—I let her lead me to join Kirby and Victoria, making four points around the circular table. Brittany had been installed like this, but with just Kirby and Tara present, and I'd felt no real sorcery then, which was why I wasn't having a complete freak out.

"With this sign," began Kirby in a pro forma tone. Jenna unclasped the pledge badge from my shirt and looped a little gavel charm through the pin.

"And with this flame"—the chapter president struck a match and lit a white candle, like at the pledge ceremony— "we install you as president of the pledge class, and charge you, by the North Star you wear as your emblem, to guide and represent your sisters, in all things and in all ways Sigma Alpha Xi."

The three of them gazed at me expectantly. Was I supposed to say Amen? So say we all? Then I realized Kirby was holding out the candle. I was supposed to accept it.

When I'd insisted to Justin that the only way for me to get to the bottom of the Sigmas' power was from the inside, this wasn't what I had in mind. Yet as I looked around the circle, at their studying expressions, I realized it was a test of faith.

Of course it was. But not between me and the Sigmas.

*Here I go again*—stepping off the ledge, trusting everything to turn out right. I reached out and took the candle, and accepted all things Sigma.

Amen.

✳   ✳   ✳

When the alarm pierced my sleep on Monday morning, I hit the snooze button and rolled over, pulling the covers over my head. The erased feeling was worse than ever. Instead of a neatly excised spot in my psyche, there was a raw, torn hole where a dream should have been. When I took stock of the situation, I tried to look on the bright side. At least now I *knew* I was blundering around in a fog.

The second alarm went off, and I went to the shower and soaked my head under the hottest water I could stand. After I'd come home from pledge meeting, I finished my column— Victoria was not going to be happy about my writing that our alumni mixer looked like an episode of *Desperate Housewives*—and tried to figure out why it disturbed me that Brittany had been kicked out of the sorority. She was annoying but harmless, and she really bought into the whole Greek thing.

So why get rid of her, other than to clear the way for a more favored candidate? Was it that she was bossy? Or because she was disobedient? Maybe all these inane tasks and absurd rules were really a test not of commitment or "sisterhood," but obedience.

Mulling it over, I dressed in jeans and a purple sweater, dried my hair, and put on some lip gloss. When I was done, I still had no answers, and all the good the hot shower had done in clearing my head was wasted.

Muddled and fuzzy again, I grabbed my books and my satchel and left for my first class of the day—journalism with Dr. Hardcastle. I felt the need for industrial-strength caffeine, and swung by the campus Starbucks for a latte, then hurried to the arts building through the morning chill.

As I walked, the fuzziness fell away, replaced by a vague unease. It couldn't be the three espresso shots making me jumpy—I'd only had time to drink down two of them at most.

By the time I reached the classroom, I felt wound like a

clock. And when Professor Hardcastle came in and pointed to me, I wasn't really surprised.

"You. Quinn. Go over to the journalism lab. Take your books and do whatever Mike tells you."

I didn't ask any questions, just grabbed my stuff and went, dropping the remains of my latte into the trash can by the stairs. I had adrenaline to carry me to the fourth floor and down the hall at a double-time pace.

The air seemed to thicken as I neared the lab. With a hand on the doorframe I swung into the room, where the staff worked in hushed voices. Weaving through all that anxious industry, I went to Cole's office and found Mike sorting through files.

"What's going on?"

"Cole didn't show up this morning." Mike ran his hands over his cropped black hair. "He's not answering his phone or e-mail, and none of the stuff he usually has waiting on Mondays is here."

I edged past the assistant editor and sat in the chair, logging on to the computer with Cole's pass code, which he'd given me to use after Hardcastle griped that a freshman was spending too many hours in the lab. "He last accessed this file—tomorrow's edition—on Friday. Will that help you?"

"It's better than starting from scratch. Can you put it on the public server?"

I moved the file then jotted down the pass code in case he needed it again. "Has anyone gone to Cole's place to check on him?"

"I was planning to, once I got things going here." He looked at me as if the idea were his own. "Could you do it?"

Try and stop me. "Where does he live?"

Mike gave me directions to an off-campus apartment and I headed there with dread eating at my insides. Maybe it was nothing. Maybe he and Devon had gone away again, and had car trouble getting back. Maybe they eloped. But my heart banged against my ribs the same way I banged on the apartment door.

"Cole!" I shouted through the window and rapped on the glass. Just as I'd decided to get the manager or call the police, the door swung open.

"What?" he growled, squinting at the sunlight. He was almost unrecognizable, with several days' growth of beard and cadaverous shadows under his bloodshot eyes. On Thursday he'd appeared fine, but now, only four days later, he looked as if he'd spent a month in a cave.

I swallowed my shock. "Why didn't you answer your phone?"

His gaze was feverish, glazed. "What do you want?"

"You didn't show up this morning. I was worried about you."

"I'm working." He left the door open and retreated into his apartment. When I followed, he said absently, "Don't step on any pages. They're in order."

I tiptoed through a minefield of paper, all covered with notes scrawled in a bold, assertive script that bore only a slight resemblance to Cole's neat, professional printing. Reference books towered on every flat surface; sticky notes covered the wall by the desk.

"Have you slept at all?" I tried to sound calm and not completely freaked out. "Eaten anything?"

"Don't need to." He sat down at the computer. "Can't. Have to get this out before I lose it again."

I stepped over a pile of fast-food wrappers. "Cole, I think you're sick. Ill, I mean."

"I'm fine, if you'll just go away and let me work."

"Come with me to the Health Center, and then I'll bring you back here to write."

"No!" He jumped out of the chair, shaking me off. "Haven't you ever had an idea so incredible, so glorious that it burns inside you, and you have to pour it out or be completely eaten up?"

I followed him, trying to reach any part that might still hear reason. "I know it feels that way, Cole. But the book will still be here after you rest—"

"I have to keep working." He began moving around the room, rearranging piles of paper.

"No, really. You have to stop."

"Don't you understand?" His voice was plaintive, almost pleading. I put my hand out to him, to restrain or reassure. He caught it, brought it to his chest, and laid my palm against his heart, beating as fast as a bird's. "I can't stop."

Fire raced up my nerves. *Inspiration* was too mild a word. This was the forge of creation, the blazing gift of da Vinci or Michelangelo. Of Shakespeare or Beethoven. Of all of them together, in one human body too fragile to hold the terrifying genius that had been ignited there.

My dawning realization brought a smile to his face. "I knew you'd understand, Maggie." Then his knees buckled, and he collapsed.

I leapt forward, but all I could do was keep him from

hitting his head. My fingers felt scorched where I touched him, but it wasn't figurative this time. All analogies aside, Cole was burning up. His skin felt desert-sand hot.

Laying his head down gently, I ran for the phone and dialed 911. The dispatcher was able to call up the apartment address while I told her Cole's symptoms as best I could: blistering fever, seriously altered mental state, and, finally, unconsciousness. She read off a list of instructions for me in case he started having a seizure, which I prayed—*really* prayed, as respectfully as I could—wouldn't happen.

When I hung up, I soaked a dish towel in the kitchen sink, then bathed his face until the paramedics got there. They would think he was sick, or on drugs, or maybe even crazy. But there was no mundane explanation for this.

Cole had been touched by sorcery, and the price for his fit of genius had been more than his body could pay.

# 30

The emergency-room resident had a brisk demeanor, very businesslike.

"We think it's meningitis." She briefed me outside Cole's curtained cubicle while I folded my arms tightly and tried not to shiver in the frigid, antiseptic air. "I've started him on broad spectrum antibiotics, and we'll do a lumbar puncture. You've called his girlfriend? What about any family?"

"Devon may be able to help you, and if she can't, his parents' number should be on his school records." She nodded and made a note. I'd found Cole's wallet and brought it with me, so they had his social security number and his insurance card—hopefully everything they'd need to help get him better.

"So . . . he hasn't regained consciousness?"

The doctor didn't look up from her clipboard. "No."

"That's not good, is it."

It wasn't a question, and she didn't answer it. "I'm going to start you and the girlfriend on prophylactic antibiotics, and possibly the students in his dorm as well."

I tucked my icy fingers more tightly under my arms. "He doesn't live in a dorm."

"What about anyone else he worked with?" she asked.

"I can get you the names of the newspaper staff, but he's been keeping to his office a lot."

"That could be part of the infection, if he kept the lights low. Light sensitivity is—"

The crash of the double doors from the waiting room interrupted her. I turned to see Devon pushing off the restraining hand of an orderly and quickstepping toward us. Her blond hair was a mess, flecked with the same multicolored paint that spattered the oversized shirt she wore.

"Where is he, Maggie?" Her blue eyes were wide and bright with frantic worry. "Jenna just said—"

She broke off, her gaze focused on the curtain behind me. Ignoring the doctor, she shoved it aside and crossed to the bed to touch Cole's face, as if that were the only way she could believe it was him. Her countenance shattered, the pieces dissolved into helpless tears. Sinking to her knees, she pressed her face to his hand and cried as if her heart had been ripped out.

"Miss—" The doctor glanced at me, and I supplied a

name. "Devon. We're treating him now. Calm down and I'll explain what's going on."

Devon continued to sob, giving no sign she'd heard. I crouched down, putting my arm around her. "Come on. There's a chair right here. We'll pull it close, and you can listen to the doctor."

Her slight weight lay against me, her strength all turned to grief. "It doesn't matter." Her choked words were almost too muffled to hear. "It's my fault. I just love him so much."

I glanced up to see that the resident was consulting with a nurse, and took the chance to whisper in urgent secrecy. "What's going on, Devon? I can't help if I don't understand."

"It doesn't matter." Her voice had become a mournful drone. "It's done. They'll save him or they won't."

A pair of sneakers appeared in my line of sight, and I followed the scrubs up to the face of Dr. Disapproval. "If she doesn't calm down, she can't stay here."

Devon pulled herself together after that last, fatalistic whisper. She drew back from me, wiped her streaming eyes, and stood up. "I'm all right."

Her withdrawal was more than physical. I felt her defenses going up, and I knew she'd tell me nothing more now that she had her wits about her. The grip was tenuous, but unless it slipped, my time was wasted there.

✳   ✳   ✳

I'd stolen Cole's keys when I stole his wallet, but I hadn't turned them over at the hospital. I planned to remember to do that after I'd checked out his apartment.

The paramedics had made a mess of his piles of paper. I

picked some of them up, glancing at the notes. From what I could tell with my grasp of not-entirely-current affairs, Cole was writing a thriller based on the international politics of oil. Sort of like that George Clooney movie where he grew that awful beard. What I didn't get was what Devon had meant when she said that she was his muse. I didn't see the connection between cute, artistic Devon and OPEC.

Laying that aside, I started searching for any clues to what might have happened to him. I riffled through his bedroom, under the mattress and under the bed itself, and through the medicine cabinet. I checked his desk, the kitchen, beneath couch cushions. Nothing out of the ordinary; no poppets, voodoo dolls, talismans. *Nada.*

My phone rang, the caller ID flashing the number for the journalism lab, and I answered. "Maggie? It's Mike. How's Cole?"

"Not so good. They're thinking it may be meningitis."

"That sucks. Poor guy."

"Yeah. You're going to be getting a call about a prescription for preventative antibiotics."

"Wow. I never thought I'd get that kind of call in regard to a guy."

I reminded myself that he didn't know how serious this was. "That's more than I need to know about your personal life, Mike. Did you call just to check on Cole?"

He got down to business. "Listen. I was going to finish my article on Saturday's football game with some quotes from the trainer who came up with the defensive strategy. Coach attributes the win to him. But now I'm doing Cole's job, so I need you to call this guy and ask him about it."

"I guess I—"

"Great." He gave me the name and a phone number. "Sooner the better, Maggie. Thanks."

He hung up before I could say anything else. I looked at my watch. It was midafternoon, I'd missed biology, and at this rate I wouldn't make it to my last class, either.

What the hell. I dialed the number Mike had given me and Troy, the student trainer in question, answered quickly. I explained who I was and what I wanted, and he laughed.

"I can't believe Coach is giving me props for that. I just came up with the idea, and he was like, hey, this is great. And I was like, whoa, I'm just a student trainer. I thought, they won't listen to me, but I couldn't not say it, you know."

I deciphered that into English, jotting on a legal pad from Cole's desk. As I did, something struck me. "When you say you couldn't *not* tell the coach your idea, do you mean you felt a responsibility to the team, or . . ."

"Well, yeah. Like, I want to win. But also—and this is weird, right? It was one of those ideas you know is really great, and you'll just pop if you don't say it. You know?"

Yeah. I think I did know.

"Thanks. I hope I'm not keeping you from class or anything."

"Nah. I took the day off. I was feeling kinda crappy yesterday. Probably too much partying, right?"

"But you're okay now?" He assured me he was. "Do you know a guy named Cole Bauer? Ever take a communication class?"

"You're, like, joking, right?"

"You live in a dorm?"

"Yeah. Is this going in the paper?"

"Um. No. This is just for, um, demographic research. Thank you for your time . . ." I glanced at his name. "Troy."

I hung up and tore off the page, then sat back, looking at the pieces of future bestseller littered around the room. Supernatural inspiration. There was something there, something important, but it stayed elusive. And Cole didn't have time for me to chase down dead ends.

✳ ✳ ✳

I decided that exposure to meningitis was a good enough reason to skip class, so I spent the rest of the afternoon in the journalism lab, helping Mike get up to speed on Tuesday's edition of the *Report.* Fortunately, since he asked me to prepare something on meningitis, I had an excuse to call the hospital for updates on the patient's condition. ("Unchanged," all afternoon.)

In the end, however, the doctor called *me.* Cole's lumbar puncture was positive, and I was to start taking the Cipro they'd given me as a preventative.

Meningitis, Wikipedia told me, was an infection of the membranes covering the brain, and it could cause all sorts of things, including brain damage, hearing loss, and, oh yeah, death. (That's when I paused in my research to take the antibiotics.) The disease was particularly contagious in close living quarters, like college dorms.

Lovely. I called the university Health Center and spoke with a nurse practitioner who told me that yes, they were aware of the situation, and they were working with the community hospital, outbreak prevention, blah blah blah.

I jotted down a few quotes, then asked, "Do you have any

record of the last time a BU student was diagnosed with meningitis?"

"Hang on." The tapping of a keyboard came over the line. "It was about twenty years ago. Oh dear."

"What?"

"One boy died, and another one was in the hospital for two weeks and had to drop out of school."

"Did they live in the same dorm?"

"Let's see. Not the same dorm, but the same fraternity house."

"I don't suppose it was Gamma Phi Epsilon."

"There's no note of the name."

"Great. Thank you, Ms. Stevenson. You've been a big help."

I hung up and stared at the computer screen for a long while. The date she'd given me, twenty years ago, would have been about the time that Victoria and Juliana were in school. And for the first time, it dawned on me that my mom would have been, too.

Typing like a madwoman, I entered the information from the Health Center and the quotes from the nurse practitioner into the article, called the hospital one more time ("Status unchanged"), and uploaded the draft to the server.

"Mike," I called, grabbing my jacket and book bag, "article's ready for proofing. I need to run home for a few minutes before meeting tonight."

He didn't look up from the screen, but I saw his hand appear over the monitor and wave.

On the walk to the Jeep, I tried Devon's cell again, then Justin. Neither answered. I called Lisa, too, but got her voice mail as well. I tried not to imagine anything ominous in it, but it was hard not to when I had no idea what was going on except that it was bad, and getting worse all the time.

✳ ✳ ✳

Mom was fixing a snack when I got home—a sandwich of peanut butter, sweet pickles, bacon, and mayonnaise. On toast, with a glass of milk on the side.

"It must be an obedient-stomach day," I said, going to the fridge for a Coke.

She sat on a barstool, elbows on the counter, as she took a big bite of sandwich. I didn't know who this woman was, who'd replaced my stickler-for-manners mother. "I have to eat while the eating's good."

Eyeing her plate, I said, "I'll take your word for it."

"What are you doing home?" She wiped a drip of mayo from her lip with a ladylike dab of her napkin. That was more like her. "You don't usually come home before chapter meeting."

"It's been a weird day." I leaned against the opposite cabinet. "Listen, Mom. Do you remember two Gamma Phi Eps who got meningitis while you were in school?"

She took a sip of milk, her expression thoughtful. "Yes," she said, then with more surety, "yes, I do. I was a sophomore, I think."

"I don't suppose you remember who they were dating."

"Goodness, how would I know that?"

"Well, they were Gamma Phi Eps, so . . ."

"So chances are they were dating Sigmas." She bit into her sandwich and chewed it, and the question, over. "No, wait. They *weren't* Gamma Phi Eps."

I leaned back in surprise. I was sure I'd been on the track to something.

Mom reminisced, smiling at things past. "We were all so jealous of the SAXis. Homecoming, Greek Week . . . It was always Sigma Alpha Xi and Gamma Phi Epsilon."

"And that didn't seem odd?"

"That they were so lucky? Not really. Do we have any potato chips?"

I got them out of the pantry, and she put a few in her sandwich. "There was something, though, now that you remind me, about their being jinxed."

"Jinxed?"

"Yes. I think the Deltas started the rumor, because they were always coming in second in everything." Her face lit with a click of memory. "That's right! Those guys who got sick weren't Gamma Phi Eps, but they *were* dating Sigmas. That's when the joke started. It was those guys, and a Phi Delta broke his leg, and then everyone came down with food poisoning after a SAXi party. A couple of the guys even ended up in the hospital with dehydration."

"But this jinx. It didn't stop the frat guys from wanting to date them?"

Mom shook her head. "It was a mark of status. The SAXis' boyfriends were chapter presidents, football captains, fellowship recipients . . . I guess when you think of the good things that happened to guys that dated Sigmas, it pretty much balanced out the bad. So they couldn't really have been jinxed, right?"

I didn't answer. She laid down her sandwich and looked at me closely. "Right, Maggie?"

"Sure, Mom." Funny how much concentration it can take to read a Coke can when you don't want to look at your parent.

"Oh, Maggie." The maternal unit in question sighed. "You're not in the middle of something *weird* again, are you?"

Picking up my satchel, I headed for the stairs. "Weirder than my being in a sorority in the first place? Come on, Mom."

Question evaded, I went up to my rooms, hearing her call up to me: "Did you clean up that mess?"

"Sure!" I yelled back, staring right at my self-ransacked bedroom. Dropping my bag onto the study sofa, I went to close the French doors. Out of sight—

The door swung shut and there, two inches in front of my face, was the answer. Crimson and indigo, compass and North Star. Even a stupid octopus. The door decoration had been there since the night I pledged, turned back against the wall.

Out of sight, out of mind.

# 31

**MightyQuinn:** I'm such a *moron*!!!

**0v3rl0rdL15a:** You're not a moron, you idiot.

**MightyQuinn:** How could I not SEE this?

**0v3rl0rdL15a:** That's the whole point of it. Did you soak the door thing in the bathtub like I told you to?

**MightyQuinn:** Yes. I used a whole carton of salt.

**0v3rl0rdL15a:** Table salt or sea salt?

**MightyQuinn:** Are you sure you don't think I'm a moron?

**Justin578:** No one is a moron. Can we get back to business?

I'd gotten Lisa and Justin online—despite the fact that he hated IM for anything but brief exchanges—because they were both in semipublic, and a phone conversation about sorcery was bound to attract the attention of their classmates.

As soon as the door decoration—which I'd seen on Holly's door, too, so I wasn't special—was submerged in the salt bath, I'd felt something like when your ears pop in an airplane, a change in the pressure around my head. And clarity. Finally, I could think and talk about the Sigmas without the muffled, wool-headed feeling.

I considered the plethora of crimson and indigo decorations in every SAXi room I'd seen, and wondered how many girls never questioned their good fortune, accepting it with perfectly normal Greek elitism. But that led to more questions. If you accepted something suspicious without question, did that make you guilty, or just stupid?

Either way, it didn't change what I knew, now more than ever, I had to do.

**Justin578:** Just help me out here, Lisa. Tell Maggie she has to get out of that sorority.

**Ov3rl0rdL15a:** I don't tell Mags what to do. You can try if you want to.

**MightyQuinn:** Hello! I can see you guys.
**Justin578:** OK. Just say that she doesn't
  need to be *inside* the sorority.

He wasn't going to like her answer. I didn't, either, but I was prepared when Lisa typed . . .

**0v3rl0rdL15a:** Just a little longer.
**Justin578:** How much?

A pause while we waited for her to type.

**0v3rl0rdL15a:** I've almost got the
  components of the spell identified. Then
  I'll know if it can be broken from outside
  or if she has to stay in the circle.
**Justin578:** How long to initiation?
**MightyQuinn:** Maybe two weeks.

It had seemed so far in the future, like I had all the time in the world. And now the end of the semester, and of pledgeship, was almost here.

And speaking of time, I had to get to the Sigma house for the chapter meeting. I couldn't afford to be late, now that I was pledge president and all.

**MightyQuinn:** I've got to run. Can't be
  late for meeting.
**0v3rl0rdL15a:** I'll call you tomorrow,
  Mags.
**Justin578:** Just be careful.

I typed a quick acknowledgment to both of them, and logged off. I didn't need Justin's reminder that I needed to keep my wits about me. Not only did I have to keep my normal façade going, now I had to make sure no one guessed that I'd neutralized their secret signal-jamming device.

✳ ✳ ✳

I had to park a block away from the Sigma house—every chapter on Greek Row had meetings on Monday night—and arrived at the door flushed and out of breath. The girls were already lined up in the foyer, alphabetically by class. I joined the freshmen, sliding in beside Holly.

"You okay?" I asked. She'd been elated yesterday, probably at thwarting her mother. But today she seemed like a guitar string, tight enough to vibrate if you plucked her.

"Yeah. Mom's still here." That served as her explanation.

Ashley, at the front of our line, turned back to tell me, "Some of us are going to the hospital after meeting. If you want to come."

"Thanks." One of the juniors glared at us, and I lowered my voice. "But I'm not sure they'll let you in to see him, since he's in bad shape."

Ashley frowned. "Who are you talking about?"

"Cole." Her look was blank. "Devon's boyfriend. Who are *you* talking about?"

"Brittany. She was in a car accident yesterday. She'll be okay, but her leg is broken in about three places."

A clammy chill started in my gut and spread out. I looked up at Holly, and she avoided my eye.

When Sigma luck ran out, it ran out big-time.

✳ ✳ ✳

The chapter meeting began as normal, but the girls seemed subdued, sitting stiffly, their chatter muted.

Holly's mother was indeed still there, sitting with the other alumnae advisers. Victoria had on her game face, all political smiles and gracious nods; Juliana was annoyed, but pretending to be amused by her rival's presumption of superiority. The tension between them telegraphed clearly to the assembled SAXis and put them on edge.

And then there was Devon's usual chair, sitting in empty accusation. I reminded myself that I was there to help her and Cole, but if I'd just wised up sooner . . .

Kirby started the meeting with a rap of her gavel. "Some rumor control before we start. The Standards Board met this weekend, and I'd like to thank our alumnae advisers, including our legal counsel, Ms. Juliana Hughes, for their time. In a completely unrelated event, one of our pledges has decided to resign, and Maggie Quinn is the new pledge president."

The actives murmured and Kirby's frown deepened, especially when her eyes found me among the pledges. Impatiently, she pointed to the seat beside Tara. "You're supposed to be over there, Maggie."

She held the meeting so that my first act as pledge president was to cause a delay of game while I changed chairs. I had to go around the seniors, and as I did, the doors—which are supposed to stay closed once the meeting has started—flew open. Devon, wild-eyed and pale, stood framed on the threshold.

"He's gone." She squeezed the words out of a throat broken with grief. "Cole's gone."

No one moved or spoke; in the horrible stasis of the moment, her words refused to compute. Then she swayed on her feet, and I jumped forward, wrapping my arm around her. Her sorrow snatched away my breath. How was she still standing?

"I killed him," she whispered, her eyes fluttering closed.

"What?" My brain still refused to assimilate the first shock. It flatly rejected that phrase. "What do you mean?"

"She doesn't know what she's saying." Jenna had gone to the girl's other side. "Come on, Devon. We'll take care of you."

She shook her head, violently. "No." When her eyes opened, she focused behind Jenna, where Kirby and Victoria and Juliana had come forward while the rest of the chapter watched in silent distress. "No. I'm done with you."

Kirby sheathed the steel in her voice. "You're upset, Dev. You've suffered a terrible loss. But don't say something you'll regret."

"Regret?" She stared at the older girl, a knife's edge of bitter outrage in her tone. "Re*gret*?"

"Dev, don't." Kirby reached out, laid a hand on her arm. "We tried to tell you."

Devon wrenched from our grasp. "I regret the day I met *any* of you." Her voice climbed into the rafters of hysteria as she backed as far from them as she could, pressing her back to the wall. "You did this. You *made* me what I am. Well, you can all go to Hell!"

A great sob wracked her, and she threw back her head, face contorted with anguish, tears slipping into her hair. "You will, you will," she keened. "But you'll take me with you."

She slid down the paneled wall, crouched in a heap of misery. Jenna knelt, and Devon accepted her arm around her shoulders. When Kirby took an impatient step forward, Jenna's head came up, eyes flashing a warning.

Juliana, arms folded, turned to Victoria. "I see how well you've managed things." Ignoring the other woman's death glare, she stepped forward like an auburn-haired icicle.

"Devon. Control yourself immediately."

It wasn't the voice of a mother or the voice of authority. It was the voice of *power,* and it vibrated along my nerves and settled at the top of my spine, resonating in my brain. My jaw went a little slack with it, and the command was not even aimed at me.

Devon stopped her hysterical sobbing. She raised her head and looked at Juliana, hatred and fear in her eyes, body taut with grief and useless rage. But silent.

"That's better. Now go to your room. Jenna will go with you."

I stepped forward. "I'll go, too."

"No." Juliana was implacable. "Jenna is sufficient."

"Devon is my friend." I set my chin. "And so was Cole."

Two flags of color appeared on Juliana's cheeks, the only sign of warmth I'd ever seen in her. As her anger grew, so did the ice in the air. This was the alpha. The queen bitch. And I had just disobeyed her in front of the whole chapter.

Probably not one of my smarter moments.

When she spoke, it was for my ears only. The rest of the room seemed to retreat beyond reach of voice or aid. "Do not think," Juliana began, her eyes glittering like the sun on a glacier, "that your ability grants you any special powers or protections. Not from me."

"I can see that would be a mistake."

She studied me the way an entomologist might a bug. "I have not yet figured you out. You reek of do-gooder, but yet you've accepted what Sigma Alpha Xi has to offer. You seem the model, if somewhat sarcastic, pledge, but I think you are fooling them all. Yet Victoria wants to add your power to ours. She says we need you."

"It's always nice to be needed." There was something about her eyes. Something *other* that spoke to the primal part of me, the part that recognized a predator.

She tilted her head, an animal-like expression of consideration: *Do I eat you now, or later?* "Perhaps we do. But we need you obedient. So think about the things you love, Magdalena Quinn. And do not cross me."

It was my full name that did it. Prickles of bone-deep fear marched over my skin like ants. The murmuring of the girls reached me once more, and the strange, isolated feeling of our conversation dissolved.

The triad—Kirby, Juliana, Victoria—returned to their places and rejoined a sober membership. Jenna met my gaze as she led the silently crying girl away. I watched them go, feeling in my soul that I'd failed Devon twice.

# 32

"What could you have done, Maggie?"

Justin watched me pace his tiny apartment. Wall to wall took me only eight steps, and my legs aren't that long.

"I don't know." Frustration choked the words. "Something. I should have just stolen the book. Maybe there would be something in there to tell me what the hell is going on."

"You did the logical thing. If the Sigmas found their grimoire missing, they would have done anything to find it."

*Think of the things you love,* Juliana had said. I shuddered, even in the safety of Justin's home.

"I should have known." Back and forth I paced. Arguing

about what was done and unchangeable was easier than facing my fear of failing the next task, whatever it might be.

"Not even you see the future, Maggie."

Forward and back, running my hands through my hair. "I should have found the spell sooner. I thought I had until initiation. It never occurred to me that someone would die while I was out *partying* with the Sigmas."

He blocked my path, forcing me to look at him. I raised my eyes to his, which were warm and dark, melting with compassion that I didn't deserve. "You did not cause this to happen. They did."

Tears stung and blurred my vision. His handsome, earnest face disappeared behind a watery haze of guilt and grief. "I couldn't stop it. I didn't even *see* it. What's the point of having my Sight if I couldn't save him!"

Justin wrapped me in his arms, tucked me tight against his chest, making me feel sheltered and forgiven. "Evil is deceptive. You fight it, you do the best you can. Sometimes you fall short."

He pulled back and met my gaze again, brushing the tears from my cheeks. "But you have to get over yourself. You can't get back into the fight until you do."

*Think of the things you love.*

I loved that he didn't deny my feelings, he just told me to get over it. I loved that he was chivalrous to a point just shy of chauvinism, but still held me accountable to fight the good fight. I loved him for being quixotic and square, holding himself to a higher standard, but not thinking less of those, like me, who made a mess of things.

He could have stopped me when I rose up on my toes and

pressed my lips to his, but he didn't. I think he considered it, because he froze for a moment, not in horror, thank God, but indecision. And then he pulled me close, and kissed me back.

*Friends don't kiss like this.*

There was nothing chaste or amiable about it. His hands cupped the back of my head, fingers threading through my hair. I wrapped my arms around him, kissed him with my whole body—my whole being. My nose was stopped up from crying, and I couldn't breathe and I didn't care, because if I pulled away to take in oxygen, this glorious moment might end.

It did. Justin put his hands on my waist, pushed me back just a little, his eyes dazed in what must have been a reflection of mine. "I'm still the TA for your history class."

An incredulous laugh bubbled out of my throat. "This is your big objection?"

"No." He drew me back in. "I'm just getting that off my chest."

And then he kissed me again, and it didn't seem possible that it could be better than the last one, but it was. For a lawful good square, Justin knew a lot about kissing. Granted, I didn't have a huge basis for comparison, but I didn't have to be a rocket scientist to recognize an explosion when I felt it.

I don't know how we got to the couch. I don't know how we ended up horizontal, tangled in each other, our breath loud in the silence but still drowned by the pounding of my heart. His fingers danced across my ribs, and I gasped at the tickle. He started to pull away but I caught his wrist, kept his hands where they belonged, against my skin.

I suppose that's how I lost my shirt. The more of him I touched, skin against skin, the more I could feel him in my blood, like a drug, like a shot of tequila. The denim of our jeans rasped as we wrestled closer still. He nuzzled the curve of my neck, the line of my collarbone. I kissed his shoulder, the indentation of muscle in his bicep, and he trembled. A rush of power zinged through me. I was invincible. I could have it all.

When his fingers touched the clasp of my bra, I wanted to shout *Yes. Do it.* I wanted it more than anything ever, but more than that, I *deserved* it. I'd waited all this time and I was *entitled* to this.

The very foreignness of the thought was a splash of cold water. And I heard my voice like a stranger's: "Stop."

That was *so* not what I wanted to say.

Justin stopped, of course, but his hands shook. I moved away, all the way to the other end of the couch, before I could change my mind. "I need to think."

"Yeah." He sat up . . . slowly . . . and rested his elbows on his knees and his head in his hands. "Okay."

I'd reduced him to one-word answers. Which was fair, I guess, because I was incoherent myself.

"This feels weird. I mean, I want to do this, but my head feels strange."

"I know." He sat back, looked at me with an expression of chagrin. "Too fast," he said, still monosyllabic. Still breathless.

That was only part of it. I was old enough to vote and in love with the guy, so it wasn't as if I would cry if my untested virtue died a timely death tonight. Except that I was getting a feeling—maybe it was my intuition, back in the game after two months on the bench—that I knew why the pledges had a proscription against sex. The strangeness of my thoughts, driving and hungry, made me think this wasn't solely between Justin and me.

"Let's get out of here." He rolled to his feet. Handing me my shirt, he pulled on his own. "I can't think with you sitting there."

Probably one of the nicest things he'd ever said to me.

✳ ✳ ✳

As I don't go to church much on Sunday, it seemed particularly weird to be there on a Monday night. Especially after the way I'd spent the last hour of it.

"You pick the weirdest places to take a date."

Justin looked down at me in amusement as he pulled open the heavy, carved wooden doors. "You're one to talk."

Good point. When you almost die on your first date, you shouldn't cast stones. I ducked under his arm to enter. Automatically, my hand went to the font just inside, and I dipped my fingers and crossed myself. Some things were just like riding a bicycle, I guess. Spectacles, testicles, watch and wallet. Jimmy Lopez had taught me that when we were kids. He'd thought it was the funniest thing ever, but I guess you do when you're an eight-year-old boy.

I'd grown up in this church, and the wooden pews and stained-glass windows formed my idea of what a sanctuary should look like. It was a warm, solid place, and despite my lingering feeling of trespass, I was aware of a peaceful welcome, too.

Footsteps echoing on the stone floor, I followed Justin

down the side aisle to an alcove. Under an icon of the Madonna and Child was a rack of votive candles, each in a red glass holder. A few already burned; I reached out a finger and touched the fluted glass edge of one, then another. Someone's mother, dying in hospice care. A husband, lost to cancer.

This was becoming natural, the sixth sense integrating with my others. The thought came to me that this may be a Sigma gift, too. Maybe not the Sight itself—I'd had that already, except the *Dead Zone* thing—but the skill I'd developed. Or maybe it was because I'd gotten so much practice around them. Nothing like battlefield training.

The strike of a match made me look up at Justin as he lit two candles, side by side. They flared brightly as he touched the match to the wick, then flickered in tandem. His parents. I glanced up at him, but his gaze was turned inward; not sad, exactly, but poignant. My fingers reached for his, and he squeezed my hand tightly.

"Have they been gone long?" I asked. He'd never spoken of them.

"Since I was ten."

"Does it help?"

He handed me the matchbox. "It can't hurt. Sometimes rituals have deeper power, sometimes they just give us comfort."

I thought about Cole as I shook out a match and struck it. Remembering his friendly nature and his talent and potential, I held the match and let the flame creep closer to my fingers.

*I hope you're at peace, Cole. Forgive me for not seeing until it was too late. I swear, I'm going to stop these girls from harming anyone else.*

It did help. But not as much as solving this mystery would.

✳   ✳   ✳

That night, it was as if the dream had been waiting for me, long past patience. It drew me down swiftly, as soon as I closed my eyes, with no time to prepare.

I stood in the empty Sigma Alpha Xi chapter room; the phi spiral on the floor, instead of being flat, inlaid wood, descended into the ground. Standing at the outside arm, I felt the cold reaching up from below, from the dark well of earth.

*Okay, Maggie. You're not going to find out what's going on from up here.*

I stepped onto the path, spiraling down and down; I kept to the outer edge; the other side dropped into nothingness. The cold intensified as I descended and the natural light faded, until I was seeing only by the frigid pale phosphorescence that came from the spiral itself.

Dream time was stretchable, like Silly Putty; I walked until my feet were blistered and my skin was numb with cold. How long was this going to go on?

Indefinitely. Phi was an irrational equation. Self-symmetrical, to the infinite power.

The realization brought me to a halt, and in the same instant, an icy wind roared from below, whipping my hair and tearing at my skin. I pressed myself back against the spiral wall, shielding my watering eyes. In the center of the well, a frosty vapor formed; wisps of winter breath that twisted together into something . . .

No. It was some *thing.* No shape of man or beast, but a *creature* nonetheless.

The wind became sleet. I squeezed my eyes closed as ice lashed at my cheeks. Just a dream. The glacial storm flayed my skin, and I clung to that thought. A thing of spirit, not of body. My muscles cramped, my limbs drew in to protect my vital organs from the cold. I tried to scream, but the howling gale snatched the sound away as I tried to force myself to . . .

\* \* \*

*Wake up.*

In my own bed, I lay curled in a tight, shivering ball, too painfully cold to move, too miserable not to. Reaching over, I grabbed the fallen quilt from the floor and pulled it around me, my teeth chattering in the silent room.

This was what the thing on my door had kept me from seeing, this frozen well connecting the Sigmas to an infinite power. I'd been thinking *Faust,* and Mephistopheles. I should have been thinking *Inferno.* The center of Dante's Hell was not fiery, but frozen.

Not just capital *E* then. Capital, boldface, italic *E.* And I was going to have to find a way to stop it.

# 33

At seven the next morning, I let myself into the Sigma Alpha Xi house. The atmosphere was heavy with slumber, and I headed for the stairs. I had to maintain my cover—until Lisa finished her translation, or until initiation—only I didn't want to lose anyone else in the meantime.

But Devon's room was empty.

Not just vacant. Unoccupied. Her bed was stripped, her walls naked. Her closet and bookshelves, bare. The seaside mural was the only evidence that she'd ever been there at all.

I stood in the doorway and cursed—mostly myself, for

not coming back last night. Then I turned to go, and found Kirby standing in the hall behind me.

"Looking for Devon?" she asked, arms folded.

"Yes." I kept my hands at my sides and my cloaking device set on harmless. "I was worried about her."

"Don't be." She reached around me and pulled the door shut. "She decided to go home."

"But there are only two weeks left in the semester."

"She's devastated, as you can imagine, and she wanted to be with her family." Kirby looked me in the eye, and I felt a Juliana-esque chill, slight but distinct. That was new.

"Was there anything else you wanted to know, Maggie?"

The way she phrased the question said I'd reached the bounds of justifiable curiosity, at least in the Kirby camp.

"No, ma'am. Thank you."

I left the house and headed for the Jeep, unsure what to do next. Journalism class was one option, but Hardcastle was hard to listen to even when I wasn't distracted by life-and-death matters.

Journalism made me think of the *Report*, which reminded me of another inspired guy I'd talked to yesterday. It was a long shot, but I felt better about those since despelling myself. Grabbing my cell phone, I scrolled through my recent calls and found the number I wanted.

He picked up on the fourth ring. "Mmph."

"Troy Davis? This is Maggie Quinn from the *Ranger Report*."

"Wha?" A fumbling clatter. "What time is it?"

"I have one quick question. Do you know any Sigma Alpha Xis?"

"Whaaa?" Still barely coherent. "None of them would have anything to do with me."

"What about a blond girl. Short hair, pointed chin. Bossy."

"Oh, her. *Legally Blonde* Girl. Yeah." He sounded more sleepy than lascivious. "We just, like, hooked up last Thursday at a club, you know?"

"Thanks." I hung up and drummed my fingers on the steering wheel. Cole had writer's block when he and Devon were on a break. Troy the trainer had a great idea after hooking up with Brittany—who had said she liked football guys.

I was just closing my mental fingers around the next variable of that equation when the phone rang.

Justin spoke as soon as I answered. "I think I've found something." His voice rang with excitement, and my heart sank.

"Are you okay?" I asked. We'd only made out. How badly could he be affected?

He kind of laughed at the question, which was both reassuring and not. "Where are you? Do you have class?"

"Why?"

"Let's meet at your gran's place. I think she can help."

"Gran?"

"Wake up, Maggie. Let's get to work."

He hung up without once saying the word *careful*. Now I was really worried.

\* \* \*

Gran was not only up and finished with her treadmill time, but she also had a pot of tea steeping, with three cups set out, when Justin and I arrived.

She poured as she listened to Justin's question, then sat

back and looked at us. Him. Then me. Then back to him. I could feel myself blushing all the way to the tips of my ears.

It didn't help that he looked as though he hadn't slept at all. Not scary bad—who hadn't pulled an all-nighter once or twice? But still.

Finally, Gran took the spiral notebook he'd brought and peered at the handwritten entry. "Liannan Sidhe." Then she studied us again, her eyes narrowing. "How did this come up in conversation, then?"

"Hypothetically," I assured her. "We just need to know more about it."

She made a doubtful face. "I never told you about the Liannan Sidhe?"

"No." She'd told me the Sidhe—"shee," she said, slurring the *sh*—were Irish fairies who lived under hills and danced in fairy circles that trapped the unwary. There were the Dannan Sidhe, the bright folk, and the Bain Sidhe, who, if you saw one, you were basically screwed. But I'd never heard of this variety.

She poured a mug of tea, added sugar, stirred it. Obviously trying to kill me with impatience.

"Liannan Sidhe are female fairies who inspire creativity in human men who they . . . Well, let's say love."

Granspeak for *hooking up,* I guess.

"So, it's like a muse," I said, remembering Devon's word.

"To a fearsome degree." She sipped her tea. "The inspiration of genius, but it burns the man out like a candle while the Sidhe feeds on that creative energy."

"Why couldn't you have told me about that when I was a kid?"

"Well, I didn't want to scare you out of being creative. Besides." She cleared her throat delicately and glanced at Justin. "There's the sexual component."

He blushed, and discovered something very interesting on the ceiling. I tried to keep my own mind on the line of inquiry. "So these fairies sleep with men, feed off the creative energy, and then . . ."

"The man usually dies."

"Dies?" asked Justin, not blushing now.

Gran nodded, and I narrowed my eyes at her. "Are you sure this isn't a cautionary tale? Don't go into the woods or the big bad wolf will eat you?"

"I'm only telling you what I heard as a girl."

"How come all these things that lead men to their deaths are always female? Mermaids drowning sailors, the banshee, this Liannan thing . . ."

Gran took a rather coy sip of her tea. "We are the deadlier of the species, darling."

Justin laughed, and I gave him the hairy eyeball. "More like the stories were written down by men. When you write your book, you'd better dig up some male tempter to balance things out."

"I'll do my best," he promised, still smiling as his eyes met mine.

More blushing, this time from me. Not that it mattered. If the Sigmas really had transformed me somehow, I wasn't going to be able to get near Justin. Maybe ever. The Sigmas had screwed me over big-time. So to speak.

"Why do you need to know this?" Gran had gone back to staring, now with twenty percent more suspicion.

"Research project." Justin lied without a blink. It seemed I'd contaminated him.

Gran knew whom to blame. "Magdalena Quinn . . ."

I decided it was time to get out of there. "Gotta run. Journalism class. Hardcastle would love an excuse to throw me off the paper."

Justin grabbed his notebook. "Thanks, Granny Quinn."

She caught his hand before he could go. "You, go home and sleep at least four hours. And no more fooling around with Maggie until she fixes whatever is wrong with her."

"Gran!"

"Yes, ma'am," he said without hesitation.

She let him go, and we headed out to the driveway. I couldn't look at him; I might combust with embarrassment.

"I'm sorry," I said when we reached the Jeep.

"I'm not."

"You would have been if I'd killed you."

"Maybe."

I shot a look up at him; he was smiling slightly, in a way that nearly had me blushing *again*. "It's not funny."

"No. It's really not." He opened the Jeep's door for me, but his grasp on it was tight, as if he was holding on as much for support as for courtesy.

I stared at his white knuckles, and let the thought catch up with me, the personal repercussions of all this. The Sigmas had done something to me. And I had done something to Justin.

"Hey." His voice drew my eyes up to meet his reassuring gaze. "I'm all right, Maggie. A nap between classes, and I'll be good as new."

My mouth curved in a rueful smile. "How can you always tell what I'm thinking?"

He shrugged. "I've always been good at reading people. Especially when I . . . know them pretty well."

That was interesting for two reasons: (a) "know" had more than one connotation, and (b) he definitely changed the direction of that sentence.

We exchanged good-byes and I started the car, flexing my hands on the steering wheel the same way I gripped my renewed determination. I had to figure this out. There was no other option. Forget the long-term adverse effects of a karmic imbalance on the space-time continuum. Forget that my budding romance was now on ice. If I didn't fix this, I was going to end my days a dried-up, lovelorn virgin with a houseful of cats.

✳ ✳ ✳

"It's all about sex."

I'd gone to Dad's office to confer with Lisa long-distance; it had been the only private place on campus I could think of. Dad was in class, the door was locked, but I still expected lightning to strike me for saying s-e-x while at his desk.

"It's *always* about sex, Mags." Lisa's tone was dry, and the sound of shuffling paper underscored her voice. "Are you just finding this out?"

"Um, in regard to the Sigmas? Yeah."

The rustling stopped abruptly. "Maggie Quinn. Have you been a bad girl?"

"No! Of course not." Her silence was disbelieving. "Okay, not exactly."

Lisa sighed. "You'd better tell me what's going on."

I brought her up to speed about Cole and Devon, the guy Brittany had hooked up with, and—quickly and without going into detail—about Justin. Then I told her about the legend he'd come up with in his inspired state, and Gran's confirmation of it.

"Okay," Lisa said, when I finally paused for breath. "That makes what I've got here fall into place."

"You figured out the spell?" A glimmer of hope sparked in my chest, followed by a stab of irritation. "Why didn't you warn me?"

"Like it's my fault you picked *now* to give up on eighteen years of chastity?"

"Can we get back to the magic? Am I right? Is it like the Liannan Sidhe, but stealing luck instead of life force?"

More rustling over the phone, then the slide of a computer mouse. "More or less. Are you at your laptop?"

Swiveling in the chair, I tapped the trackpad to wake up my screen. "Okay."

An IM window popped up with a link. On my click, a browser window opened, showing one of the pages I'd photographed.

"This is part of the initiation ritual. Luckily, you got the important stuff."

"Sigmas are very lucky."

"Whatever. These symbols at the top—the same as are on the lamp and censer—are for transformation. But there are also things in the spell for binding and amalgamation."

"What's that in nonwitchspeak?"

"It means that the individuals become part of the whole. What's yours is mine, basically."

"Does it go the other way, too? What's mine is yours?"

"Not so much." I got another IM link and this page showed me a diagram of a familiar looking spiral. "This is—"

"On the floor of the Sigma house." And in my dream. "A focaccia spiral thing."

"Fibonacci. It's a representation of the golden ratio, but it's not exact. It's supposed to be like fractal geometry— self-symmetrical, which means that at whatever level you look at it, it's a repeat of the smaller or bigger picture. But the Sigmas' deal isn't like that, exactly. It's weighted toward the center."

A new diagram appeared, one of the same spiral, but three-dimensional, so it looked more like a funnel . . . or the well that I had seen in my nightmare.

I ventured a guess. "So the psychic juice sort of runs to the center."

"Right. If these girls really are sexual karmic vampires, then what they take in goes toward the top. I'm guessing that's the alums. The longer you're in, the more you get."

"Like a psychic pyramid scheme."

"Essentially. The younger girls—meaning the college students—have more sex and there are more of them. While the bulk of the energy comes from them, the load is spread out, so that no one girl draws too much from one hookup."

Before I'd called her, I'd looked through my pledge book, noting which actives had boyfriends, and which of those had any particular status or accomplishments. A few seniors and juniors had steadies—guess which fraternity they were in— but the rest of the girls were . . . let's say *shopping*.

I checked my understanding. "So, as long as a Sigma just

hooks up with a guy once or twice, he's okay." Lisa confirmed this. "But if she goes too often to the same well . . ."

"Don't think water," she said. "Think electricity. The sex generates psychic energy potential; the Sigma draws it off, creating a current. If you exceed the capacity of the human design, the wiring burns out."

Talk about metaphysics.

"And the inspiration before the burnout?" I asked.

"The part of the generated potential that isn't drawn off."

My headache kept getting worse. It seemed that for every question answered, three more popped up. "So . . . that's what happened twenty years ago? The jinx, I mean?"

"I'm sure. It might have started with just a few girls who somehow found this book and did the transformation spell—either not knowing or not caring that they were screwing guys over in more ways than one. Then someone got the idea of sharing the wealth to reduce the current, and modified the arrangement to include the whole sorority."

"Victoria, I think." Eavesdropping behind Devon's door, I'd heard her talk about long-term plans. "It was probably not so much about sharing as about not attracting so much suspicion."

"True. Not to mention that whoever's at the center of that spiral gets the most bang for her buck."

"Then, how is Gamma Phi Epsilon immune?"

"It looks like Victoria pulled them into the pattern, protected them from burnout. It's the why that I don't know."

I remembered the article about Peter Abbott, president of his fraternity. "Victoria's future husband was a Gamma Phi Ep."

"Of course. A little old-fashioned, but does get rid of the black widow problem."

That explained why everyone was so freaked that Devon was going steady with Cole; it was the ultimate un-protected sex.

"So, what's the big deal about pledge celibacy?" I'd given this some thought. "If we're the youngest, and we haven't gone through the initiation spell, then we shouldn't draw much current at all, right?"

"Finally, you get around to asking me that. Or didn't you wonder why you whammied Justin just by making out?" She left a leading pause. "You *did* just make out, right?"

"Yes! You're not my mother. Why would I lie?" Except in leaving out about how easy it would have been to let that for-eign hunger slip its leash. "Well?"

"First, tell me more about this pledging ceremony. You were at the center of the spiral, right?"

"Yes." I stared at the funnel diagram on the screen. "Oh my God. Where the energy is strongest."

"Right. That ceremony set in motion the transformation part of the spell. It takes a lot of power, so you're connected to the center until the change is complete. Think of it like a negative electrical potential in the middle of a highly charged dynamic—"

"Lisa, let's pretend I'm not, on a good day, almost as smart as you. Just cut the crap and tell me what that *means*."

"Sure. It means you guys suck the most." I rolled my eyes, even though she couldn't see it. "Next question?" she said sweetly.

"How do I break the spell?"

She sighed. "I'm still working on that."

"Can we just destroy the grimoire?" I asked. "If nothing else, it would stop the ritual. Stop them from making any more Sigmas."

"But it wouldn't put everything, or every *one*, back to normal. It would only destroy the power-sharing structure, which would make things worse, not better." I heard more fidgeting noises from her end; not industry this time, but stalling. "There's one more thing, and you're not going to like it."

"Unless you're about to tell me there's no way to reverse the transformation—"

She made a short, derisive sound. "Please. No one out-evil-geniuses me. We'll break the spell."

*We,* she'd said.

"No. It's about the power source. Not the karma suck, but the transformative and binding power."

She didn't continue; she didn't really have to. The weight of personal history lay heavy on the line.

I said the words for her. "It's a demon."

"Yeah." She breathed easier once it was spoken. "The pages you gave me don't show its name. That's the biggest hitch in figuring out the countermeasure."

"Lisa, all you have to do is help me work it out. You don't have to be near the thing. It's my deal this time."

She didn't even address that. "How long until initiation?"

"End of next week, I think. Sometime during dead days."

Ah, life's little ironies.

"Dad bought me a plane ticket home for Thanksgiving," she said, "so I'll see you this weekend. We'll work it out then."

"Okay." I hung up and stared at the screen, my head full of information, unsorted and chaotic. One thought, though, lay on the surface.

Victoria had been married to Peter Abbott for eighteen years. But on the flip side of that was Juliana Baker-Russell-Hattendorf-Hughes. So it seemed they hadn't gotten rid of the black widow completely.

✳ ✳ ✳

When I got to the journalism lab for my usual Tuesday-afternoon duty on the *Report,* Mike avoided my eye and sent me to see Professor Hardcastle. Somehow, I didn't think this was going to be good news.

I hitched my satchel higher onto my shoulder and headed down the hall, my sneakers squeaking on the newly polished linoleum. Dr. Hard-ass looked up as I came into his cluttered shoe box of an office, then turned back to his computer.

"Quinn. Right. That Phantom business stops now. I don't want to deal with the complaints and letters."

"Okay." I don't know why I said that, when it wasn't okay. The column had an end date. This was like canceling a TV series right before May sweeps.

But churning with the anger and disappointment in my stomach was a sudden fear. A yellow flag had just gone up. Luck is not supposed to happen in reverse.

"You can submit photos and stories for consideration," he said, "but you're off the staff. And don't expect any more favors. You were Cole's pet project, not mine."

"Yes, sir."

"That's all." He waved me out, his eyes still glued to his screen.

I left the office and stood in the hall, not quite sure what to do next. Newspaper staff was the thing that kept me from going postal, kept me focused on something besides the waiting game with the Sigmas.

With the thought of the sorority, something clicked in my head. The Sigmas giveth, and the Sigmas taketh away.

*Think about what you love, Magdalena Quinn.*

I didn't even bother reaching for my phone. I just took off for the history building at a dead run.

# 34

I slid to a stop at Dad's office door, grabbing the frame to keep myself upright as my exhausted legs tried to buckle. My face burned with exertion and my heart pounded so hard, I thought my eardrums might blow out. Fitness hadn't gotten me there, only adrenaline.

Justin was at the computer, and on the phone. He glanced my way, doubtless alerted by my gasps for oxygen, and didn't look surprised to see me. Just carefully neutral and calm.

"She just came in, actually." He spoke into the phone, talking about me. "Don't worry, Dr. Quinn. I'm on it. You want me to call your mother?" I staggered into the office, worry ratcheted up to panic. "Okay," he told Dad, and hung up.

"What?" I demanded. It came out as more of a plea.

He stood up and came around the desk. "Catch your breath, Maggie."

"Is it Mom?" My stomach ached like I'd swallowed a handful of tacks. "The baby?"

"At your mom's checkup, her blood pressure was really high. They've admitted her overnight for observation and—"

I started for the door, all action, no thought. Justin caught me by the shoulders, made me stop and listen.

"Everything is okay, Maggie, but they're watching her closely. Here's the room number." His hand slid down my arm to capture my fingers, keeping me from running off while he grabbed a Post-it from the desk.

"I have to teach your dad's class, or I would drive you over there. Are you calm enough to manage?" He bent to hold my gaze, expression inarguable. "Maggie?"

"Yeah." That didn't sound very convincing, so I said it again more firmly. "Yeah."

The dazed, distant feeling resolved into the here and now. Justin saw that in my eyes, and released me. But not before he touched my hair and promised, "I'll be there as soon as I can."

✳   ✳   ✳

The elevator ride to the OB floor of the hospital was the longest in my life. I hurried down the hall, checking numbers, passing carts full of flowers and rooms full of laughing, giddy people. How could they be so happy when worry was trying to claw its way out of my gut like a cat from a bag?

Finally I found the room, and tapped on the open door. "Mom?"

"Magpie!" She smiled at me from the bed. I ran and hugged her tightly until she gave a laughing protest. "I'm not dying, sweetheart. We're all okay."

"The Quinnlette, too?"

"Yes. I just have to stay in bed until tomorrow, while they poke around and see if my blood pressure goes down."

"Can I do anything?" I asked. "Get you anything?"

"No, sweetie." She squeezed my hand in reassurance. "Your dad went downstairs to get me a few magazines from the gift shop. My biggest problem is I have nothing to read."

"So you're really okay?"

"I feel fine." Which was not the same thing. She didn't look ill. In fact, with her hair in a ponytail and her face free of makeup, she could almost be one of my classmates. A slightly annoyed classmate. "Sit down and stop hovering."

I did, talking to her about inanities until Dad came in, his arms loaded with periodicals. "Why didn't you call me?" I demanded.

He gave me a stern look. "Hello, Maggie. Glad to see you, too."

I gave him a hug and a proper greeting, then asked again. "Why no phone?"

"Couldn't get through. You must have been in one of the older buildings."

Pulling my phone from my pocket, I checked. Four bars of signal and no voice mail waiting.

"Honestly, Michael," said Mom, "did you buy every magazine in the place?"

I left her in Dad's care and slipped out of the room, finding the nurses' station at the hub of three pastel-colored halls. "I want to talk to someone about Laura Quinn, room three-eleven."

A nurse with dark skin and steel gray hair sized me up; when I didn't flinch, she grabbed a chart and flipped through a few pages. "What's your name?"

"Maggie Quinn. I'm her daughter."

"Your mother's blood pressure is still quite high. We're keeping her in bed and monitoring her condition."

"What does that mean, quite high? My blood pressure goes quite high every time I watch the news."

She raised a we-are-not-amused eyebrow. "Yes, but you're not pregnant, I assume. If you were, it would be called preeclampsia, and that can be a very bad thing."

All my bravado drained away, and I clutched the counter with white-knuckled fingers. "You mean she might lose the baby? Or . . ." I couldn't say the other possibility.

The nurse's expression softened a bit as she closed the chart. "Your mom is okay for now, and so is the baby. We're keeping a close eye on them both. She'll probably be on bed rest when she goes home, maybe blood pressure medication. The numbers aren't so high right now and there's no significant protein in her urine, so that's good. But she's got a way to go to full term."

"Okay." I closed my eyes and assimilated that. "Okay," I repeated, as if that would make it true.

"The main thing is to give the fetus as much time as possible to grow and for her lungs to develop."

I nodded, understanding what she was saying. My sister was a ways from being able to survive on her own.

Thanking the nurse, I wandered farther down the hall, not ready to go back to my parents just yet.

*Think about what you love, Magdalena Quinn.*

It was one thing to threaten me. It was another to have my nature altered to the point where I was facing a life as the spinster cat lady. But to drag my mother and unborn sister into things? That was fighting dirty.

Next week was Hell Week, the trials of sisterhood leading up to initiation. I was scared and pissed off, but I could only go forward, so I focused on the pissed. The SAXis were going down. I was going to use what was left of my Sigma luck against them, and I was going to show them a thing or two about how to handle demons.

# 35

Wednesday night, I had just enough energy to sprawl on the couch with Justin and watch a mindless Thanksgiving special while we recovered from the efforts of getting the house ready for Mom's return. He and Gran had consolidated all their folklore knowledge to protect the house: doors, windows, and hearth. Justin washed the porch with a concoction that an Irish woman had sworn to him would keep witches away.

Gran had put together little bags, like sachets, and told me to put them under Mom's pillow and mattress. "What's in them?" I'd asked after an experimental sniff.

"Angelica root, mostly. My own granny swore by it." Next she handed me a jar of bath salts. "Get her to have a nice long soak with these, too."

I might be able to manage that, if I passed it off as aromatherapy. Hard enough getting her to wear the medal I'd gotten her—St. Margaret of Antioch, patron saint of pregnant women. I was covering all my bases.

"The house is as secure as we can make it," Justin assured me. "She'll be safer here. Home is a sanctuary."

I agreed. "And hospitals are nasty."

We sat side by side on the couch, our knees touching. I was aware of him in a vivid way, but too tired to do anything about it, even if I weren't worried about putting him in a coma.

"Think you can get some rest this weekend?" he asked, interlacing our fingers.

"Yes. Holly said she and Juliana are headed back to Chicago until Sunday." I gave a tired laugh. "Hell is closed for the holiday."

I would need the downtime, for rest and preparation. And turkey. Not to mention pumpkin pie. I had to keep up my strength, after all.

✳  ✳  ✳

Lisa sniffed the air as soon as I opened the front door, and arched a brow. "Been practicing your herbology?"

"Gran," I said in explanation, and invited her in with a gesture. "I saw you stumble on the front walk. Are you okay?"

"Stepped on a loose rock." I could never hide much from her, and she slanted a wary look at me as she came in. "Why?"

I pointed to the porch before I closed the door. "Witch repellent."

She turned to stare at me, her expression carefully blank. "Does that mean it doesn't work very well, or that I'm not very much of a witch?"

I studied her for the first time in three months. She'd lost weight, and she hadn't been hefty to begin with. Tall and lean in her jeans and leather coat, her chestnut hair falling in a silky curtain around her shoulders, she looked composed and powerful. But there was a shadow on her. I could See it written on her heart, indelible and absolute.

"What do you want it to mean?" I asked, keeping my own answer out of my voice.

She looked away first, something that never would have happened with D&D Lisa. "I think we should get to work."

✳ ✳ ✳

We went upstairs, wasting little time on pleasantries— how's your mom, fine, etc.—and got down to business. Lisa had brought a black duffel bag with her, and we sat on the bed with her visual aids laid out for my instruction.

"The spell is divided into three parts," she explained. "Binding, transformation, and amalgamation. You'll have to break each one. First is the binding. It closes the circle and makes the members one unit for magical purposes."

"Do they lose free will?"

"Not exactly. It's more like a permanent version of that charm on your door."

I got that. "Complacent and unlikely to ask questions." She nodded. "So, the girls wouldn't necessarily know what's going on?"

Lisa met my eye levelly. "What sane person would think the reason they're lucky and successful is an elaborate contract with a demon? Does that excuse them for not questioning it? I'm not the one to answer that."

She flipped to a new page of her notepad, closing that door firmly. "Moving on to part two. Transformation. This is the part that empowers or transforms the girls to be able to draw energy from the guys."

"Which you said began at the pledge ceremony."

"You get a gold star for paying attention." She pointed to her drawing, where stick-figure girls were arranged at the center of the spiral. "Part two completes what was started when you pledged. It's not permanent until then."

I hadn't taken this into account. An exit. "So, if I didn't go through initiation, I'd go back to normal?"

"I think so. The problem is that there's a backlash effect. That's likely what happened to that girl who got kicked out."

"Brittany."

"Right. As long as you haven't been channeling too much energy, you would probably survive it."

Part of me wished I didn't know that, even with the worrisome word *probably,* I *could* get out of jail free. "Part two," I prompted, turning the subject back to initiation. "Transformation is finished, and the pledges become karma vampires."

"Right. Straight up, no power sharing." She turned to the next page, where her notes were completely indecipherable. "Only it doesn't stop here. Part three is amalgamation, which ties the knot tighter. That's the pyramid scheme part. All the energy—which is all magic is, at its essence—that the actives collect from the sex feeds upward through the pyramid. As below, so above. Basic alchemy."

"So do all the alums stay connected to this scheme?"

"The binding is permanent, unless broken by a counter-spell. Each time they initiate more Sigmas, it refreshes all three parts of the spell. An alumna wouldn't have to be there every time, but she'd get a bigger piece of the pie if she came back every now and then."

"Okay." My brain was full. "So, do we know why Peter Abbott isn't dead after eighteen years married to Victoria?"

"This is the ingenious part." She spoke with real animation, the weight of her baggage lightening in her enjoyment of the puzzle. "Remember I said that sharing the wealth reduces the draw on an individual. Hook up with a guy once or twice, he might ace his test the next day, feel like he's got the flu, but no harm no foul."

"Well, I wouldn't say *no* foul. You're still taking something that isn't yours."

"Yeah, but it's a renewable resource. As long as there's recovery time . . ." She looked up from her notebook and saw my expression. "Okay. Maybe some foul."

"Maybe a lot of foul if you fall in love with someone and can't sleep with them." I was mostly thinking about Devon. But not entirely. "How did Victoria get around that?"

"It's so simple. She funneled some of the karma power to the Gamma Phi Ep house, protecting them from the effects of the drain. It's a current converter fueled by their own stolen energy, feeding their own stolen energy back to them."

"So, the guys have no clue?"

"It's completely passive on their part." A smile curved one corner of her mouth. "Well, not completely passive."

"Don't need a mental picture, thanks."

"Prude."

"Yes. So how do I break this down?"

Lisa went back to her notebook. "I'm reasonably confident I've got the components right."

"Reasonably confident?"

"Well, the modifications are the problem. I know all the pieces, and I know how *I* would combine them. But neither of us has been through Victoria's version."

I sighed. "We need Devon. She's got no loyalty left. I'll bet she'd tell us everything she knows."

"Do you know where home is for her?"

"Birmingham. How many Brinkerhoffs can there be in Alabama, I wonder?"

"Not a clue," said Lisa, though I could see her storing the information as she got back to business.

"Basically everything that the Sigmas do, you have to counter. They bind, you break." She began removing things from her duffel bag. "It may be as simple as this." She held up a pair of silver embroidery scissors, laid them down, and pulled out some more vials. "Salt or salt water. Lemon oil. Valerian. Black or red pepper."

"It's like cooking."

"Spells are all about combining the right ingredients plus a power source. So . . . yeah. Kind of like cooking. Only they're using hellfire in their furnace."

"I know. I've seen it in my dreams." Her busy hands stilled and she looked at me, maybe sensing I had more to say on the subject. I steeled myself, because speaking this aloud seemed to make it more real, and more frightening. "It's not the same as Azmael."

Lisa considered that, filed it away. "Worse?"

I shook my head, not really denying or agreeing. "Different. Formless, elemental. Powerful. Deep, raw power. How am I going to counter that?"

"Everything they do, you do the opposite." Reaching across the bed, she grasped my pendant, holding the tiny crucifix tightly between her fingers. "Time to put your money where your mouth is."

✳ ✳ ✳

By one in the morning, we had concocted a plan. It was either brilliant or insane. Funny how there's so little middle ground in these things. The logical parts were all Lisa. The insane parts were mine.

Lisa threw everything back into the duffel bag, zipped it, and set it on the floor. "Keep that with you. You think the ritual will be at the end of the week?"

"Yeah." I linked my hands overhead and arched my back in a stretch. "We're not supposed to know exactly, but they've told us all not to go anywhere on the weekend."

"Okay." I could see the intricate wheels in her brain turning. "My plane leaves at about eleven tomorrow morning. I've got two papers due and finals start on Tuesday." She offered this like an apology.

"I never would have thought up this plan on my own. Even with Justin's help." Maybe we could have come up with something, but not this quick and this detailed. Lisa had said it herself. No one could out evil-genius her.

She slipped on her jacket, pulling her hair from under the collar. "He's going to help you with this, right?"

"Somehow. I'm still hoping to convince this other pledge, Holly, to help me, too."

"Okay." We walked down the stairs, through the dark house to the front door. She stood with her hands in the pockets of her coat, still *thinking.* "I'll be in touch this week. Be careful, okay?"

"I will."

"And keep Justin nearby."

I smiled slightly. "You don't even like him."

"Not the point. I trust him, which is more important." Hand on the door, she turned back again. "Maybe I can fly back after my test . . ."

"How will you afford another ticket?" I said it bluntly, because I desperately wanted her to do just that, but knew it couldn't happen. "Gandalf taught Frodo a lot, but in the end he had to go into Mount Doom alone."

"But Frodo had Sam."

I laughed, but it was fond. "Lisa, you are *so* not a hobbit."

She smiled a little, too. "Good point. Be careful, Frodo."

"See you on the other side, Gandalf."

# 36

Justin and Gran had hit it off before he and I had even met, so I guess it wasn't that weird to come into Froth and Java and see them sharing a table. Especially since Justin had had Thanksgiving dinner at our house. Gran waved me to the third chair, and I took the box of Lucky Charms out from under my arm and plunked it down.

Justin looked from the breakfast cereal to my face. "What's with the box?"

I tilted my head and said with a vapid sorority-girl smile, "They're magically delicious."

"If you do that in a fake leprechaun voice," said Gran, her

accent as thick as an Irish Spring commercial, "I'll see you grounded till Christmas, see if I won't."

Justin laughed, and I grinned as I took off my jacket and sat down. "Hell Week?" he asked.

"No. It's *Sisterhood* Week." I nodded at the box. "Some Sigma has a twisted sense of humor."

"So, today it's cereal." He moved it off the table. "And yesterday your clothes were inside out. That isn't too scary, as hazing goes."

"We live in a kinder, gentler, more litigious society." I stole the corner of his coffee cake. "Most of the national sorority offices and school administrations have cracked down so hard on hazing that no one wants to ask pledges to do anything. Even to stand up when an active enters the room, or do interviews for pledge books."

"That doesn't sound so bad."

"Most sororities aren't." I'd researched this for my Phantom columns, the ones that would never be finished. "On the other hand are ones that circle the fat areas on the pledges' bodies with Sharpies so they know what to 'improve.' "

Justin sat back. "You're making that up."

I shook my head. "These are things girls have reported."

"After they dropped out?"

"After they graduated. The need to belong is so strong, they'd 'voluntarily' do things like drink a fifth of vodka and then go Christmas caroling through a fraternity house."

Gran set down her cup. "Do they not read the news, about what happens to girls? How can young women do that to each other?"

"The same way that young men dare each other to drink until they end up in the hospital. They think they're invincible." Maybe I was soapboxing a little, but it was relevant to my dilemma. "The predominant feeling on Greek Row is that they are specially blessed with luck and good looks and success. Who'd suspect that the Sigmas had contracted with Hell to make it true? The devil's best trick was convincing man he didn't exist."

Justin looked at me quizzically. "Who said that? C. S. Lewis?"

I broke off another piece of coffee cake. "Kevin Spacey, in *The Usual Suspects.*"

He frowned at the decimated crumbs on his plate. "Do you want your own one of those?" I shook my head, since my mouth was full. "How about a latte?"

At my nod, he excused himself to Gran and went to the counter. "He looks tired," she said, watching him go.

He did, but honestly, you couldn't tell that from the back. I'm just saying.

"It's not me, Gran." My classes were over until exams next week, but Justin's work wasn't done. "He's got papers to write and he's grading Dad's term papers, and he's helping me . . . Okay, maybe that's my fault, but not like you mean it."

"I don't mean it any way, miss." She looked at me hard. "Unless the lady protests too much."

"No, ma'am." After a whole semester, what was a day or two more unrequited? If I didn't reverse the Sigmas' spell, and/or sever their underworld power connection, I doubted this would be my biggest problem.

"Are you ready?" asked Gran, following my thoughts easily.

"Yes." I had Lisa's duffel in the trunk of the Jeep, and I had the Plan. The only thing I could do at the moment was wait, and play the Sigmas' game.

She laid her hand on mine, and I felt a gentle tide of

warmth. "You won't fail, Maggie mine. You are strong and smart."

"So are they, and they've got twenty years of experience, a chapter full of accomplices, and a demon on their side. I'm just one girl with a half-assed plan."

"Then why not just give up? Why fight at all?"

I looked up from the coffee cake, which I'd crumbled into bits. "Because it's the right thing to do."

"And that," she said, stroking my cheek with her cool fingers, "is why you are much more than one girl with a half-assed plan."

✳   ✳   ✳

I hadn't been on a scavenger hunt since I was ten, but that was the plan for the evening. It was as if I'd joined a Mephistophelean Girl Scout troop.

My pencil sliced through the next item on my team's list. So far we'd acquired a copper colander, a Manolo Blahnik shoe box, a rabbit's foot, and a picture of a celebrity.

"Okay. We still need a hard hat, some Silly Putty, and a bottle of Tabasco." I looked at Holly and Kaylee. We'd been ordered to the Sigma house after dinner, chosen teams—two pairs and a trio—and gotten our lists. "Ideas?"

Holly looked at her watch. "None, except we've got to hurry if we're going to beat the others."

Kaylee peered over my shoulder. "Maybe we should split up. The cafeteria will have Tabasco bottles. And I think I can get Silly Putty from my roommate."

"There's that new building going up on the north end of town," I said. "You two head back to campus. I'll get the hard hat."

"You should go in pairs off campus. That's what Tara said."

Holly took the list and folded it into her pocket. "Kaylee, you head to the cafeteria. We'll meet back at the house."

We ran to the Jeep, parked up the street near campus. I checked for traffic then pulled out, heading toward Beltline, and from there north. Neither of us spoke. Ever since Devon's breakdown, Holly had been quiet and distant, especially with me. This might be the only time I'd have to talk to her about initiation.

But how to start? *You were right, your mom probably did sex your dad to death* didn't seem tactful enough to win her over to my side.

"Holly, do you know why the pledges aren't allowed to have sex?"

"Why? Have you been a naughty girl?"

"No. Well, not yet." I passed a puttering Ford in the left lane. "Do you?"

"No." She was too sullen to be convincing.

"You said something once. About a succubus. Re-member?"

"That's crazy." She folded her arms and looked out the window. "Besides. If it was true, there'd be a lot more dead fraternity guys, wouldn't there."

So she'd thought about it, opened her mind at least once to the idea. "Don't you think it's weird your mom, who wants so bad for you to be a Sigma, hasn't told you anything about initiation?"

"She's not allowed to."

I glanced at her out of the corner of my eye as I drove. "Why not? If it's all just fake magic?"

Her head snapped toward me, and her expression wasn't so much disbelief as denial. "You're nuts."

"Okay." I backed off quickly, since it would do no good to force the issue. I couldn't afford to have her slam the mental door on me. "Just remember, you may think you have no option but to obey your mother. But you do have a choice."

She looked at me, perplexed, her arms loosening their tight fold. "You said you'd do this with me, Maggie. You're not backing out, are you?"

"No. I'll be there. And I hope we will be in it together. On the same side."

Did she get it? She seemed to understand so much, but so little. There was no telling, not even with my superpowers, what she was thinking as she subsided into silence.

✳　✳　✳

We easily climbed the chain-link fence and dropped into the construction site. It seemed I'd acquired a knack for breaking and entering.

"I'll look that way, you go there." Holly gestured vaguely. "They've got to leave some extra hard hats around for visiting inspectors and stuff, right?"

"They do on TV." Not that I would put anything on my head that I didn't know where it had been.

I pulled my flashlight from my back pocket; like any good girl detective, I kept one in the car. The construction site was full of eerie silhouettes and dangerous obstacles. Probably why they kept a fence around it, to keep kids on dares from falling into a hole or getting squished by an I-beam.

As I wound through piles of lumber, the shaft of light fell on a sawhorse table. Score. I wondered if hard hats were expensive. I felt a lot worse about stealing than I did about trespassing.

Picking the oldest-looking one, I called into the shadowed darkness. "I got it!"

A thump echoed from the skeleton of the building. I stopped. Listened. "Holly?"

No answer but the soft clink of metal on metal.

You know those scenes where you watch the movie detective go into the spooky building, and you want to shout at them not to be an idiot, because everyone knows that something bad is going to happen? Now I knew how the other side feels. It's a compulsion to go look, a twisting in your vitals that says whatever is there can't be worse than turning your back on it.

I swept the flashlight over the concrete slab, shadows taunting me just out of the beam. Another creak, and a whisper. One sneakered foot in front of the other, I went into the belly of the beast, the light bouncing over the girders like a prison searchlight.

Movement. Edging forward, I saw a great loop of chain, each link as big as my hand. It hung from a pulley overhead, swinging slowly on an intangible breeze, the metal moaning softly.

My phone rang, and a scream escaped before I could stifle it. I fumbled the cell out of my jacket pocket and answered, still scanning the site for Holly. "Hello?"

"Maggie, I've found Devon."

"Lisa?" I whispered.

Behind her voice I heard the noise of a diner or a truck stop. "I've got her with me, and we're driving back to Avalon."

"You're in Alabama? What about your exams?"

She didn't answer either of those questions. "I've explained things to her and she's explained some things to me, and we'll be there by tomorrow afternoon."

Relief and worry bubbled together in my chest. "Just be care—"

A hideous, clacking rattle shook my bones. If Marley's ghost had been a twenty-foot giant, this was the clanking his chains would have made as he visited from Hell. I whirled and saw the real chain moving, the pulley screaming as it spun, and something massive plummeting toward me.

I flung myself away as a huge tub of rivets crashed to the ground where I had been standing. My ears rang with the concussive sound; my head pulsed with it, as if the seams of my skull might shake apart. The first time Holly called my name, I could only stare at her in numb shock.

"Maggie! Are you all right?" She'd come out of the darkness and crouched beside me. I heard an echo of my name and realized it came from the phone that I'd dropped to the concrete.

"I'm okay." I hoped my answer would carry to Lisa, too.

Holly pulled me to my feet. "Oh my God. You were standing right there!" Her hands shook and her face was so pale she seemed to glow in the moonlight. "Talk about lucky."

I'd ripped my jeans and skinned my palms when I dived for safety. But all things considered, no complaints. "Yeah. Lucky."

Only I wasn't. I'd thought losing the column last week had been about Victoria's patronage, and Mom was a warning. But I thought about Brittany now, about the backlash effect Lisa had mentioned. Had my luck been revoked, too?

# 37

By the next afternoon, I'd gone to the door so many times to look for any sign of Lisa and Devon's arrival, Mom threatened to tie me out on the porch like a dog. After that, I tried to discriminate the car noises, and after a false alarm for the mailman, I heard an engine turn off and two car doors slam.

I opened the door to see that it was not the cavalry arriving just in time, but Jenna and her roommate, Alexa. With a hand on the knob, I hesitated, uncertain. Then Jenna stumbled and wiped out on the front walk, and I hurried out to her side. Stupid crusader instinct.

The air was frigid—I hadn't grabbed my jacket—and I helped Jenna sit up. "Are you okay?"

"Nothing damaged but my pride." Actually, she'd skinned her elbows and palms, and as Alexa gingerly rotated her ankle, she winced, going pale beneath her cold-reddened cheeks.

"It's just twisted," she said. "Help me up."

We did, and she wasn't so bad off she couldn't laugh at herself. "Well, that's not how I meant this to go." She grinned at me, and said formally, "Maggie Quinn, we are here to escort you to initiation into the Sigma Alpha Xis."

"But it's only Thursday," I said. "I thought it would be Friday. And nighttime."

"The idea is to make it unexpected," Alexa said, helping Jenna balance with her weight off her left leg.

It wasn't as if I couldn't escape. Even I could outrun a girl with a gimp foot. But that wasn't the issue.

"Can I at least get my jacket?" And my cell phone.

"The heater's on in the car." Jenna looked behind me, toward the house, and waved. "Bye, Mrs. Quinn."

"Have fun, girls!" Mom grinned at me as she closed the door. At least she would tell Lisa where I was. That was my best hope now. What was the point of a plan if it all went to crap when the bad guys didn't do what they were supposed to?

Jenna was warmly expectant as she waited for me to join them in the car. She turned and smiled at me from the front seat. "Stop scowling. It's an act of trust, Maggie."

God, I hated those.

\* \* \*

I sat on Jenna's bed, shivering in the sleeveless white shift she'd handed me. She indicated that the other pledges would arrive soon, too, change their clothes, and we would all wait together.

There was nothing to stop me from walking out. I could forget the Plan. While everyone was distracted bringing in the pledges, I could find the grimoire and burn it. Or maybe create a diversion or delay until Lisa and Devon could get there.

The door opened, interrupting my internal debate. I poised for fight or flight until I saw Victoria Abbott, looking smart in one of her designer pantsuits. "Are you ready?"

"Is it time?" I asked, almost not panicking.

"Just about. I was hoping you could settle an issue for me."

Warily, I edged back. "I'm supposed to wait in here."

"You have special dispensation." Smiling almost maternally, she stepped back to allow my exit into the hall. I followed her down one flight of stairs, but instead of continuing to the ground floor, Victoria pointed to the left. "This way."

My bare feet slowed as we approached the end of the hall, where Juliana Baker-Russell-Hattendorf-Hughes waited beside the yawning door of the initiation closet.

"Don't you look pretty," she purred. "Vestal-virgin chic."

"Appropriate, I guess." The temperature seemed to plummet the closer I got to Juliana. I didn't know if this was literal or if my extra senses were using this as code for *Evil ahead, get the hell out.* If so, I wished for a shorthand that didn't raise so many goose bumps.

I rubbed my bare arms, deciding to play stupid. "Why are we at the initiation closet?"

"How do you know what it is," Juliana asked, circling me like a cat, "if you haven't been here before?"

"Everyone knows it's where the chapter stores the initiation stuff. And the Christmas decorations."

Juliana shot Victoria an irritated look that would have

made me laugh if my terror level hadn't just shot from orange to thermonuclear red.

"Here is what I think, Magdalena Quinn." The glacier glint in her eye drove me back a half step, toward the open closet. "Victoria says we need you. But I think that no matter how much power you have, you are simply more trouble than you are worth.

"In fact," she said, in that voice she used when she didn't want anyone but me to hear, "some *thing* tells me you're a threat to our sisterhood. And I can't have that."

She moved inhumanly fast. Her hand flashed out and hit me hard in the chest, knocking me backward onto the bare wooden floor of the closet.

"This will keep you out of my hair for now." She stood with one hand on the jamb, the other on her hip. "And if you're very, very good, and don't make a disruptive fuss, then in all probability that water heater in the corner might *not* spring a leak in the gas line."

"Wait!" I lurched to my feet, and she swung the door closed so quickly that I ran into it, face-first. I grabbed the knob and turned it, pushing all my weight against the wood. It started to open, then slammed tight as, I suspected, Victoria added her efforts. The latch caught, and the lock clicked into place with a fatal finality.

I rattled the useless knob in disbelief. What kind of evil was this? Where was the gloating monologue on how clever she was? Where was the time I was entitled to, as the hero, to think of an escape? This was just not right.

Beating my frustration out on the door was hopeless. I would be very lucky if someone heard me, and luck, I knew, was on the Sigmas' side. But the action made me feel a little better, at least until the scrapes on my palms started to crack and bleed.

I sagged against the wood and slid down to rest. *Think, Maggie. What would Nancy Drew do?*

Nancy would work her way out of captivity with her compact and a bobby pin. I had none of my trusty supplies, and was essentially dressed in a nightgown.

Crawling to my feet, I searched for something to pry open the door, or maybe just bang louder. The most promising thing I found was a plumber's helper. Maybe I could plunge the door open.

I tossed it aside and stared at the initiation cabinet, which stood ominously empty. When Lisa and Devon got to my house, Mom would tell them where I was. But even if they *did* arrive in time, how would they find me? I was certain no one would be checking the closets.

What would the other girls think? Would Holly consider looking for me? Or would she think I'd reneged on my word?

I walked to the carton of toilet paper, and after a thoughtful moment, pulled off one of the flaps. Sitting with my back against the door, I flexed my scraped hand until the sting brought tears to my eyes and blood welled from the splits in the scab.

It might surprise you how much blood it takes to write "Help" on a piece of cardboard. I left off the exclamation mark, figuring that was implied. Then I worked the stiff paper under the door, the best distress beacon I could manage.

*God, maybe luck is on the Sigmas' side, but I really hope that you are on mine.*

With nothing else to do, I settled down to wait.

✳   ✳   ✳

I dreamed of the vanquished demon Azmael, and its noxious, rotten egg smell. Its miasma invaded my nostrils, my throat. Vanquished, not destroyed, it lurked and waited, and sent out putrid tendrils to choke and poison.

A cough woke me. My own. I shook off the disoriented half-doze and then realized the odor, at least, was real. Jolting upright, I scanned the dark corners of the closet, but nothing moved. No *otherness* seethed.

But the rotten-egg smell remained.

Of course. The gas water heater. Juliana raised the probability, and it happened. She was the queen, and all karma led to her. Damned Sigmas and their damned luck. Juliana was going to kill me with it.

I crawled to the heater, keeping low. Surely there was some kind of safety valve. I found a knob and twisted it, but had no idea if I'd just made things better or worse.

Again I coughed, my lungs trying to expel the poison. Retreating to the door, I lay down, pressing my nose and mouth to the gap at the bottom.

*Think, Maggie, think.*

Footsteps in the hall. At that moment, I didn't care if it was the Sigmas or not. I didn't care if they dragged me to their initiation, and if I could never touch another guy, at least a convent was better than being dead.

"Hey!" I shouted, then started to cough. I grabbed the edge of the cardboard distress flag, sliding it back and forth. The mud brown color wasn't eye-catching, but maybe movement . . .

The footsteps hurried closer. I heard the rattle of some tool against wood, then a splintering groan. The door popped open with a shotgun crack, and I looked up to see Lisa standing with a crowbar, and Devon behind her.

"Thank God." And I meant that. I might not be eloquent, but I was fervent.

Lisa pulled me to my feet. Her face was pale and thin, and there were dark shadows under her eyes. I wondered if she'd slept at all since she left DC. "Nice outfit," she said.

"Nice crowbar," I wheezed.

"Thanks. Your friend knows where they keep things."

Devon offered a ghost of an ironic smile. "Lucky, huh."

I closed the closet door the best I could, considering the splintered latch. "There's a gas leak. Get something to stuff under the door." Eyes widening, she dashed into one of the rooms and brought out a couple of wet towels.

"They're going to know you're in here," I said, wondering why there weren't people running already.

"Devon is still a Sigma," Lisa explained. "She doesn't register as a trespasser. She invited us in, so that gives us a little grace."

"Plus," said Devon from the floor, where she was stuffing the towels under the door, "the chapter room doors are closed. I think the insulation works both ways."

"Wait." My brain wasn't quite up to speed. "Us?"

Lisa checked her watch. "Justin is downstairs. In three minutes he causes a distraction. Then we've got to get in there and reverse this spell."

"Hel-lo! Gas leak. We have to get everyone out."

She swung the black duffel bag from her shoulder and handed it to me. "If they start the spell, you must do the counterspell. You have to return things to their normal flow. Things aren't meant to be out of balance."

"Excuse me?" I searched her face for a sign she was joking. "*Who* has to perform a counterspell?"

"You do."

"I thought you came back to do it."

She shook her head. "I'm here to help you. We all are."

"Lisa." Even my voice shook with the trembling of my confidence. "I've never done a spell before."

"Neither had I." That shut me up. So did the look in her eyes as her gaze held mine. "Maggie, you *have* to do this. The butt-kicking of a righteous woman availeth much."

I didn't feel righteous. I felt like throwing up.

"Remember," she coached me like a prizefighter about to go into the ring. "Stick to the Plan. Reverse the transformation, undo the binding, cut the power supply. Whatever they do, do the equal and opposite. Basic math. Positive and negative numbers . . ."

"Cancel each other out."

She nodded. "Just feel your way. That's what you do. I'll help you."

Devon joined us. "So will I, Maggie. I trust you."

"Great." I managed a wan smile. "Everyone trusts me but me."

"That's right." Lisa shoved the bag into my hands. "So stop whining and let's go."

Nothing like winging it against the forces of darkness.

The fire alarm split the air with a brain-melting buzz. My heart bounced around my rib cage like a Super Ball.

"Distraction!" Lisa shouted. At least, that's what I read on her lips, since my fingers were in my ears trying to keep gray matter from leaking out. "Time to go."

# 38

B*y the pricking of my thumbs.*

We three weird sisters ran for the stairs, two sets of sneakers and my bare feet clattering down the hardwood steps. Justin met us in the empty foyer, gesturing at the closed chapter-room doors.

"Can't they hear the alarm?" he asked.

"It's started." The words fell from my lips with dead certainty. The collected consciousness behind that portal built like clouds before a storm, charging the air with an electric potential. Even through the wood, I could feel the ebb and flow of energy, stinging my skin like nettles.

*Something wicked this way comes.*

"Once the ceremony starts," said Devon, "no one can go in or out."

I yanked on the brushed nickel handle, which was cold to the touch but utterly unyielding. When I looked expectantly at Lisa, she frowned back. "When I said I'd help you, I didn't mean I could pull a Hermione Granger on the door."

"Right. But you could try the crowbar."

"Oh." She looked at it in surprise, and I realized that despite her show of confidence, she was scared, too.

Justin took the tool from her. "Let me be the chauvinist here." He slid the business end into the gap in the double doors and applied his weight to the lever. The wood creaked and groaned, then gave with a pop. The portal flew open, and thick, fragrant smoke poured out.

No reaction from inside. It was as though what was across the threshold existed in another plane entirely.

"What about the gas?" Devon asked with a cough. "The candles, and the incense . . ."

"Gas?" Justin shot me a look.

"Leak upstairs," I said. "We tried to contain it, and it's got to fill the third floor before it comes down here." I hoped.

"Let's do this," said Lisa, her expression grim and set.

I held my breath and plunged through the door and into the smoky darkness. My companions charged in with me like matinee heroes, then stumbled to an anticlimactic halt at the static scene, silhouetted by flickering candles and wreathed in smoke and mist.

Girls in crimson shifts and bare feet ringed the outer

arm of the spiral, crimson candles in each right hand, the left raised, palm up, as if making an offering. A red cord looped each wrist, running from one girl's left to the next one's right, and on around the circle, binding the sisters both literally and symbolically.

Their stillness was eerie. Only their mouths moved as they sang a song of unity, a melody that seemed to thicken the air.

At the heart of the coil were the pledges in their white togas, swaying with the chant, their expressions dazed and unseeing. Around them, at the four points of the compass, were Kirby and Jenna, Victoria and, across from her, Juliana, the high priestess. She wore a flowing crimson robe trimmed in gold, and in front of her was a table—no, an altar—with the lamp, the censer, and the book. She made a gesture over the incense, and it curled up and out in a widening circle toward the girls.

I had to get in there and counter the transformation, but as I started for the opening of the inlaid design, a growing resistance opposed me until I was pushing against an invisible, immovable force.

At my feet, the spiral was the most obvious pattern, but I could see another inlaid piece closing the gap, sealing the outer arm into an ellipse. Justin joined me, his cheeks red, as if windburned. The fire alarm rang in my ears, even though the Sigmas couldn't seem to hear it, and rather than shout over the sound, I nudged Justin's arm and pointed downward.

He drove the iron crowbar into the wood, gouging a fissure, severing the line on the floor. The invisible barrier tore open, and it felt like I'd flung open a door to a storm of freezing rain and wind.

I tightened my grip on the strap of the duffel bag, and stepped into the metaphysical tempest. The energy raised the hair on my arms like a static charge. The incense was thicker, too, and I could feel something icy and inhuman in the smoke that curled around the girls' bare ankles and caressed their skin.

The first Sigma I came to was Michelle, a sophomore from Denver. She gazed forward like a sleepwalker, chanting along with the others. Rummaging in the duffel, I found the tiny silver scissors and snipped the cord that linked her to the girl beside her, undoing the first step, the binding. Michelle blinked, but didn't move until I dumped some black pepper into my hand and blew it into her face.

The reaction was immediate and violent. I wasn't quite quick enough to dodge her sneeze. But then she wiped at her streaming eyes and nose and looked around in cognizant fear. "What . . . ?"

"Fire," I said. "Get out of here." She blinked in confusion, and Justin, who'd come into the circle with me, turned her toward the door and gave her a gentle push.

I let him make sure she got out, and moved to the next girl. Lisa intercepted me, took the pepper for herself, and handed the scissors to Devon. "We'll do this. Get to the middle."

She and Devon got to work; I braced myself and pushed through the remains of the protective outer ring. The full force of the inner circle lashed at me like psychic sleet; I could hear a second chant now, a long, liquid phrase that licked unpleasantly at my ears.

Jenna's voice faltered in surprise when she saw me; Kirby snapped at her, "Keep chanting." The girls were east and west on the compass that was worked into the heart of the spiral, encompassing the pledges. Victoria was south, and to the north, at the altar, was Juliana.

Victoria's eyes were closed in concentration, and Juliana ignored me completely. To interrupt her position or her rhythm would risk breaking the spell.

I tried to remember all of Lisa's contingencies and instructions. Equal and opposite. Dropping my duffel at the southern end, directly behind Victoria, I took out what I needed. Wooden bowl. Dried herbs. Lighter, which I stuck in my bra to keep handy.

The chanting didn't change; I had no warning before a high heel came down on my hand, pinning me to the floor. Only Victoria Abbott would wear pumps with a toga.

"I wanted you to join us, Maggie." Her gentle disappointment was completely at odds with the tasteful two-inch heel digging into my palm. "Why did you have to betray me?"

"Maybe it was after you let Juliana lock me in the closet to die." I spit the words through teeth clenched in pain. "That doesn't establish a whole lot of *trust*."

I drove my shoulder against her knee, only meaning to unbalance her, but I heard something snap. She collapsed, holding her leg and shrieking in agony.

"Oh God." She writhed and howled, and I stared at her, horrified at what I'd done.

Kirby hit me from behind and my body met parquet with a bone-jarring crack, driving the air from my lungs. She seized my hair and yanked; I grabbed her wrist to stop her from tearing my scalp as she hauled me across the floor, back out through the spiral. I wheezed and squirmed and dug in my heels, desperate that she wouldn't drag me out. If I lost this battle, it would *not* be in a girl fight.

Fumbling a hand in my bra, I found the lighter. The flame sprang to life, and I hauled myself up by my grip on Kirby's wrist and held the fire to her arm. Flesh sizzled; she dropped me with a shriek of surprised pain and I hit the ground, leaving a hank of hair behind. In a blind rage she kicked at me, but I rolled away and scrabbled back to the bag.

She lunged, her mouth twisted in fury, her fingers raised like claws. I flung a handful of cayenne pepper into her face, and she stumbled back like I'd maced her, screaming and wiping at her eyes.

I rested my hands on my knees, panting for breath, getting my bearings. Devon and Lisa were working their way around the circle, snipping cord and waking the girls. While one came out calmly, another came out terrified and sobbing. Next, I searched for Justin, who was carrying a struggling girl toward the door while she beat on him in blind confusion. It was hard to see through the incense smoke, but it looked as though Justin's nose was bleeding, and Lisa might have a black eye. Devon just kept cutting the cord.

"Have you gone crazy?" I looked toward Jenna's voice and found her kneeling beside Victoria. Her mentor lay curled in a ball of pain, and Jenna pulled her head into her lap and yelled at me, as much in fear as anger. "What the hell is wrong with you?"

I resumed gathering my supplies. "Don't even go there, Jenna."

Her gaze was stricken, accusing, and honestly hurt. "I thought we were friends."

"We are." I was honest, too. "And friends don't let friends make deals with the devil."

"*What?*"

I ignored her for the moment. In all this chaos, Juliana had never stopped chanting, and the pledges stood like wax figures, transfixed, bound for the transformation.

Dropping the bundle of herbs into the wooden bowl, I flicked the lighter and set them to smoldering. Marjoram and basil, sage and clove. This was the second undoing, the retransformation.

Juliana's incense was the scent of seduction, of perfumed harems and dark, secret places. It was the perfume of power and wealth, of worldly pleasures.

*My* incense smelled of Thanksgiving dinner, of home, of protection and family. It was the scent of things bigger than ourselves, of intangible treasures. As the smoke wafted over the inner circle of pledges, I saw them quiver, as if stirring in their sleep.

Lemon oil, to restore and renew. I dripped some into my bowl and blew across the embers. Kaylee and Nikki raised hands to their eyes. Mugwort, smelling of clean, damp earth. The rest of the girls woke up, shaking off the dazed funk the way a dog shakes off water.

The process had reversed. And Juliana knew it. She stopped chanting, slammed the ornate brass censer down on the altar, and glared at me through the smoke. "You, *child,* are really beginning to piss me off."

"I have that effect on people." I still had to finish one thing, but I couldn't move from my position, south to Juliana's north, and my comrades were still freeing the last of the Sigmas.

"Holly!" Putting my trust in her, in the independent spirit under her mother's manicured thumb, I tossed her the vial of lemon oil. She caught it, and I pointed to my forehead. "Put it here. It will cut the last connection—"

"Holly Eleanor Russell!" Juliana snapped in a very maternal voice. "Don't you move."

Holly whipped her eyes back and forth between us, suspended on a thread of indecision. Then, squaring her jaw, she turned from her mother and went to Kaylee, dotting the girl's forehead with the oil. Immediate effect. The ballerina-sized brunette started cursing like a sailor and ran for the door.

The rest of the pledges didn't question, just fled as they were released. Jenna ducked as Nikki hurtled over her and Victoria in her haste. Finally, only Holly remained, and she, too, turned to go.

"Freeze!" Juliana's command halted her daughter as if she had rooted to the spot.

The equation, hanging in balance, tipped back to Juliana's side. The pledges were free, and the actives were safe. The pattern was scattered, and chaos was as random as it ever had been or would be. All except here, where the inner circle remained.

"Will someone please tell me what the hell is going on?" Jenna demanded.

"Did you never tell them, Juliana?" I threw it across the circle, keeping her attention on me. "You're a lawyer. Wouldn't lack of full disclosure invalidate the contract?"

"What contract?" demanded Kirby. Her eyes were red and swollen, and they widened as she saw Devon come into the circle of candlelight. Justin and Lisa followed her, rebalancing the pattern: four of them, four of us, and Holly in the middle.

I looked at the woman on the floor beside Jenna. "You didn't tell them, either, Victoria? I thought you cared about these girls."

"I do." Her makeup was streaked and her face contorted with pain, but she managed a veneer of composure. "Juliana found the book and set up the spell. But I was the one who worked it out so that no one had to die, and we could all of us benefit."

"Cole died." Devon shook with rage as she stepped toward Victoria. "Cole died because of what you Sigmas made me."

"No. Because you couldn't follow the rules. Your sisters tried to tell you, but you wouldn't listen. Did you think love would conquer all?"

Devon still had the scissors in her hand, clutched like a weapon. Victoria's mocking tone goaded her forward, but Lisa's voice stayed her. "Don't, Devon."

She looked up at her like a lost little girl. "I'm already a killer, so what does it matter?"

Gently, Lisa took the scissors from her. "It matters. Believe me."

"My God." Juliana's voice was all contempt. "Just *shut up* already. I offer you the world, and all you do is whine."

The grimoire had, through all this, squatted like a living thing on the altar. Now Juliana pulled it closer, and flipped back the sleeves of her robe. "I was tired of sharing anyway. Holly, come here."

The girl moved like an automaton. Her mother didn't

glance at her, just turned to a new page in the book. Raising her arms, she started speaking again, a chanting drone of renewed vigor. The flame on the altar lamp jumped and danced, and I felt the power surge from someplace deep and elemental, beyond human reckoning.

Justin had joined me, standing close by my shoulder. "What's going on, Maggie?"

"I don't know." This wasn't in the parameters. The air was turning colder, growing thick. Devon and the Sigmas darted their eyes warily from Juliana to me as Lisa came to my other side.

With a contemptuous disregard for all of us, Juliana lifted the censer. The smell had turned bitter and noxious, like stale ice and refrigerator coolant. Cold rolled out with the smoke, raising goose bumps on my skin. It crept into my bones, along with the realization of what she was doing: calling the thing that lay hidden at the heart of the pattern.

Equal and opposite.

My backup plan was really more of a desperate improvisation. I blew across the wooden bowl in my hands, fanning the red embers to tiny flames that fought against the clammy air. Kicking the duffel to Lisa, I said, "Time to pull a rabbit out of your hat, Gandalf. Justin, there's a piece of notebook paper in there. I need you to hold it for me."

The glass on the pictures around the room had started to frost. Devon drew her jacket closed, Jenna and Kirby rubbed their bare arms, and Victoria huddled into herself. Standing beside her mother, Holly's lips were turning blue.

Juliana's voice became harsh, rasping out the sharp, cutting words of her chant. Staring across at me, she pulled

Holly's arm to her and picked up a bronze dagger from the altar.

"Don't!" I started forward, without a clue how I could stop her. Justin's hand held me in place, kept the balance from tipping even farther.

"She's mine to use," the woman said. "They're all mine."

"You can't own people," I argued. "And Hell can't take them—her—without her consent."

I heard Jenna's indrawn breath, and felt the cold intensify in answer to my naming.

"They chose to be what they are, regardless of how they were created." Juliana paused, as if she were listening to instructions whispered through her soul on an ill wind. When she spoke again, it was with cunning. "But you can trade places with them if you like. You have real power, and I would get a lot of bonus points for you."

"Give me a break, Ice Queen," I said, "do I look like an allegorical lion to you?"

She smirked. "I didn't think so." Without warning, she put the tip of her blade to her daughter's thumb and cut until blood flowed freely. It dripped into the censer and hissed on the embers of incense. The smoke poured out like fog, flowing down the altar and across the circle. Frost spread in the wake; it rimed the tablecloth, the floor, and came toward us like a diamond-hard tide.

I held out the bowl toward Lisa and she dropped in nuggets of frankincense and myrrh. The resin caught immediately, flared ruby and amber in the rude wooden vessel. "Paper, Justin."

His eye scanned the handwritten page. "Are you out of your *mind*?"

"Look." I used enough bravado to convince both of us. "I don't even *want* to know what she's summoning over there. So excuse me if I go straight for the big gun."

Jenna dragged Victoria away from the encroaching frost; Devon—after palpable indecision—ran forward and grabbed Kirby, pulling her behind Justin, Lisa, and me—a strange sort of trinity if there ever was one.

Raising the bowl, I breathed across the smoke, sending it out carrying the first words of my own spell.

*"Veni Sancti Spiritu."*

*Come Holy Spirit.*

Justin crossed himself, and Lisa whispered, "Amen."

# 39

The frost slowed, but kept creeping toward us. Juliana gritted her teeth and growled a guttural string of words. She could have been ordering a metaphysical pizza for all I knew. I had just enough Latin to get through my own invocation. Catechism class was finally paying off.

*"Veni, Creator Spiritus!"*

I said it more strongly now, since the first tentative whisper hadn't called down a bolt of lightning at my audacity.

The infringing ice covered the floor, a sea of frosty white. We stood on a shrinking peninsula, and my bare feet cringed from the burning chill.

*"Mentes tuorum visita."*

*Come Creator Spirit. In our souls take Thy rest.*

The incense in my bowl glowed, as if fanned by intangible breath.

*"Imple superna gratia."*

*Come with Thy grace and heavenly aid . . .*

The frost stopped, inches from my toes.

*"Quae tucreasti pectora."*

*And fill the hearts which Thou hast made.*

Holly crumpled, like a puppet whose strings had been snipped. Just as abruptly, the ice retreated, a fast-motion thaw melting the ground for the coming spring.

It converged on Juliana, ran up her robe and over her chest to her bare arms and neck. For a moment she was encrusted, like spun-sugar candy. Then the frost sank into her skin, and what looked out of her eyes was no longer human.

"Uh, Lisa?" I held the bowl in two shaking hands. "Did she just absorb that . . . whatever . . . into herself?"

"Yeah." She sounded as poleaxed as I felt. "That's unexpected."

"Why isn't it cancelled out?"

Justin answered. "The blood. You've got to—"

"You *bitch.*" Victoria had gained her feet, lurching on her wretched knee, eyes fixed on Juliana's face. "You're still hogging all the power for yourself. You were never satisfied with an equal share."

Juliana—or what was left of her in there—stared at the other woman with disdain. "Like you would know what to do with it, Vicky. You never did want to go all the way with anyone *really* powerful."

Jenna tried to pull her back, recognizing the danger—maybe even Seeing it for what it was. "Victoria, please. She's not . . ."

Victoria shook the girl off, limping forward. "We were partners when we started this. And while I've nurtured this sisterhood, built it into something lasting and strong, you do nothing but take take take . . ."

Juliana's hand came up in a dismissive gesture. "Whatever. Most people *like* instant gratification. Peter, for example."

*"What?"*

Now her expression was just catty. "You don't really think *you* inspired his meteoric political success, do you? With your prissy little pantsuits and your camera-friendly hair?"

Victoria slapped Juliana across the face. The Juliana-thing reciprocated by flinging her across the room with one hand. The congressman's wife hit the wall with a plaster-cracking thud and fell to the floor.

The thing turned her—*its*—gaze, blazing with cold, on us. Distantly, I heard fire trucks approaching. Had they taken that long, or had that little actual time passed? It seemed as if we'd been waging battle for days.

"Still have those scissors, Lisa?" I held my thumb over the bowl.

Justin pushed my hand away, put his in its place. "She didn't use her own. You shouldn't, either."

"I'm not sure I can hurt you," I said honestly.

Lisa opened the scissors and put the silver point to Justin's thumb. "Get on with it."

"What are you doing?" The transformed Sigma Prime demanded an answer, but I heard alarm thrumming through the voice.

Her agitation renewed my confidence. "Basic math, Juliana. An equal positive and an equal negative equals zero. A gift for a theft."

Lisa cut the pad of Justin's thumb and I caught three drops of blood in the bowl. They flashed as they hit the incense, and the resin heated up, red-hot, then glowing white. The bowl itself caught fire, and I dropped it.

Flame sped across the floor, encircling the witch in a fiery prison. Her clothes began to steam, then her hair, then her breath, fogging like a winter day. Juliana seemed to deflate, then collapsed to the parquet. The steam around her rose into the air and the flame followed it, entwining the trails of vapor and banishing them with angry, defeated hisses.

Hammering at the door. The firemen were trying to get in. Justin crossed the circle to Holly, lifting her limp body into his arms. "Can everyone else get out okay?"

"What about Victoria?" Jenna asked.

"Let the firemen move her," I said. "Juliana, too." Her body now a heap on the floor, she looked smaller.

They ran for the door. I ran for the grimoire, not trusting *luck* to destroy it. My hands closed on it, then I snatched them back with a yelp of pain. The thing was burning cold. Grabbing the tablecloth, I scattered the altar paraphernalia and wrapped the book enough to grasp it. Then I turned and saw Juliana—not lying where she ought to be, but standing between me and the door.

"You little bitch." She had the bronze knife in her hand. Her eyes were feverish with madness. She hadn't just looked into the abyss; she'd invited it in to set up house. And now she was hollowed out, nothing left but instinct and old patterns.

"Give me the book." She raised the knife, which suddenly seemed huge.

I lifted the heavy tome as a shield, not interested in heroics or victory, only in survival. "Let's get out of here, Juliana. The firemen are coming."

She slashed and I jumped back, staying out of reach of the blade. The fire was spreading, purifying and consuming. I tried again to reason with an unreasoning shell of a woman. "There's a gas leak, Juliana—" She hacked at me, and I skittered back to where the fallen oil lamp had spilled, and I held the book over the flames. "Put down the knife, or I'll drop—"

The blade sliced across my arm and the book tumbled from my fingers.

It didn't even hurt at first. I watched, shocked, as bright red blood welled, dripped down my skin, fell to the floor. A lot of blood. Enough to make a little pool.

I sensed more than saw her come at me again. Dodging, I slipped on the blood and crashed to the ground, hitting my head hard enough to make my vision blur. Crawling across the floor, leaving great smears of blood, I searched for something to defend myself.

My hand closed on cold iron. The crowbar. As Juliana bent and grabbed my injured arm and dug in her nails, I swung.

I swung with all my strength. I swung like a major leaguer.

I swung like someone who wanted desperately to live through the next five minutes.

The impact knocked the metal bar from my weakening fingers. It didn't matter. Juliana collapsed on top of me, pinning my legs. I couldn't tell if she was breathing or not.

Neither did I want to know. The woman—witch, demon, whatever—had tried to kill me. And as I lay in a growing puddle of my own blood, it occurred to me that maybe she had succeeded.

# 40

I woke up in the hospital.

On the plus side, I wasn't dead.

On the minus side, I had no idea how I got there, what day it was, or why an army of dwarves had taken pickaxes to the inside of my skull. I was also attached to an IV in one arm, which was scary, and the other was swathed in bandages and pain, which was worse.

A soft snore made me turn my head. Justin was stretched in a recliner, sleeping with a book on his chest. He was cute asleep. I hadn't thought I'd ever find that out.

"Are you awake?" a nurse in Christmas-colored scrubs whispered from the doorway.

"Yes." My mouth felt like that same army of dwarves had marched through it in their dirty socks. She must be a good nurse, because she anticipated this, and held a cup of water with a straw to my parched lips.

"Is that your boyfriend?" she asked in a teasing tone.

"Yeah. At least, I think so."

"Yes, I am," said a groggy voice from the chair. Justin sat up, rubbing sleep from his eyes. "I am," he confirmed.

That was nice. That was nicer than all the luck in the world.

He rose and came by the bed. "Your dad was here earlier, while you were getting the transfusion."

"I got a transfusion?" Alarmed, I looked at the nurse, who made a soothing noise and patted my blanket-covered knee.

"You're fine. You just lost a lot of blood." She lifted my splinted arm and looked critically at my fingernails. "Can you wiggle your fingers? It may hurt."

It hurt like the devil himself was crawling out of my wrist. But I did it.

"Excellent!"

"Do I get a cookie?"

"No, but you can have a Vicodin."

"Bring it on."

When she left Justin continued to hover, finally taking my IV hand and holding it as if I might shatter.

"I'm not going to, you know."

"What?" he asked, understandably confused.

"Break."

He let out a long, slow breath. "I thought you had. When the fireman carried you out of the house, covered in blood . . .

Dammit, Maggie, I thought you were right behind me. I never would have left you. I never should—"

"Hey." I squeezed his hand as hard as I could with a needle stuck in me. "I know you're a white knight. Now get over yourself."

He looked surprised, maybe a little offended, and finally amused. "Yeah. Okay."

We stayed that way for a while, holding hands, just . . . *being.* And then I had to ask. "Juliana. Is she . . . ?"

"She's here in the hospital."

"Alive, then?" I didn't feel relieved yet.

"Psych ward."

My heart squeezed and it got hard to breathe. "Because of the crowbar? Did I . . . ?" God. Had I broken her brain?

"No," he assured me firmly. "She woke up from that and started raving. She's under restraints and observation. Probably will be for a long time."

"And Victoria?" I asked, tentative for a different reason. I'd always suspected her, always knew she wanted to use me. But it was a twisted kind of self-interest; she thought she could make things good for everyone, no losers, as long as everyone followed the rules.

"Her neck and spine were fractured. She'll live. That's all they're saying for the moment."

I closed my eyes, a new kind of pain subsuming all the physical misery. "I feel like I failed at saving them, too."

Gently, his hand stroked my hair. "I know. But you can't save everybody."

"You saved me." Lisa spoke from the doorway, tentatively, her coat over her arm. "I'm pretty grateful for that."

"Hey! Come in here." I tried to push myself up, with no success.

She edged into the room. "Are they giving you any decent drugs?"

"Soon, I hope."

Still unsure, she glanced from Justin to me. "Should I come back later?"

"No." He grabbed his book from the chair. "Sit down if you want. I can leave you guys alone."

"Please don't," she said politely.

I figured this could go on for hours, so I interrupted, giving her a narrow-eyed stare. "Did you blow off your exams to come help me?"

"Can I get you a Coke or something? You want some water?"

"Don't dodge the question!"

She ducked her head and stared at the floor so long, I thought she wasn't going to answer. Finally, she shrugged. "A's are overrated anyway."

"Oh, Lisa."

"It's no big deal. A couple of incompletes. I can make them up."

"But your scholarship," I said, sorrow and gratitude mixed in my voice. "Your GPA."

She raised her eyes and despite her guard, I could read the raw emotion there. Something fundamental had altered in the last few days. Her soul was still wounded, but it was as if a nasty, dirty field dressing had been ripped off, exposing the injury to clean, healing air.

"It's not just that I owe you for saving my life last spring," she began. "Though I do. But after everything, you trusted me again, when I thought I'd never even be able to trust myself." She looked across the bed at Justin, who was trying to pretend he wasn't in the room. "And you did, too, Sir Galahad. Though you don't have to like it. It means . . ."

She trailed off, and after a beat, Justin supplied the answer. "Redemption."

"Atonement," she corrected, though I suspected they were both right. "A chance, anyway. Even if it takes the rest of my life." She glanced at me, deliberately shifting her mood. "Which might not be that long, if I have to keep saving your butt."

"Saving *my* butt?" I protested. "Whose idea was that invocation?"

"Who was locked in the closet when I got there?"

Justin cleared his throat. "Personally, I think pulling the fire alarm was an inspired idea. Even if the house burned down anyway."

I looked at him in surprise. "The whole house?"

He nodded. "To the ground. The prevailing theory on the news is that Juliana Hughes did a Mrs. Rochester on the place."

"Oh my God." I sat up, ignoring the ice pick between my eyes and the fire in my hand. "I need a newspaper. And my laptop. I don't believe this. I was *right there,* and I *still* got scooped for the story. *Again!*"

Justin laughed and shook his head, but he handed me a copy of the *Avalon Sentinel* all the same. No wonder I love him.

# 41

There's this principle in witchcraft—at least the New Agey, rainbows-and-light kind—that everything you do has the potential to come back on you three times as bad. Payback's a witch, I guess.

Kirby got caught cheating, and was expelled from the university with only nine credits left to complete her degree. Alexa, Jenna's roommate, lost her slot in medical school and her boyfriend dumped her for a plastic surgery resident.

Jenna's boyfriend also dumped her, but not before making her an STD statistic. She told me about it over coffee at

Froth and Java after everyone had gotten back from winter break. Those that were coming back, anyway.

"At least it could be cured by antibiotics," she said. "It could have been much worse."

"I'm glad it wasn't." What can I say? *G* and *E* aren't always absolute. I hope I never see them that way.

She cupped her mug between her hands. "We—the SAXis—knew we were lucky, and special. And I followed the rules. Heck, I only had two hookups until I met David, who was a Gamma Phi Ep. I figured, who was getting hurt?"

"Do I need to answer that?" Just because I don't judge doesn't mean I let people delude themselves.

"No." She shook her head. "Poor Devon. Have you heard from her? Do they think her hearing will come back?"

"No. It's permanent nerve damage from the meningitis."

The doctors had thought it weird that her illness had been delayed so long after the incubation period. But they'd dismissed it as a coincidence or a fluke, which is what rational people did when confronted with the irrational.

"Poor Devon." Jenna repeated it softly, guiltily. "She was so out of her league. Over her head before she knew what was going on."

Maybe that was why she was only deaf and not dead like Cole. Though I doubt she saw that as a good thing right now.

The alums, having had more use of the Sigma power, were taking harder hits. One movie-star trip to rehab made barely a blip on the national radar, but I checked it off my list, along with a couple of CEO firings and insider trading scandals.

The wintertime bustle of Froth and Java continued, heedless of life changing events. Jenna and I said we'd get together for lunch, and we might, but I wasn't really expecting her to call. It takes a lot of history together before the investment in a friendship outweighs seeing in the other person the constant reminders of your bad decisions.

Lisa and I, for instance, would never have the same relationship that we did before. But now I had hope that *different* didn't mean *worse*. We had to stay friends. Who else could I call and say, "I think my calculus teacher might be an agent of the devil." (Not really. But his idea of homework was pretty infernal.)

After Jenna left, I sat back, looking through the window at Congressman Abbott's office across the downtown street. Victoria was in a wheelchair, with only partial use of one hand. Speculation said Abbott would finish the last year of his term and return to private law practice, ostensibly to take care of her, though possibly because his campaign contributions didn't bear scrutiny. Funny how the universe can set itself right when otherworldly forces aren't skewing the balance.

Juliana now lived in an expensive sanatorium, which is what they call a funny farm when its residents are rich and high-toned. Since Juliana had been declared non compos mentis, Holly now had control of all the Baker-Russell-Hattendorf-Hughes financial resources, which meant that not only was Juliana in a padded cell, Holly held the checkbook that kept her at the Riverview Sanatorium instead of the Illinois State Hospital.

The door to the shop opened and Justin came in, bundled against the January chill. He sat down and unwrapped; I slid my mocha across the table to him. "Mmm," he said appreciatively, warming his hands on the paper cup. "Toasty."

"How'd your meeting go?"

"Well, my thesis subject was approved. Apparently your dad told the committee I wasn't crazy."

"That was nice of him."

"It was." He grinned at me, and I grinned back. We had to stick together, those of us who saw past disbelief.

"How's Lisa?" he asked, following my train of thought with his usual accuracy. "Settled back in at Georgetown?"

"Yep." I retrieved my drink.

"Are you guys really planning a road trip for spring break?"

"Probably. Worried?"

"Not about you two. God help any evil thing in your way." He rose and grabbed my coat from the back of my chair, holding it out for me. "Ready?"

"Yep." I slipped my arms in and reached for the mocha. The pain reminded me to switch the cup to my left hand before I dropped it. Mostly I had trouble grasping things. The physical therapist said I might always have weakness in that hand. I guess there goes my promising career as a concert violinist.

Justin put his arm around me as we stepped out into the blustery day. "Excited?" he asked.

"I can't wait for you to meet her. She's not much to look at, but boy can she wail."

"No worries about her lungs, then."

"Nope. She'll probably outtalk me someday."

"I doubt that," he said as we reached his car, then kissed away my indignation.

Brigid Joanna Quinn had been born on January second

at four-fifteen in the afternoon, a few weeks early, but healthy and . . . Okay, not beautiful. But I understand they all come out looking that way.

As for me, I was pretty sure the effects of the Sigma Alpha Xis had dissipated. My dreams had returned to what passes for normal. I hadn't had any more ambush visions, but sometimes when I touched things weighted with memory or emotion, it seeped in. So I guess that's really me, and not a special Sigma gift.

The grimoire had burned; at least, I woke up in the hospital with the recollection of it dropping into the pool of lamp oil, and flames rushing up to consume it. Hopefully a real memory and not a product of blood-loss delirium or wishful thinking. But it *felt* finished, and I had to trust my instincts until there was evidence to the contrary.

Holly was the only ex-pledge not coming back to school in the spring. She'd called me after the new year to say she was going into training to try out for the U.S. Women's Soccer League, now that she had the resources to follow her own dream and no mother standing in her way. I would be following her dream, too, for a while, to make sure she wasn't extraordinarily lucky in her quest. The work of a psychic supergirl is never done.

But for the moment, I had nothing better to do than stand in the freezing wind, wrapped in my boyfriend's arms, warming up from the inside out. Sometimes, you are just in the right place at the right time, and nothing in the universe is entirely random.

# ACKNOWLEDGMENTS

Sometimes I wonder if I talk to myself because I'm a writer, or if I'm a writer because I talk to myself. Here are a few of the people who keep me from being any crazier than I already am.

My agent, Lucienne Diver, and my editor, Krista Marino. How great is it that I get to work with people I genuinely like and admire? I'm also extremely lucky to have the support of so many people at Delacorte Press. You guys rock.

My BFF Cheryl A. Smyth, who knows the voices in my head almost as well as I do.

My wonderful, talented friends Candace Havens and Shannon Canard, who know I'm a dork and still let me hang out with them.

The DFW Writer's Workshop and the North Texas Romance Writers of America, two fantastic organizations. And a sundry bunch, for various encouragement, kindness, and inspiration: A. Lee Martinez, Michelle Nordahl, Delilah Peeler, Carole Millard, Ashlea Robertson, Haley M. Schmidt, Father Sherwood, Amy Frost, and the Camp Crucis Girls Cabin Circle.

My husband, Tim, and my family—especially Mom and Pete. As they say in *High School Musical:* We're all in this together.

ROSEMARY CLEMENT-MOORE loves history, Jane Austen, vintage embroidery, Dance Dance Revolution, BBC America, and the Sci-Fi Channel. She can tap dance, make balloon animals, sail a boat, and rappel from a cliff. In college she was in honors choir, ROTC drill team, and a sorority she prefers not to name, even though, as far as she knows, they were not in league with the devil.

Rosemary lives in Texas with her husband and her dogs. She loves to hear from readers, who can visit her Web site at www.readrosemary.com.

09 08